SAM GAO

ALL AT ONCE

THE TIMEKEEPER'S DAUGHTER
BOOK 5

CHAPTER ONE
MARIA

I turned twenty last month, but my birthday cake reads "19" in big, blue frosting numbers. When you're a time traveler, the subject of birthdays becomes complicated, to say the least. Technically, I'm still a few months off from turning twenty. I told my boyfriend as much, and while he said I'm being ridiculous, he still decorated the cake with "19" instead of "20." Isn't that sweet?

I've never been a big birthday person, and frankly, I don't like cake very much, either. Don't get me wrong—I don't *dislike* it. But I don't go crazy for it the way everybody else seems to. It's been flung at my person too many times. Once, Shane McKay frosted a brick and threw it at me. What a waste of buttercream. Thankfully, he missed my face and hit my chest. I was wearing thick silicone bra inserts, so I barely felt the brick bounce off and land not-so-safely on Hannah Dwyer's foot. And there was another time, in the group home, when Sarah Sweeten—the least sweet person you'll ever meet—snuck into my room and shoved leftover birthday cake in my ears, just because I told our social worker that Sarah was still dating a college student who was on probation.

So, yeah, not a lot of great cake-related memories.

This particular cake, however, is the best I've ever eaten —not just because Rhys is the one who made it. It's not too sweet, and the peaches are from a famous family-owned farm a few hours inland. Rhys was inspired by an episode of *The Great British Bake Off* last month, when my birthday actually was—but we had to put off the party due to finals.

To no one's surprise, the cake is a massive hit. By the time I go back for seconds, the entire sheet is reduced to a pile of crumbs.

With the cake finished, I take it upon myself to clear the plates and start doing the dishes. Everyone is hanging out in the backyard, though we don't have enough seating, so most students brought their own folding lawn chairs. Frankly, I don't know half the people at this party—I think they just came for the free food. Nothing draws a crowd of college students faster.

I've never had this many people at a birthday party in my honor, on account of being a total social leper for most of my life. My popularity has boosted significantly since last semester, going from being hated by the general student population to being a total nobody. I couldn't be happier. It's better to be forgotten than remembered for the wrong reasons. At least now when people say, "Mar, who?" it's out of ignorance, not spite!

Sliding the unflattering rubber gloves on, I turn the kitchen sink all the way to hot. The back door jingles, and my sister Tasha comes in with a stack of plates I must have missed and grabs a towel hanging from the oven handle.

"Having fun?" she asks, knowing full well that I'm now

exhausted from socializing with all these strangers and I'm ready to go to bed.

"I think it's starting to fizzle out," I reply. I don't actually know if that's true, but I read an article in *Cosmo* last week about manifestation and putting my wishes out into the universe or whatever. It sounded like a load of BS, but when I mentioned it to my therapist, she thought I ought to give it a try. She's the expert. "Thankfully. I need to get some shut-eye. I've got training in the morning."

"Right. I still can't believe it." Tasha sighs, leaning against the granite countertop. She's so dramatic, she should major in acting, not marketing. She's certainly got the looks for it—acting, I mean. She's always been gorgeous, but in a natural way. I, on the other hand, need a full makeup kit just to achieve "alive and awake."

Tasha has long, dark curls to her waist and dark, warm-toned skin that glistens under the kitchen lights. She's tall and leggy, and Isabelle says that the only reason Tasha's never dated anyone seriously is because men are intimidated by her looks.

Men aren't really intimidated by my looks. I'm average in terms of appearance, but makeup helps. Regardless of what I do, I'm still firmly in the girl-next-door category. You know what I mean—mousy brown hair, 5'4", somewhat stubby legs. I'm no supermodel, so guys have never been too scared to ask me out. My self-esteem isn't the best, either. The only thing that's unique about me now is my eyes—and not in a good way. Last semester, they went from dark brown to bright yellow, which is just as attractive as it sounds—which is to say, not at all.

This is a fantasy novel, right? But I couldn't get a cool iris color, like pink or purple, or even gold. Nope, I get lemon-rind yellow, which really doesn't suit my coloring. But I've given up on colored contacts. Besides, Rhys thinks my eyes are cool.

Well, he didn't say "cool" exactly. He said "ravishing," which now that I think about it was probably sarcasm.

"You can't believe what?" I ask Tash. "That I exercise regularly?"

She shakes her head. "No, that's not it."

"That magic exists? That one of my biological parents was a snake?" I continue. "That I can time travel, sort of?"

"Nope, wrong again."

"Uh." Those were the only big-ticket items I could think of.

Tash took the news well—better than I did when I found out. Granted, she, along with the rest of my family, was taken into my living room by a professor at Southeastern and told, very gently, about magic. I learned about magic after a demonic cult tried to kill me and launched a hostile takeover of the cruise ship I was trapped on. Not a fun time.

"I just can't believe that you landed such a hot guy," Tasha continues, staring out the window. I would be offended if she weren't completely right, as per usual.

I follow her gaze, spotting Rhys and his sister, Siraye. He always looks polished and neat in crisp white button-downs and slacks. He just got a haircut, so the silvery blond locks no longer reach his shoulders, and instead brush just past his ears.

Tasha is human, so she can't see his elongated elf ears. She has trouble sensing magic—it's some sort of natural human glamour that keeps them oblivious, for the most part. Which is a shame, because I like his ears.

Well, not his ears specifically. It's more accurate, and

more embarrassing, to say I like everything about him. But I'd probably die if he ever found out. Selma Hyatt, an older girl in the group home who taught me everything I needed to know about boys, told me that men like a little mystery. You've got to keep them on their toes, because the moment they find out how much you like them, it's over. Then again, Selma never met someone like Rhys—mostly because she's human, and Rhys is a trueblood elf. Oh, and he was born over 300 years ago. So there's that.

Rhys must sense me watching him, because he turns toward the kitchen window and smiles. Stupidly, I melt a little. I can't help it. We're still in the honeymoon phase, according to my friend Ava. According to Ophelia, who is very much not my friend, it's only a matter of time before I screw things up. What does she know?

Tasha's eyes shine with amusement. "You didn't land just one hot guy, but two."

"The first time didn't work out well," I remind her. Besides, I can hardly say that I "landed" Archer. We kissed a few times, not even with tongue. He hated me far more than he ever liked me.

"You're friends, though." Tash gestures to Archer, who stands on the opposite side of the yard.

Archer is like the hot-guy-next-door, which is distinctly different from the girl-next-door. The girl-next-door, like me, is average in a charming way. (Not that I'm calling myself charming.) The guy-next-door is undoubtedly hot, and while he might seem available due to the proximity, he's just out of reach.

Archer has sandy blond hair, blue eyes, and a great body. I might not want to date him, but hello, facts are facts. He works out often, usually with me. Not to mention, he's got that brooding, unapproachable thing going on. He'd be perfect for a hero in a YA romance novel. For me? Not so much. We clash on a romantic level, but platonically, we get along. He doesn't hate me anymore, which is always a good basis for a friendship.

"We're *friends*," I confirm. "But that's it."

"Did they fight over you?"

"No." Things were over between Archer and me before I got involved with Rhys. That hasn't stopped Rhys from disliking Archer pretty strongly, which can be kind of funny at times. Even without me thrown into the mix, Archer and Rhys are like oil and water. "I wouldn't want them to."

"Really? I think it would be hot."

"It's June in Georgia. It's hot enough around here."

"You're so funny. Have you ever thought about doing stand-up?" she asks.

"I know you're being sarcastic, but yes. If you must know, I've considered it."

"Right. Let me know how that works out for you."

"Unfortunately, I have some 'saving the world' to do. There's not a lot of time for much else," I say. Tasha rolls her eyes.

The party comes to an end at two in the morning, with the last of my friends stumbling drunkenly back to their dorms.

My friends aren't the only students staying on campus for the summer. A bunch of students are either here to train, earn extra credits, or they volunteered to help me save the world. Apparently, a good number of shadowborn have hero complexes. They might be total strangers to me, but they're still willing to help fight against Neil and his merry band of timekeepers.

I'm not entirely sure they understand just how threatening Neil and the timekeepers are, but Theodas assures me that he wouldn't trick one of his students into anything. He disclosed what the stakes were when enlisting students for the cause, and apparently, the majority of the students he asked to help agreed. It pays to be the chancellor of a magic college, I guess.

Rhys stays behind to help me clean up, even when I insist he doesn't need to. He assures me he wants to, because if he doesn't, there's a chance I'll forget to put out the fire pit and the whole house will be up in flames by tomorrow morning. He likes to exaggerate.

When we're finished, we sit on the big wooden swing on the front porch (after it's been dusted off for spiders). I lay sideways, leaning my head against his shoulder. It's quiet, dark, and we're alone… It's the perfect opportunity to fool around, right? But Rhys is from an era where hooking up just doesn't happen, unless you're married. He doesn't even like going to my room unchaperoned.

"Did you enjoy the party?" he asks.

"I enjoyed the cake," I say, "but I think my partying days are over. You've successfully domesticated me—congratulations."

He snorts. "*You*, domesticated?"

"Yep. The next thing you know, I'll be wearing a frilly apron and baking my own cakes."

"Will you be providing medicine for the inevitable food poisoning?"

"Hey, I'm not that bad of a baker."

"Your bread could be considered a biochemical weapon," he quips. "Also, I have no interest in…*domesticating* you. You aren't an animal."

"I don't mean it like that! You've cured me of my wild ways. Again, congratulations. You've achieved what every girl who dates a bad boy wants to do—you've changed me," I say dramatically, "with the power of love."

Rhys looks down at me, his face dangerously close. "Is this your subtle way of comparing me to a heroine in one of your romance novels?"

"Maybe, but you don't have to put it like that." Given the free time I've had lately, I've gotten into reading some of Allegra's bodice-ripping historical romance novels she keeps in her room. They're more entertaining that I previously thought, and I'm probably something of an expert on Victorian-era England now.

"I find your enjoyment of such books entertaining."

"Being called 'entertaining' when you're not an entertainer isn't a compliment."

"English is my second language," he replies, but I know he's full of it. His English is perfect, possibly better than mine. "Should we converse in Elvish instead?"

"No thanks." I don't need to humiliate myself—my mid-year resolution is to avoid embarrassing scenarios. Right now, I'm on a two-week streak. In Victorian romance speak, they'd call that a fortnight. "Where'd Siraye go?"

"She's returned to the house. Tomorrow morning, she has errands to run in the Veil," he explains. "She intends to help our efforts against Neil and Astaroth, albeit from the shadows."

Our efforts. It's stupid, but I love how he's included himself in my fight against Neil and the timekeepers. It makes me feel like we're partners, like I'm not dealing with this alone and dragging everyone I know along for the ride.

Having Rhys' sister on our side is good for both of us.

For one, she used to be an elf princess before the monarchy was dissolved. She's wealthy and well connected. Two, Rhys spent an inordinate amount of time away from her, due to my time-traveling antics. I feel better knowing they're reunited again, especially since they were so close in the past. Having a sister myself, I get it.

"How is David faring? He left before the cake was served. There is a piece for him hidden in the back of the fridge," Rhys says. "I put a note with his name on it. The container is opaque so others will not eat it."

Hearing my brother's name causes my entire body to tense up. David shut himself in his room after dinner and didn't come out for the rest of the evening.

Two years ago, David witnessed our foster father, Luke, get shot in a drive-by. Understandably, David hasn't been the same since. He went to therapy for a while, but it's still difficult for him to process. Isabelle thought getting a therapy dog would help, so two weeks ago, we went to a shelter and picked up the unfriendliest golden retriever in the world. David named him Buck, because he had to read *Call of the Wild* for summer reading.

Buck likes everyone but me, and he especially likes David. Whenever I get too close to my brother, Buck barks like crazy. Tasha thinks it's hilarious.

The dog is admittedly cute, when he isn't making so much noise. But putting a dog in a father-shaped hole unsurprisingly hasn't helped. And, admittedly, I'm probably the reason David has been so down lately.

At first, my family didn't understand why Luke was killed. The police couldn't find the killer or any motive for the shooting. Last month, I had to tell them Luke died because of me—not an easy conversation. Neil wanted to prove that he would do anything to force me to comply with his demands.

Isabelle says it's not my fault, and my therapist, Dr. Jones, says we need to work on my tendency to blame myself and not think logically through situations. But I know that if I weren't in the picture, Luke wouldn't have died. It's a simple fact.

For David, learning the reason behind the shooting caused all his feelings about the incident to bubble up. I don't blame him for being a bit withdrawn, but that doesn't make it any less difficult to watch. My brother used to be so happy and innocent. In some ways, I wanted to protect that, because no one had the courtesy of doing the same for me or Tasha when we were younger. And now look what I've done.

"David will like that," I say. "I think he's doing better recently. I saw him smile yesterday when we were watching *Mean Girls*."

"Will we be continuing our movie marathon tomorrow night?" Rhys asks. We've been watching a bunch of movies and television shows because he wants to be more "modern- ized" to understand me better. I told him it was sweet but unnecessary, but Rhys insists he wants to.

We've also been watching a lot of nature documentaries, which is the least sexy thing I can think to do on a "date." I don't know if that actually counts as a date, since we hang out in the living room with my family coming in and out. Sometimes, we don't even sit directly next to each other.

"We could," I say. "But I was hoping we could do some- thing special. Just the two of us. Like, maybe we could have a picnic on the beach."

"You hate the ocean, and the sand," he points out. "You

hate the outdoors, in general. The other day, a fly landed next to you and you knocked an entire tray of freshly-squeezed lemonade over."

"I'll endure it for you. Besides, too many of our dates get interrupted by my family," I say, trying not to sound too desperate. "We'll sit on the sand with a blanket and have a good time, I promise."

"*I* will prepare the food."

"That would probably be best, yes." Unless he's in the mood for instant ramen.

He nods. "I should go home. You need to get some rest."

"I'll walk you back."

"No need. We can talk in the morning." He gives my hand a squeeze and gets up, pressing a kiss to my forehead.

After he leaves, I walk back inside, only to find Tasha and Isabelle in the living room near the window. They were supposed to be asleep! No lights were on!

"Were you spying on me?" I ask, though I already know the answer.

"You two are adorable," Isabelle gushes. I'd accuse her of teasing me, but I think she really means it. Her cinnamon curls are pulled into a bun atop her head, and her warm eyes glow in the kitchen light. "He's a keeper, Mar. He's so polite."

Yeah, Isabelle is Team Rhys all the way. They share recipes and shit, which is kind of sweet since he asked her to teach him how to cook all my favorite meals. He doesn't do anything remotely inappropriate when we're alone, and in front of others, he's the perfect gentleman. Not to mention, he's intelligent and wealthy, being a former prince and all. Of course my mother would like him.

"Do you *love* him?" Tasha teases.

"Oh, shut up," I grumble, trudging to the kitchen so neither can see how red my face is getting. "I'm going to bed. Good night."

"Good night," Isabelle chirps, sounding far too cheerful this late at night.

I head down to my room in the basement, but Tash follows. Doesn't she have anything better to do? Ever since she arrived on campus, she's been warding off hordes of guys. Funny, when I come to Southeastern as a human, people think I don't belong here. When my sister comes, it's like every student here wants to protect her. Damn pretty privilege.

"Are you going to tell me what's wrong, or am I going to have to guess?"

"Nothing's wrong," I say, surprised she would even ask. Am I not the picture of happiness? Aside from the stress of having to prepare for a final confrontation with Neil, and the pressure of being the only one who can save the world from time-traveling snakes, my life is great. I have friends, I ate cake, I have a sweet boyfriend, my family is reunited... Everything is perfect.

"Okay, so I'm guessing, then," Tasha says. "Let's see. Is it...your boyfriend is too hot and your hormones go out of control whenever you see him?"

I stare at her, horrified at how well she knows me. But the last thing I want to talk about with her is my raging hormones. "*No.* Rhys and I are doing fine. We're going on a date tomorrow. And training with Archer is going well. My blood magic is coming along. We're still trying to find Astaroth and Neil, and Nic is MIA, but at least Allegra is on the road to recovery. Everything is fine, okay?"

"You're so convincing!"

"Just go to bed already."

Tasha shrugs. "Sooner or later, I'm going to figure it out. And when I do? Well, I have two years of meddling in your love life to catch up on."

"Yeah, yeah." I wave my hand. "I'm looking forward to it."

RHYS IS RIGHT—I HATE THE OCEAN, AND I'M NOT A FAN of the beach, either. But this is supposed to be romantic, damn it, so I suck it up and set the blanket down on the grass.

It's disgustingly hot out, even at sunset, and it's too windy for candles. I use them to hold the corners of the blanket down, instead. Rhys is still getting the picnic basket ready, but he texted me and told me he'll be on time. Which means he'll be a few minutes early. He told me once that he always tries to be early because he doesn't want me to wait for him.

True to form, Rhys arrives three minutes ahead of schedule with a wicker basket. The wind makes his hair look purposely tousled, like one of those Calvin Klein models. Not that I'm thinking about his underwear or anything.

"I made quiche," he tells me, setting the basket down. He settles beside me, handing me a plate with a slice of quiche wrapped in Saran. He brought silverware, too—the real stuff, not the plastic utensils I would have brought. "It is the only dish I know how to make that tastes good lukewarm."

"Good God," I mutter, taking a bite of quiche. It practically melts in my mouth. "You need to stop doing this."

"Pardon me?"

"Being so perfect all the time," I inform him. "Your consideration and attentiveness are making me look bad."

He chuckles, even though I'm not kidding. We're both new to romantic relationships, but Rhys is flawless at it. That seems to be a trend with him—he's good at everything he tries. Meanwhile, despite the number of romance books I read on a weekly basis, I'm a terrible girlfriend by comparison. All I brought today was a stupid blanket and some candles I stole from the dorm house.

Sometimes, I don't know what Rhys sees in me at all. With his looks and personality, the dating pool should be wide open to him. He's also a former prince, which comes with a huge inheritance. He'll never have to work a day in his life, and he's going to live thousands of years.

"Seriously, how are you so good at everything?" I mutter.

Rhys leans back on his elbows, packing our empty dishes back in the basket and handing me a bag of home-made chocolate-chip cookies. "I can hardly claim to be perfect."

"You are! Even your misuse of emojis is cute," I say with a groan. Rhys got a cell phone last week at Siraye's insistence—she wanted to be able to send him funny cat videos, and he has a hard time saying no to his sister.

"They are difficult to see on the screen," he argues. "These phones are too small for an old man like myself."

I roll my eyes. "You're hardly old. You're, what, a few years older than me now? Besides, you've adapted really well to modern times, given the circumstances. Me, on the other hand? I could barely ride a horse in the past."

"You could not ride a horse at all," he corrects, putting our empty plates in the picnic basket. Moving it aside, he lays down on his back. I flop down beside him, close enough to feel his warmth, but not touching him. The sun is just about to set over the horizon, the sky a wash of pinks and purples.

"Your horse hated me," I grumble. "I could see it in its eyes."

"Perhaps the horse sensed your reptilian heritage. Maybe this is why you and Buck do not get along."

"That's a mild way to put it. But whatever. I still much prefer the present. I was a horrible time traveler."

"I enjoy modern conveniences," Rhys admits, which is a relief to me. "Pinterest is very useful. There are many incredible recipes on there, and you can access them without cost."

"And hot showers," I say. "The only thing I kind of liked about the past were your letters."

He wrote hundreds of letters to me while we were apart. Let me tell you, a letter is way more romantic than a text. Especially when Rhys thinks the emoji with the straight line for a mouth is a "neutral" expression, and ends all his texts with it.

"It never occurred to me that they would be meaningful to you," he says. "I wrote them because I missed you."

"I know. I'm sorry."

"Maria, I told you, your apologies are un —"

I bend down, pressing my lips to his before he can finish. Rhys kisses me back, his lips warm and soft against mine.

The way he holds me is careful, gentle, like he's afraid to shatter me.

He's holding back, as always. I pull away, a jumble of words I'll regret later rising in my throat, but before I can spit them out, something roars in the distance. I freeze, turning around. Another roar sounds, low and guttural, and we spring to our feet.

A lion breaks from the tree line in front of us. It's feral, with black goo dripping from gaping holes in its ribcage. One of its legs is broken, the bone sticking out as it prowls toward us. With dead black eyes, it snarls at us before lunging.

CHAPTER TWO

Over these past four books, I've been attacked countless times, and I've never been prepared. That's led to: getting multiple head injuries, which is possibly the reason why I'm such a head case; getting shot at; having bricks thrown through my window; getting the crap beaten out of me; being forced to drink some old demon guy's blood. That's *not* an all-inclusive list, but you get the picture. After all these incidents, I've learned something: always be armed. Even on dates.

I lunge for my canvas tote and pull out a few pre-prepared spell bags. They require blood to activate, but after much negotiation, I promised to only use my own blood in emergencies. I keep a bottle of pig's blood in my purse. Scrambling, I use the dropper to activate the little pouch, dying the muslin red before tossing it into the air.

Light explodes from the pouch, and I throw an arm up to shield my eyes. The downside of awesome night vision is being more sensitive to light. But flash bangs are the easiest type of spell bag to make, and they're pretty effective.

While the feral is momentarily stunned, Rhys picks up a stone from the ground. As a trueblood elf, he can manipulate nature to a small degree. It takes more time here in the mortal realm, but he manages to morph the rock into a spear the length of his arm. He launches it at the feral with deadly accuracy, the pointed tip sinking into its eye.

The lion snarls, jerking back. I pull another spell bag out and drop blood onto it, tossing it in the air. This one is purely experimental, but I felt I needed to up my game with these. I've been practicing all sorts of combat combinations, but due to their deadly nature, testing on other students is a no-go.

As soon as the bag hits the feral, a barbed silver net unfurls, wrapping around the creature tightly and pinning it to the ground. I want to revel in my success, but Rhys pulls my hand. There's no time to waste.

Screams tear through the air, and my mind immediately goes to my family, who are very mortal, which leaves them vulnerable. I need to reach them, but they're on the other side of the island. I insisted that we have our picnic somewhere secluded, so we could enjoy some much-needed alone time without distractions. I'm regretting that now.

"We need to find the rift and close it," I tell him, though he already knows. My legs burn as we race uphill through the dark.

My night vision is good, but Rhys' isn't. I scan the surrounding area as we run, but there are no other ferals in sight. Still, that net won't hold the feral on the beach forever. And we'll have to pass through the woods to get back to campus.

"Stay by me," I tell Rhys, slowing down. As we near the trees, I scoop up a branch from the ground and hand it to him. He begins working his magic on it immediately. The surface of the wood smooths and lengthens, with the tip sharpening to a point.

We make our way through the trees, with no direct path to campus. It's not difficult to find my way through, since I can just follow the litter on the ground. Smashed red SOLO cups, napkins, beer cans, and cigarettes mix with fallen leaves, reminding me that despite all the magic on the island, it's still a university. Magic or not, college students like to party.

Once we clear the woods, campus finally comes into view. Unfortunately, so does another feral, crash-landing in front of us with as much grace as a ballet dancer with two broken feet. The two-headed bird-like creature shakes itself off, its wings so rotted and skeletal it's a wonder the thing got a foot off the ground. Its beady black eyes stare at me, both heads twitching. When it snarls, its razor-sharp beak opens, revealing two rows of shark-like teeth. I'm not sure why the creature evolved to be this deadly, and I don't have time to ponder it as it bolts for us. Rhys and I roll out of the way at the last second, each going in opposite directions.

The two bird heads keep us both separated, and Rhys manages to keep his at bay with his spear. Me, on the other hand? I'm barely managing to keep myself out of reach. Its neck is long, but it can't lunge for both of us at the same time now. I circle around it, trying to maintain my distance.

Rhys spears one of the heads through the throat, but the feral doesn't die. Instead, the spear gets stuck, and he's left empty-handed.

The bird roars, a sound I expected to come from a lion or a tiger, not a…whatever the bird is. Its feathers might have been colorful once, but now they're a mottled grey.

The feral illness does something to all the beastbloods it infects, causing a sort of zombification to occur. The disease spreads through bodily fluids, and for shadowborn, it's fatal. Within twenty-four hours, you're infected and rotting from the inside. That is, if it doesn't kill you immediately.

There's no cure, and while I haven't ventured to ask, I'm not sure what it would do to *me*. Somehow, I don't think being the pseudo-daughter of a timekeeper makes me immune to becoming a feral. I'd rather die immediately than become a zombie.

The monster darts for Rhys. Everything happens within a matter of seconds. I grab a spell bag, spilling the bottle of blood on my hands as I fumble to activate it and throw it at the bird. It hits the feral square in the ass and glows upon contact.

As it shrieks in pain, Rhys manages to roll out of the way just in time as it writhes on the ground, its blood boiling. The black goo leaking from its mouth begins to bubble and steam — not a pretty sight.

"Mar!" Archer shouts, jogging toward us. His blond hair is in disarray, and his eyes go wide once he sees the feral on the ground. He hands Rhys a sword, turning the hilt toward him. "Are you both okay?"

"We're fine," I reply, taking a big step back as Archer beheads the bird for good measure. Rhys cuts off the second head, not to be outdone. "What the hell is going on? Where are all these ferals coming from?"

Technically I knew where they were coming from — the Veil.

Beastbloods aren't supposed to be able to open rifts into the mortal realm, though. Only truebloods have been able to in the past, using bladed weapons. Some have figured out that they can open rifts if their claws—or in some cases, beaks—are sharp enough. Recently, ferals have been working together to come to the mortal realm in hordes. In other words, it's been a total shitshow from every front. As if I didn't have enough to deal with regarding Neil and the timekeepers.

"A few rifts have opened across Kingsmarch," Archer explains quickly. "One opened in my living room. It's utter chaos."

"What about my house?" Not only is my family there, but I'm keeping Karina Swan in the upstairs bedroom.

Karina is special in the same way I am, which is to say, fate is fucking us royally—and it's not using any protection. I'm not really sure how *she's* supposed to destroy the world, but I know it can't be worse than becoming a womb for the timekeepers.

The timekeepers wrote some sort of "grand design," a roadmap for how everyone in the universe is supposed to live. They're omniscient, with a caveat: for some reason, they can't see Karina Swan. She's their "blind spot." That's according to a talking tree in the Veil, which is always a reliable source of information. To be fair, it hasn't steered me wrong yet.

The tree said a lot of things, most of which I failed to write down. The basics are, I'm supposed to destroy the mortal realm by popping out snake eggs, and Karina is also supposed to destroy the world. I'm not too clear about the specifics on her side, and she's been unconscious so I haven't gotten a chance to speak with her since saving her life.

I'm not supposed to be able to do that. I did it once, with Rhys, but the timekeepers "allowed" it and used their Time Agents to fix any paradoxes that might have occurred from it. But with Karina, I went back in time a few months, found her, and brought her to the present.

I guess I managed to avoid a paradox because everyone thought she was dead, anyway. They couldn't even find a body. It's not like I changed anything major, that I can tell so far. No black holes have opened up.

The timekeepers haven't shown up since I saved Karina, which is either a coincidence, or the Wisdom Tree was right —the timekeepers can't interfere in my life if I have Karina around.

If only she'd wake up.

"Georgia went to the house to settle things," Archer says quickly. "It should be okay for now. But we need to hurry."

"Less talking, more running," I confirm. "Got it."

But even if we run at top speed, it's still ten minutes away. Southeastern is laid out like a town, with most of the buildings being Victorian houses. The lawns are sprawling, and it's easy to get lost when the walkways and paths are too far away from the houses to see the signs outside.

Archer knows the way, though. As ferals and students battle it out around us, we attempt to avoid the fighting as best we can.

The other students should be used to this by now, as fucked up as that is. That's another reason why so many students stayed at school over summer break—to fight the ongoing feral crisis around the country. There are five magic schools in the US, and each is assigned a territory. If you couldn't guess already, Southeastern is assigned the southeast.

Ferals have attacked the school once already since the summer began, but not this many at one time. Still, the students have trained all their lives to fight monsters, so I imagine they can handle themselves.

That is, until the dragon arrives.

I see its head first, poking through a rift. It struggles to get its body through, but by sheer force, it tears a rift taller than all the houses on campus and barrels through with a snarl.

It doesn't have any teeth, but that doesn't make it any less intimidating. Smoke pours from its mouth and nostrils as it advances on the lawn.

Cursing, I hand my tote to Rhys. "My hands are too bloody. Can you get me the blue bag with the red ribbon?"

"Are you planning on doing something dangerous?" he asks, knowing full well what I'm planning. But after David was kidnapped by Nic and I ran off on my own to save him, Rhys and I made a pact: no more doing stupid things without telling him. If I want to get myself killed, I have to consult with him first.

"Reckless *and* dangerous," I say honestly. "But you have my back, right?"

He sighs and tosses me a spell bag.

I rub my bloody hands on the surface to activate it, running ahead to get closer to the dragon. If I'm going to get this to work, I need to throw the bag in the dragon's mouth. Shrapnel will explode inside it, hurting it, but probably not killing it. Still, if I can slow it down, it gives Rhys and Archer a better chance at finishing it off.

I've long since accepted that I'm not going to transform into Xena, warrior princess, anytime soon. Or, if you want a more recent reference, Katniss Everdeen. Unlike my shadowborn peers, and my trueblood boyfriend, I've been training inconsistently for a little over a year now. Before this whole ordeal, I thought it would be a lot easier to pick up fighting skills. Unfortunately for me, it's not. At this point, all I can do is support those I care about with my magic.

The dragon opens its mouth and I toss the bag inside, but the dragon's reactions are faster than I expect. Its rotting tongue rolls out, flicking the bag away. The spell bag, upon contact, activates.

I roll out of the way as shards of metal and glass fly from the bag. At least I know my spells are working. But it's kind of hard to be happy when your own spell backfires on you. The dragon roars, taking most of the damage. Pain explodes in my shoulder as a piece of glass hits it, and I gasp from the impact. Smaller pieces hit my back, and I'm essentially a human pincushion.

The dragon isn't distracted by its injuries like I'm distracted by mine. Before I can recover, it's swinging its skeletal paw at me.

Wait, is a dragon's hand called a paw? It's not really a hand, but it's not furry like a paw. When I think of that word, I think of puppies and kittens. Well, dragons are kind of like dinosaurs, right? And dinosaurs are ancestors of chickens. And chicken have feet. So is the dragon going to crush me with its foot?

Ah, the things we think about in the face of death.

The foot, paw, or whatever doesn't end up crushing me into dust. Rhys launches his sword through the air, slicing through the dragon before it can step on me. I use the extra time to roll away, pulling the large piece of glass from my shoulder, which is pretty nasty and covered in my blood. This shirt has to go in the garbage, because as soon as I get the glass out, blood gushes down my back. It will heal, but it's also going to stain.

Rhys runs to me, not bothering to hide his concern. He takes one look at my back and blanches. "We need to find shelter and a first aid kit. Come on."

"We can do that once we get to the house," I argue, glancing at the dragon. Every little movement sends spasms of pain down my spine, but I grit my teeth and put on a brave face. Or a constipated face. They look very similar. "We can't fight that thing alone."

"An open wound could be fatal on a battlefield of ferals," Rhys insists, holding my wrist. I'm just glad he's not sweeping me into his arms, because as I've told him, I hate being carried. It's embarrassing and, frankly, uncomfortable.

"We need to go," Archer shouts, heading toward us. "Come on, let's get the others and regroup—"

But we don't need to get anyone else.

In the distance, I see a girl. I don't recognize her at first. All I see is a curtain of long, dark hair as she walks past the streetlamps. A trail of monsters follow her, but they aren't feral. They're regular beastbloods—no black goo, no snarling, and no rotting flesh.

She heads toward us, her head held high and her back straight. She exudes confidence and grace just by the way she moves, like she's gliding across water. The dragon roars upon seeing her, but she merely glances at it, unfazed. She stops in front of it, crossing her arms and staring at me. There's nothing dangerous in her eyes, nothing to indicate she's going to attack me. She's not even armed. But chills roll over my entire body, and my instincts tell me to get as far away from her as possible.

The dragon growls and moves forward, but as soon as it

takes a step closer to her, its entire body seizes. And, like a tower of cards, it folds at her feet. The signs of rot slowly begin to fade, the black goo and smoke receding as its grayish green scales slowly begin to return to a shimmering iridescent blue. Even its exposed bones grow flesh to cover them, fully restored.

The girl tilts her head, drinking me in. For a moment, no one moves, no one speaks. All I can do is stare, caught by her hypnotic gaze.

Finally, she breaks the silence.

"Who the hell are you?"

CHAPTER THREE

While the shower has improved Karina's appearance, it hasn't improved her mood. She looks expectant and stone-faced as she sits at the dining-room table, waiting for my boyfriend to heat up a plate of leftovers for her.

I take a seat across from her, but if I lean in too close, all the hairs on my arms stand up. It's a physiological reaction I can't explain, because she doesn't *look* scary. She looks... proportionate. Which is a weird way to describe someone, but it's more illustrative than the first thing that pops into my mind, which is that she is the most beautiful person I've ever laid eyes on.

Her facial features are in perfect harmony with one another, like an architect mapped out the size and shape of every feature to complement each other. It's hard to look away.

Her eyes meet mine as Rhys puts a plate in front of her. She's clearly noticed my unabashed staring, her dark eyes narrowing. Up close, I can tell the color of her iris is gunmetal grey, almost metallic. She looks at me like a lion would an antelope.

She hasn't said much since coming downstairs, and neither have we — "we" being me, Rhys, David, Tasha, and Isabelle. I wouldn't know where to begin. "I saved your life, just FYI" would sound kind of pompous, and I can't get down on my knees and grovel for her help. Mostly because my back is still killing me from earlier, and if I bent down, I wouldn't be able to get back up.

I try to break the awkward silence with an introduction. "So, as I said earlier, I'm Mar. And you're…Karina? I mean, your name was listed as Katherine — "

"My name isn't Katherine. There was a clerical error on my file, stupidly enough. How long have I been out?" Karina asks, sounding a little like a valley girl. She turns to my family, seated at the other end of the table, and holds her hand out. "Can you pass the pepper, please?"

David gives it to her, a blush creeping up his cheeks as their hands brush. I'll have to have a talk with him about that later. I imagine it will go something like, "I know she's hot, and yeah, I might have a bit of an aesthetic crush on her myself. Anyway, this is a bad idea, because not only is she way older than you, but she's probably going to start the apocalypse."

That's going to go over well.

But back to her question. I can't exactly go into the whole time-travel thing right away, especially when I myself don't totally understand it. Instead, I say, "It's June."

"*June?*" Her voice raises in both pitch and volume. Uh oh.

"Yeah, but — "

She stands abruptly, pushing her chair back. "I need a phone. Do you have a landline?"

"Wait," I say quickly. "We aren't done here."

She glares, setting my nerves on edge. If I were in her place, I'd be a little kinder to the person who's putting a roof over her head and food in her stomach. Gratitude is apparently a foreign concept to her.

David takes his phone out of his pocket and unlocks it, handing it to her. She grabs it from him without so much as a "thank you" and spins away, dialing a phone number. She snarls something into the phone in some foreign language and hangs up, dialing two more numbers before giving up.

Which reminds me, I probably should have taken her phone when I searched her dorm last month. Damn. I know I looked at it, but I must have put it down and forgotten about it. In my defense, there was a lot going on at the time.

"Thanks," she mutters, handing the phone back to my brother. Clearly she didn't get the answers she was looking for. "I never thought I'd say this, but I need to get back to Northeastern ASAP."

"Wait a minute," I say, holding up my hands. "Can you just hear me out first?"

She crosses her arms. "Not to sound ungrateful, but I have to leave. There are people waiting for me."

"You were pronounced dead," I explain. "Everyone thinks you're dead. But I need you, and you have time, so—"

"Everyone thinks I'm dead?" she hisses. It makes me second-guess which of us is the descendent of the snake here. Her tone would make every mean girl from my high school run for the hills.

"Yes," I say in a small voice. I know I shouldn't be intim-

35

idated by her, but it's instinctual. I felt the same thing with Ophelia when we first met, except with Karina, it's about ten times worse. "I'm a time traveler. I went back in time to save you. I had to bring you back to the present because I didn't want to cause a paradox."

"That doesn't even make sense. How did taking me out of the timeline not cause a paradox? Are you even sure I was supposed to die?" she demands.

"Yeah, I'm pretty sure. And it didn't cause a paradox, otherwise we'd be having this discussion in a black hole. Probably. I don't know what would actually happen if a paradox was created, but I don't think it would lead to anything good."

"You don't even understand your own powers?" She sneers. She might as well have called me useless, which isn't untrue, but it's still hurtful.

"I saved your life," I say desperately, confirming there's no way to mention that without sounding like an asshole.

"Did I ask you to?" she challenges. "No, I didn't. We're strangers, so if you saved my life—"

"I did."

"Then you must have had some selfish reason for it. We've never met, and it's not like you just came across my dying body and took me in out of the kindness of your heart." She's spot on, but I don't like the way she puts it. It's almost like she's blaming me for helping her. Just because I have semi-selfish reasons—is saving the world really selfish? —doesn't change the fact that I saved her. I don't expect her to kiss my feet or anything, mostly 'cause that would be gross, but she could at least be a little nicer.

"It's a long story," I tell her, not bothering to hold anything back. I summarize what's happened so far, from the Wisdom Tree, to Neil Abbott's involvement with Astaroth, to her status as a "blind spot." Rhys has to jump in, because my explanation is all over the place. When we finally finish, Karina's plate is cleared and she moves on to a bowl of mac and cheese. Her stomach must be a bottomless pit.

"So essentially, you need me because the gods of fate are trying to destroy the mortal realm," she says. "And they want to use you to give birth to an army of time-traveling snakes?"

"Unfortunately, yes." But hearing it aloud makes it sound pretty pathetic. "I would really like to avoid laying eggs, so if you could help me out, that would be swell."

"How would I do that?" she asks. "I understand what you've said. Kind of. But you still didn't answer my question. How exactly am I supposed to help you?"

"You're the blind spot. The timekeepers can't see your fate, for some reason, which means they can't predict your movements. That can extend to those around you. But if you can tell us what type of magic you use to evade the time-keepers, that would help us out a lot."

"Look, it's not that I don't want to help you," Karina says, though her tone implies otherwise. "I can't. You don't understand—I'm not shadowborn."

"If you aren't shadowborn, then…what are you?" I don't know how to phrase that question politely.

Karina sighs. "Okay, so from what I gather, you aren't supposed to exist, right? You weren't part of the original plan. But have you ever stopped to consider why that is?"

"I'm not following you."

"These timekeepers are gods of fate. And according to you, they're omniscient, which means they can see and control pretty much everything that's going to happen through all of time. They shouldn't have needed to edit their plans because they are all-knowing," Karina explains. "But what if something threw a wrench in their plans? You say I'm a blind spot, but there's nothing special about me. Other than the fact that my hair is naturally silky and frizz-free, even with the cheap shampoo you keep in your shower."

"That's not really special," I point out.

"Have you looked in a mirror lately?" She rolls her eyes. Ouch. "Anyway, rifts were open to the mortal realm for the first time in the 1800s. I bet that's what threw off their plans. They can't see the fates of mortals."

"That's a good guess, but it's a pretty far reach without any evidence."

"I don't need evidence, I have logic." She taps her head. "Something you seem to lack."

"This isn't a roast," I say.

"I know, but you make it really easy."

It's apparent to me that we're not going to get along. Great, just what I need—one more person on my case.

"I don't think the timekeepers can see mortals well," Karina continues. "And they probably can't see any mortals with magic at all. Hence why I'm a blind spot—I have powers, but I'm not a descendant of the Veil."

"A mortal with magic?" I repeat. I didn't think that was possible.

"I totally can't believe you're making me explain this. Seriously?" She flips her hair over her shoulder. "Magic exists in the mortal realm, too, but it's different here. It's called chi. Like in *Dragon Ball Z*."

My face is blank. "I've never seen that. Is it a movie?"

"It's an old anime," David supplies, adjusting his wire-frame glasses. "Chi, or ki, is basically life force energy. Every living being has chi."

"At least someone around here is cultured," Karina says, giving my brother an approving nod. "I'm a cultivator—I can use chi to make myself stronger. Truebloods can't use chi in spells, and I wouldn't be able to use your Veil magic."

"That's why Ethan called you the mortal monster," I realize.

She sniffs. "That's insulting. I'm not a monster, any more than you, Medusa."

"Technically, Medusa wasn't part snake. Her hair was made of snakes," I say snidely, unable to help myself.

"Oh my gosh, you're *so* smart. Do you want a prize before or after you pop those snake eggs out of your ass?"

"They wouldn't be coming out of my butt, and if you knew anything about biology, you'd know that!" I snap.

"As productive as this argument is," Tasha intervenes, "we should probably circle back to the main point. Karina can't teach you to become a blind spot because that's something inherent she was born with, right?"

"Technically, I wasn't born with magic. But yes, if my theory is right—which it totally is, by the way—then you can't really do anything about it." Karina shrugs. "Too bad for you."

"Too bad for *you*. If you can't teach us the skill, then we need to keep you around for a while until we figure out what to do next," I reply.

"If I didn't have a life, I'd be cool with hanging around here. But I'm a very busy person."

"Busy stuffing your face?" Okay, that was kind of mean. The moment I say it, I regret it. But before I can apologize, Karina speaks up.

39

"You don't have to be so jealous."

Me? Jealous of *her*? Hold on a moment while I laugh. Sure, she's hot, but her attitude is obnoxious.

"I doubt the timekeepers would actually be powerful enough to take over this realm," Karina continues. "True-bloods aren't as powerful in the mortal realm. And obviously I'm not the only mortal monster in existence. I'm sure they'll be snuffed out sooner or later."

"You would risk that?"

"It's not really up to me. As I was saying earlier, I can't help you. I don't have powers anymore."

My stomach drops. "What do you mean? What did you do to the ferals earlier?"

"I didn't do anything. But my powers were stolen, and I'm just a regular mortal now. Sorry, I guess."

My expression goes blank, and when the room falls silent, Karina resumes eating again. My last hope just crushed my one chance at saving the world, and now, she's eating my leftover mac and cheese.

Chapter Four

Karina is staying on Kingsmarch for the time being, which is a blessing and a curse. The longer she stays, the more time I have without the timekeepers watching me. At the same time, I can already tell we're not going to get along.

I've come to the conclusion, after our brief encounter, that we're pretty much opposites. She's filled to the brim with unfounded confidence, and wears her emotions on her sleeve like a child. Her manners are questionable at best, and she's proven to be difficult to deal with. After cleaning out the leftovers in the fridge, she excuses herself and goes to bed.

She won't be able to stay in Allegra's room for much longer. Allegra has been in the nurse's office while she recovers from her injuries, but she'll be back soon. The way we left things wasn't the best, and while I don't know if she hates me anymore, I doubt she likes me. But the feeling isn't mutual — I don't hate her, or even dislike her, despite the fact that she was in league with Nic for a little while.

I'll deal with the housing situation later. Now, I've called an emergency meeting in light of what Karina told me. It's the middle of the night, but with all the excitement from the ferals earlier, quite a few students and faculty members are still awake. Isabelle, David, and Tash go to bed, and we try to keep the volume to a minimum by going to the backyard.

We sit in a circle around the bonfire: myself, Rhys, Theodas, Siraye, Archer, Provost Mathers, Ophelia, Ava, Declan, and Celeste. Yeah, the group got bigger somehow. Celeste is only here because Archer is here, and I imagine Ophelia feels the same. Declan is Provost Mathers' nephew, and he's head-over-heels for my friend Ava.

Theodas is the only calm one in our group, though that could be for a variety of reasons. He and Rhys are well acquainted, having fought in an elf-fae war together. But due to time travel, Rhys looks a lot younger than Theodas. Though Theodas only looks like he's in his forties, not his true age, which is over 300.

Not only is Theodas the chancellor of the school, but he doesn't seem ruffled about anything, ever. In fact, he's whistling and roasting marshmallows, looking perfectly content while the rest of us are in full-blown panic mode.

"I've read a few cultivation novels before. I didn't think it actually existed," Theodas says, sounding almost excited.

"Are they popular?" I ask. I've never heard the term before, and a Google search didn't answer my questions.

"Maybe not as mainstream in the West, but they have an audience overseas," he explains. He's always been fascinated by mortal media, so it doesn't surprise me that he knows about this. "Cultivation as a concept has been around for a very long time. A few Chinese folk tales feature cultivation, like the Legend of the White Snake."

"So it's some sort of fantasy trope?" Archer asks. Dark circles ring his eyes and his shoulders slump slightly. On anyone else, I wouldn't think these two things would be cause for concern. But Archer is secretly very particular. He's not a perfectionist, exactly, but he likes things done a certain way. He takes great care of himself, right down to his strict diet. I don't know what's up with him lately, but I make a mental note to ask him about it later. I can't offer advice, given the fact that I'm a mess myself, but he needs to vent.

Theodas hands him a freshly made s'more, and while Archer generally stays away from sweets, he's too polite to refuse an offering from the chancellor. I've known Theodas for a while—again, thanks to time travel—so we're not as formal with each other. Though I can't imagine him being formal with anyone. He's got a carefree spirit that hasn't changed with age, and it makes him easy to get along with. When Rhys is around him, he seems more relaxed.

Archer is the picture of human suffering as he takes a bite of the s'more. I can't read minds, but his expression clearly states that this one dessert is going to set back his healthy diet by years. The man doesn't even eat *chocolate*. He told me once that he "doesn't find the taste appealing enough to warrant the calorie count." Clearly, he needs help.

"You should try to watch a Chinese drama," Theodas says. "They're kind of like soap operas, but they don't usually go on forever. There's a set amount of episodes from the get-go, so you're guaranteed a beginning and an ending. I'm a particular fan of—"

I don't catch what he says, because it's in Chinese. I didn't even know he spoke it, but I guess I shouldn't be surprised. Despite his general blasé attitude, at his core,

Theodas is a curious intellectual. His area of focus just happens to be movies, and apparently, he doesn't limit himself to English-language films.

"Do you think what Karina said about the timekeepers was accurate?" I ask. "That they can't see her because they can't see humans with magic?"

Siraye chimes in, nibbling on a graham cracker like a hamster. "It makes sense to me, but it does add another layer of complexity to the issue at hand."

Theodas nods in agreement. "If cultivation exists, who's to say other things don't? Pantheons of gods? The Matrix? We could all be in a simulation right now."

"Regardless, that hardly changes the timekeepers' plots to subjugate the realm, and Maria," Rhys points out. "Allowing war to break out between the mortal monsters and the timekeepers could cause massive amounts of collateral damage to the mortals without magic, and our own allies."

"A war is not something the timekeepers desire. They wish to rule." Siraye puts a hand on her brother's shoulder, offering a small smile. "We will not let them, of course. But some truebloods might not see things the same way. Even if they do, I imagine they will have...doubts...about working with a mortal monster such as Karina."

Karina isn't a great person, true, but I hardly think it's because of her mortal monster status. Does she even count as one now, without her powers?

"I want to speak with Karina," Theodas decides. "How are you going to keep her here, Mar?"

"You're asking *me*?" Karina doesn't seem to like me, and the feeling is mutual. I have no clue how I would convince her to stay here.

"You are the leader of this little group."

"No she isn't," Archer, Ophelia, Ava, and Celeste say at once. It makes me feel super good about myself.

Archer clears his throat. "No offense, Mar."

"Full offense. She's physically weak, and she has no experience coming up with a battle strategy," Ophelia snaps. "You don't even know how you're going to take care of Neil yet, do you?"

Ava gives me a sheepish smile. "Sorry, Mar, but Uncle Theodas is kind of the one pulling the strings with this one. You're kind of just…here. Which is totally cool, since I don't know who else I'd spend time with by the pool. All my other friends are gone. You know Georgia went to Greece with her family?"

"You might be the main character in this pathetic little story," Celeste rants at me, "but you're clearly not leadership material. You're just not smart enough, and clearly you aren't charismatic."

That's true, but she doesn't have to be such a jerk about it. I don't have the guts to say this to her face, of course, so I shoot her a very disapproving look instead.

"Celeste," Archer warns.

I shrug and immediately regret it. My back and shoulder haven't healed completely from the glass yet. "She's not wrong. And I don't view myself as a leader."

"At least you have a little self-awareness," she says snidely, which is her only tone of voice.

"*Thanks*."

"What does it matter if you can time travel? What have you done with that power that's so special? Nothing."

"You know what, Celeste? When someone thanks you sarcastically, usually that's a cue to shut up," I snap.

"Maria could be an excellent strategist," Rhys tells her indignantly, his expression cold enough to freeze an ice pop. "Her abilities are far greater than yours."

Well, I don't know how true that is. Rhys must have his rose-colored lenses on.

"Yeah. And she's got street smarts. Like Annie," Theodas adds with a grin.

"Please don't compare me to the redheaded orphan."

"This is gettin' off track," Provost Mathers drawls.

"Aw, don't worry, Richard. You're still my favorite redhead." Theodas goes to pet Mathers' hair, but the provost ducks away and straightens his bolo tie, trying to maintain a semblance of dignity.

"I would like to speak with Miss Swan," Mathers says, changing the subject. "She sounds like an interestin' character."

"Interesting" is a nice way to put it. "Bitchy" would be more accurate.

"It's been a long day," Theodas says. "Let's get some sleep and circle back tomorrow. There's still a lot of cleanup work to do, and the ferry's been destroyed, so we're all trapped here for now."

That's just great. At least Karina can't run off on her own with the ferry being out of service. She strikes me as the type who would do that.

Granted, I barely know the girl. But I don't need to have a long, overdrawn conversation to understand that she's got killer self-esteem. You can see it in the way she carries herself, the way she speaks with such self-assured confidence. I doubt she'd run away from anything. On the contrary, *I* want to run from *her*.

I've never gotten along with people who are as self-assured as her, because usually, they're extremely arrogant with no skills to back up their illusions of grandeur. Karina, on the other hand, might not have magic—but she's beautiful, and despite her claims of being powerless, she doesn't seem weak in any sense of the word. Meanwhile, I'm over here full of power (sort of) and have no idea how to utilize it.

It's hard to articulate that without sounding jealous, so I keep my mouth shut for now. I'm not jealous, by the way. Confidence is a double-edged sword, and it pairs well with recklessness.

When it's time for everyone to leave, Rhys stays behind. He helps put the chairs back and follows me into the house.

"How is your shoulder feeling?" he asks.

"It's not bleeding anymore." Thanks to shadowborn healing and painkillers, I'm doing fine. The island is a mess thanks to the ferals, but my family is safe, and Karina Swan is awake. Whether that's a good thing or a bad thing remains to be seen.

Joking aside, I successfully saved her without any big paradoxes. I don't actually know what a paradox would do, but since no black holes have opened up and no one's been erased (that I know of), I consider the mission a win.

Karina might not have her powers, and yeah, she's kind of annoying, but...I'm glad I saved her life. I've screwed up so many times during this whole saga, and this is one thing I succeeded in. Me, on my own. The Time Agents didn't rewind time or give me cryptic clues to point me in the right direction. I saved Karina myself, against the timekeepers' will.

Unlike Rhys, who I was "allowed" to save. I'm not sure what's in store for him yet. The Wisdom Tree told me that the timekeepers allowed us to find each other, because he's my soulmate. Maybe they think they can hold him hostage, like Neil did with my family?

"Allow me to take a better look," Rhys insists. "Your bandages should be changed before bed."

"Sure. There's a first aid kit in my room," I say cautiously. "Let's go downstairs."

To my surprise, he doesn't complain or give me a lecture about being unchaperoned in a room with a bed. Then again, I doubt he wants to get the first aid kid upstairs and have one of my family members, or worse, Karina, catch him examining my bare back.

Rhys is a considerate boyfriend. We've fallen into a natural rhythm, and I like that he isn't hesitant to show concern for me. Not just when I need medical attention — though that happens more frequently than I would prefer.

I'm not just talking about opening doors for me or pulling out a chair at the table for me, either. He'd do that for anyone — it's called having manners. But if there's only one cookie left, he'll let me have it. He lets me pick the movies, he always picks up right away when I call, and he offers to accompany me anywhere I want to go without complaint. It's like he'll put my interests before his own without thinking, every single time.

I know I shouldn't be complaining. But he's so perfect, and it's like his whole life revolves around me, and it makes me feel...

Uncomfortable.

Don't get me wrong; I don't want to break up with him. I don't even want to admit this aloud, because I know what everyone would say — I'm self-sabotaging and ungrateful. I'm reading way too far into a situation and picking at flaws that don't exist. But relationships are a two-way street, right?

Trust me, I've tried to think about ways to repay him. It's important for me to make him as happy as he makes me. But the only stuff I'm good at is sexual, and Rhys and I aren't at that stage yet. I don't even know how to bring it up. I've practiced in the mirror, but every iteration of that little speech seems like I'm pressuring him. I don't want to make him do something he doesn't want to do, and I certainly don't want to embarrass him. There's enough going on in my life without the added tension of romantic issues. So I've decided to keep quiet about it for the time being, until I've saved the world.

It's easier said than done.

We head downstairs and I turn on the lights. I sit on the bed and strip off my shirt while Rhys gets a box from the bathroom. If I delude myself enough, couldn't this situation be a little romantic? Hear me out. In *Beauty and the Beast*, didn't Belle fall for the furry because he got injured rescuing her?

But I'm starting to think Rhys is made of stone, and he's not moved by my braless, shirtless state at all. He sits behind me, his expression unchanging as he gently peels the gauze away. I wince as the cool air hits the open wound.

"Does it hurt?" he asks.

"I'll live."

"So it does hurt," he says, reading my mind as usual.

"Yeah," I relent. "I was trying to seem strong. I haven't really been strong enough over this whole ordeal. I need to make up for that."

"How do you figure?" he asks.

"I won't cry outside of therapy. I won't admit something

hurts. And I'll plunge headfirst into danger and use my massive muscles to solve issues," I reason. "It's a foolproof plan."

"I take back what I said earlier about you being an excellent strategist."

"Fair."

He dabs cream on my back and begins putting the new bandages on. "But I would never call you weak, despite what you may think."

"I understand that physical strength isn't the only type of strength, but it matters a hell of a lot in my current predicament," I say. "The others had a point. I have these magical abilities, which are great and all, but look what happened when I tried to use them today. My spell bag backfired on me. I could have gotten you and Archer killed."

He snorts. "You underestimate me."

"In any case," I say, giving him a pointed look, "everyone is looking at me to decide what to do next, and frankly, I'm drawing a blank. I don't know what the hell genius strategy I can come up with to make up for the fact that I'm not strong enough to defeat Neil or Astaroth, or even Nic, if I'm being totally honest."

And there it is: the thing that's been eating at me for weeks, ever since I came back from the Veil with Karina. The closer I get to my final confrontation with Neil, the more I feel like everything is going to end. I genuinely can't see a future for myself beyond this, can hardly picture an outcome where I survive with all my loved ones intact.

Admitting that is just depressing, so I've been ignoring my feelings and drowning my sorrows in smutty books and Rhys' sweet tea. (He must put crack in there or something, because it's the best damn sweet tea in the South. And he's not even Southern.)

"Tomorrow, things will settle," Rhys promises, which doesn't make me feel any better. "We are safe for now, and with Karina, we are one step closer to ending the time-keepers for good."

He finishes bandaging me up and turns his back to me, waiting for me to get dressed. I grab a soft pajama top from my drawer and slip it on with an unattractive grunt as I get it over my head.

"Thanks," I say, embarrassed that yet again, I've shown a pathetic side of myself to Rhys. I pause before asking, "Will you stay with me tonight?"

Rhys hesitates, not turning around. "Is that a good idea?"

"If you don't want to, that's fine," I say quickly, my heart falling.

"Your mother may get the wrong impression."

"I'm twenty, now," I admit, even though it kills me a little to say that out loud. "Isabelle adores you, and she won't care what we do."

She knows I've done a lot, with guys far less mature, in places way dirtier.

"I want to ensure she knows I respect you. And I would never take advantage of you while you remain injured," he explains.

"Alright," I relent, because there's nothing else that needs to be said. I'm not going to beg him to stay, even if I want to. Where would that get me?

After Rhys leaves, I flop down on my stomach and turn off the lights.

I shouldn't complain. My family is upstairs, sleeping

soundly. I have a boyfriend who loves me—even if he doesn't want to get intimate. And I have friends who would risk their lives to help me. Everything is better than I could have ever imagined.

So why aren't I happier?

CHAPTER FIVE

Allegra and I have had our ups and downs—mostly downs, lately—but I'm happy she's coming back to the house. One, because it means she's fully healed. Two, she's coming to reclaim her room, which means Karina won't be staying under my roof any longer to irritate me.

Trust me, I've dealt with my fair share of horrible roommates. The group home in middle school sucked. After that, several of my bullies' families fostered me. Granted, I'm pretty sure they bullied me *because* I lived with them. Comparatively, Karina isn't that bad. But she's still not exactly a bottle of sunshine.

My first impression of her was spot on—she's the most vain, shallow, self-absorbed person I've ever met. She takes forever in the bathroom, using the mirror to primp and talk to herself. She'll spend a good twenty minutes blabbering at her reflection, complimenting herself and brushing her hair. Her stomach is a black hole, and she spends most of the day ignoring any attempts at conversation by going off on her own. Her general lack of consideration and annoying way of speaking is enough to make me run out of the house in the morning to pick up Allegra. Anyone would prefer Sleeping Beauty to the Evil Queen.

Granted, things are still glaringly awkward between us. Thank god the school nurse is in the room briefing Allegra on what medications she needs to take—if it was just the two of us, I wouldn't know what to say.

Unfortunately, the nurse doesn't follow us out of the building, leaving us walking side by side in silence.

Part of the problem is that I don't know whether Allegra still hates me. She doesn't look me in the eye, and it's clear from the way she walks behind me that I'm not her first choice when it comes to escorts. She probably expected Rhys to come.

Rhys served her during the three years he was trapped without me in the present. I'm not quite sure what their relationship was. Rhys tells me it was purely platonic, and he views her as a friend. I believe him, but I don't know about Allegra's feelings.

Surprisingly, I'm not insecure about it—I guess therapy is paying off. Intimacy issues aside, Rhys would never stray, even if Allegra is prettier than me. And smarter. And, up until last semester, kinder.

With further thought, it's entirely possible Rhys is with me because he has lousy taste in women. Maybe that's his character flaw.

I'd rather not be in a conflict with Allegra again, and I don't want to cause her any pain. We're not best friends, but she was one of the few people who was genuinely nice to me when I first learned about magic. And even when she hated me, she had good reason to.

"I heard Karina woke up last night," Allegra says finally. I glance at her, slowing my pace.

Allegra resembles Neil; they have the same blonde hair and emerald-green eyes. It's no wonder she grew up believing him to be her father. But Neil is her father as much as he is mine and Nic's, which is to say, we share no DNA with him whatsoever. He created us all in a lab. Allegra and Nic were unsuitable to be wombs, with Nic not having one, and Allegra being too weak to carry a trueblood fetus. They were instead used as experiments and turned into truebloods themselves. But that's a whole 'nother can of worms.

"She did," I confirm. "She's staying in your room for now, but I can have her moved somewhere else."

Allegra frowns prettily, making me wonder why Rhys *isn't* in love with her instead. She has a sort of fragility about her, like a package that has a "handle with care" sticker on it. It makes you want to protect her. Me, on the other hand? I'm like a smashed box the postman throws on somebody's front porch during the holidays.

"That's not really my main concern," Allegra says. "Did you speak with her? Did she say anything interesting?"

"She said a lot of things, none of which were very pleasant." To put it mildly.

"Archer explained most of what happened to me, before ferals attacked the island. I haven't seen him in a few days."

"I didn't realize you were talking on a regular basis." They went out, and I've always wondered if there was anything left between them. Both Allegra and Archer have assured me there isn't, not that it's my business anymore. But Archer also slept with her last year, which may or may not have changed things.

I'd be happy for them if they got back together, but now that I know Archer better, I wonder if they're even compatible. I guess that's between them.

She shrugs, which doesn't tell me much of anything. "We're friends, Mar. But he asked me a lot of questions, too, and I'll tell you the same thing I told him. No, I didn't know about Neil's plans, or Nic's, for that matter. Neither of them told me exactly what was going on, and now I feel like an idiot."

"They both manipulated you, basically from birth. Anyone in your shoes would have believed them. You shouldn't beat yourself up about it."

"Neil spoke to Nic more than he spoke to me about these things. I suppose that's why Nic knew to take the Divinities Sword. Nic's been angry at Neil for a long time." She tries very hard, and succeeds, in not calling Neil her father anymore. But I know it must be killing her inside to lose both her parents. "Neil doesn't care about Nic, and while Nic is angry at Neil, he's not the first target. You are. He needs your blood to evolve, just like you need Astaroth's to attain your true form. Whatever that means."

Astaroth already force-fed me his blood once. He needs to do it again, as "preparation" for my body to be able to contain and give birth to a trueblood. Gross.

Neil didn't fully explain this to me, but after speaking with Rhys, we have a theory. The mortality rate for human women carrying shadowborn is high, because their mortal bodies can't always handle the pressure of housing a magical being. It might be the same case with me—the truebloods want to make sure I'm at peak power, so I don't die during birth. Of course, they don't care about my life because they like me. They want to be able to continually use my body. Real nice, isn't it?

"I'm concerned about Nic, too." He's already revealed his lack of morals and his blood magic abilities. He can raise the dead with ease, and I'm sure his silence means he's plotting something big. He won't be an easy opponent by any means. "Neil, at least, I can understand."

She quirked an eyebrow. "You understand him?"

"Yeah. I don't *relate*," I clarify quickly. "But he has a solid reason for doing what he's doing. It's horrible and even I know that it's immoral, but he kindly explained everything to me while he kept me hostage, like a supervillain at the end of a movie. Nic, on the other hand, is just unhinged."

He wants power, and he'll do pretty much anything to get it. I'm not sure what comes next, but he's a one-track-mind kind of guy. Whatever his plans are, they certainly don't involve keeping me alive after this whole ordeal. Once he gets what he wants, he'll tie up any loose ends—which means disposing of me.

Because I don't understand his motives beyond that, it's hard to predict what he'll do. While I'm concerned, the inability to plan around him has caused me to shelve any delusions of grandeur when it comes to defeating Nic. I'll think of something when the time comes, which is a nice way of saying I have no fucking clue how to handle him.

When Allegra and I arrive back home, it's nearly time for dinner. I spent most of the morning out of the house, goofing off to avoid Karina. At the library, I made a decision-tree and brainstormed what-if scenarios for defeating Neil. None of them turned out well—they all ended in my death, which was disheartening and unproductive. Still, that used up a lot of brainpower, and I barely ate.

Suffice to say, my stomach is grumbling when we walk through the front door. Rhys usually comes over to eat dinner with my family as a way to bond with them and make a good impression. He and Isabelle take turns cooking. I tried to break him of the habit—he's not working for Neil anymore and I don't expect him to serve me—but he seems to genuinely enjoy it. It's no surprise that he's in the kitchen now, apron on and spatula in hand.

What I don't expect is to see him cooking with Karina.

Jealousy isn't flattering on anyone, and it's especially ugly on me. I try to remind myself that it doesn't matter, but seeing her with him, all tall and gorgeous, makes me feel weird inside. Plus, she's modified the clothes I let her borrow from Allegra's closet, cutting up the skirt to barely cover her stupidly toned legs. You know, if you're in a coma for a month, you shouldn't have toned legs. You shouldn't have toned anything.

Admittedly, whatever they're cooking smells amazing. They're so busy talking they don't even notice us until we approach the kitchen counter. Isabelle stands by the back door, a huge smile on her face. David, who's usually holed up in his room, sits and chats with them.

That's what gets me the most. I've been trying to get David to come out of his room for weeks, and now, suddenly he's interested in being social? Because of a stranger?

Even the damn dog, Buck, sits by her feet, perfectly content. Of course, he growls when he sees *me*. Stupid dog.

"Maria, Allegra," Rhys greets. "How are you feeling?"

Allegra relaxes beside me, smiling at him. "I'm better now…but is that my skirt?"

"This is your skirt?" Karina asks, lifting the corner to

show it off. "God, I'm sorry. I thought this belonged to someone's dead grandmother."

"What?" I've never seen Allegra so flustered by blatant rudeness. Even if Karina kind of has a point, and Allegra's clothes are a bit...geriatric. But that's her style! It suits her. Karina? Not so much. "You must be Karina. I'm Allegra Abbott."

"Sorry about your skirt. But you have to admit, it's an improvement," Karina says unapologetically.

"Where did you get scissors and a sewing kit?" I ask her.

"Rhys had a sewing kit in the house, and I rummaged through your drawers to find the scissors in your room. You should really lock up your things. And maybe not keep your computer password on a Post-it by your desk."

If I weren't so hungry, I'd smack her. She's only human, right? Disregarding the strange way she appeared with the ferals, which she still hasn't quite explained. If she's only at mortal-level strength, I think I can take her.

Right after I eat.

"Karina was just cooking congee," David explains, pointing to the pot.

"Congee?"

"It's rice porridge," Karina explains.

"Like *Goldilocks and the Three Bears*?"

"If Goldilocks were Chinese, then sure."

I point to the thermostat. "It's almost a hundred degrees out."

"Are you going to eat it outside?" Karina asks, making me feel stupid.

"No."

"Then we're good," Karina says, returning her gaze to

the pot on the stove. "Rhys, hand me the spoon. I think it's done."

For the first time since we've been reunited, David actually sounds excited. And happy. "Karina was just telling us about the time she cut a feral open."

"Ah, perfect dinner conversation," Allegra says dryly. My only consolation is that Allegra seems more displeased than I am about Karina's attitude, which says something.

When we first met, a lot of girls didn't like Allegra, but she was never snide or rude to them. Not that she's being rude *now*, but the look on her face makes it easy to read between the lines. She doesn't like Karina at all. Finally, something we can agree on. It's like they say: the enemy of your enemy is your friend. In this case, Allegra and I might be on the fast track to becoming BFFs.

"There wasn't much to tell about the feral, anyway." Karina turns to me, and a chill creeps up my spine the moment we lock eyes. "Are you just going to stand there, or are you going to set the table?"

Rigidly, I do as she says. Not because she's ordering me around. I'm just hungry, or so I tell myself. I put the bowls and spoons out as Tasha comes in from the backyard.

"Something smells good," Tasha says, sitting down beside Isabelle.

"It's Karina's father's recipe," Isabelle supplies as Karina begins distributing the dishes. "If you like it, Mar, I can make it for you again. Karina was kind enough to give me the recipe."

It looks like slop you'd get in prison, to be honest. It's very bland and off-white, so I don't expect it to have much flavor. Unfortunately, I'm dead wrong. Somehow, it's thick and creamy, and the pieces of chicken melt in my mouth.

Damn it.

Karina gives me a satisfied smirk, and I want to slap it right off her face, but I'm too engrossed in her food.

Allegra, at least, manages to control herself. She eats slowly, as per usual, blowing on her spoon. "Karina, how did you end up dying a few months ago?"

The question is direct, and some might interpret it as rude—especially for Allegra. But Karina takes it in stride, unperturbed.

"A lot of people want to kill me," she says casually. "I don't take it to heart, though. When you're as pretty as I am, it's only natural for people to be jealous."

Tasha actually laughs, like it's a joke. Somehow, I don't think it is.

Karina swivels toward me, changing the subject. "Rhys says you're planning on killing Neil, but you haven't gotten very far, despite thinking it over for, like, months."

"I did not say that," Rhys corrects quickly, shooting her a glance.

"I mean, that was the gist."

"It hasn't even been twenty-four hours since you woke up," I point out. "Do *you* have any genius ideas?"

"Duh. Just storm their evil lair and slaughter them all." Karina's eyes dart to David. "I mean, uh, get rid of them."

"I watch PG-13 horror movies," he tells her. "You can say 'kill.'"

"It's not nice to kill people."

"But that's what you're going to do, isn't it?"

"Yes, but I feel the need to point out that it's not very nice. Do as I say, not as I do," she explains patiently. "I mean, I know it's wrong and all. I just don't care that much."

"Thanks for the clarification," I chime in, jealousy

spearing through me. "Good to know that you're a hypocrite."

"You and I can start a club. We'll get matching T-shirts and serve cookies at our monthly meetings," she replies, without missing a beat. "In all seriousness, Mar, you should really get on this already. I'm not sure what the hold-up is. Are you waiting for their heads to be served to you on a silver platter? And that's a figure of speech, David. If you want to send a message with a severed head, putting it in a box and sending it in the mail is a much better method."

"Don't listen to her," I tell my brother sternly.

"Why? I have, like, so much good advice. Besides, he reminds me of my little brother. Except David's less of a snot rag, and his hands aren't as grubby."

"How old are you again?"

"Twenty, and I'm just getting smarter with age. That's how I know you should really spring into action and start busting heads. What are you waiting for?"

I hate how she's oversimplifying things, implying that I'm incompetent. If I could just waltz in and slaughter Neil and the timekeepers, doesn't she think I would have done it by now? I'm not waiting idly by because I feel like it. "I can't spring into action without any plan. That's a suicide mission."

"But you're a time traveler."

"Discount that power. I can't use it against the timekeepers." I've only used it twice on my own, and it probably comes second nature to them. If we start fighting with time travel, things are going to get...messy. Like, the magical equivalent of nuclear warfare.

"Mar, be nice," Isabelle chides.

I don't want to play nice, especially not with Karina,

who seems to think she can handle this shit better than I can. I'm not the one who was nearly dying on a battlefield a few months ago. Technically, I was dying in a cemetery, but everything turned out okay in the end. I handled myself. Karina, on the other hand? Not so much. *I* saved *her.*

"If you think you're so amazing, why don't you help me?" I ask her, surprising even myself with my childish tone. But I hate the way she makes me feel, like I'm beneath her somehow.

Karina grabs another helping, leaving the entire table in suspense. I think she likes that—us hanging off her every word. "As I said, I can't help you. Don't get me wrong, I love a good fight, but I have my own problems to worry about. You know, not everything revolves around you."

Rhys gives me a look, as if to say, *Don't jump over the table and strangle her.*

Oh, the temptation is strong.

It takes a few seconds for me to regain my composure. "Your problems are bigger than the timekeepers?"

"I told you last night, truebloods aren't the only type of magical creature that exists. And where there is magic, there is danger. Do you really believe that your issues are more significant than everyone else's?" she challenges.

"Um, yeah, a little," I blurt. "When we're talking about world domination, I think that trumps most things."

"I need to find my family."

"You'd let the world burn in the meantime?"

Karina's tone lowers, and her valley girl way of speaking drops completely, just for a moment. "My family is my world. If they're not around, then everyone else can burn."

"YOU WOULD HAVE SAID THE SAME THING A FEW MONTHS ago," Rhys reminds me, sitting at my desk chair.

The sad thing is, Rhys is wrong—I don't know if I could choose my family over the entire world. I have no idea what I would choose, and frankly, neither does Karina. Sure, when it's a hypothetical, she can say it with utter conviction. But if she were in my shoes, making the decisions I have to make? I don't think she'd be so calm anymore.

Instead of explaining all that like a mature adult, I say, "I might have said something similar in the past, but I wouldn't have phrased it the way she did."

"In what way?"

"Every word out of her mouth is a conversation. Like she's trying to egg me on." Not to mention, she talks like a ditz, using "like" and "totally" far too often.

Tash pulls out a dress from my closet and holds it against herself in front of the mirror. "I don't get it. You and Karina seem pretty similar."

Is she high?

"Gross, I don't want to be compared to her," I say. "She's vain and selfish, and a total narcissist."

"Yeah. You're self-absorbed and bitchy, too, hence why I think you'd make a good pair," Tasha replies, though her voice doesn't hold any malice. "Rhys agrees with me, doesn't he?"

I turn to Rhys, who says in my defense, "You are not bitchy."

"Gee, thanks. Nice to know what you both really think

of me." Though I guess they're right. I have more bad traits than good.

"You're both destined to destroy the world, and you're both fighting against your fates. You also both lost your families. At least *we* were reunited, Mar," Tasha reminds me. "Oh, and Karina has a younger sister and brother, too. I think David and her brother are around the same age. She definitely has a sweet spot for him."

"Karina Swan is many things. Sweet is not one of them."

"She has moments of kindness," Rhys says, irking me further. How does he know she has moments of kindness? They barely know each other!

"She's not bubbly, but neither are you, Mar," Tasha says. "I kind of like her. She's really open and it's refreshing. What you see is what you get—there are no games when it comes to Karina."

"What I see is a shallow Barbie, but I'll take your word for it," I say. "Okay, maybe I'm being harsh. But you've got to admit, she gives off a creepy vibe."

"I felt it," Rhys admits. "When I look at her, there is an undercurrent of something dangerous. As if a serpent has wrapped around my spine."

"Or like bugs are crawling beneath your skin!" I add, relieved Rhys feels the same way I do. At least I'm not going crazy on top of everything. "I'm telling you, there's something wrong with Karina Swan."

"You're both being dramatic," Tasha declares.

"You disagree?" Rhys asks my sister.

"She seems like a normal person to me. And she's pretty interesting once you start talking to her. Plus, she saved my life."

That's news to me. "What do you mean she saved your life?"

"When the ferals were attacking campus, Karina woke up and fought one off. She let it bite her to protect David," Tash explains. "For some reason, she didn't turn into a feral herself. She might be immune to it, being a cultivator and all. But either way, she jumped in without any hesitation to save us. She can't be all bad."

Well, that's just great. I feel like a total bitch now.

I take a deep breath and go over the facts. Yeah, Karina might not have been who I expected. But she apparently saved my family, agreed to hear me out, and she explained a key component of the timekeepers that I hadn't considered. It's not like she's choosing not to help me out—she doesn't have powers anymore. All she would really be staying around for is to be a prop. If I were in her situation, I would probably be trying to get off the island and save my family, too.

"If you cannot feel the strange aura Maria and I do, perhaps it has something to do with our Veil magic reacting to her mortal monster status," Rhys guesses.

"Am I just overreacting about her?" I ask. "Do you like her?"

Rhys is careful when he answers. "She can be abrasive, but I think she is a good person. Perhaps the two of you can come to an agreement and get along."

Well, I do trust Rhys' opinion, as well as my sister's.

"Fine," I say. "I'll make nice, I guess. Where is Karina, anyway?"

Rhys looks awkwardly away. "Allegra requires a place to sleep. Karina offered to give up the room here, so at Theodas' insistence, she will be staying with him."

"With Theodas?" I repeat. "But you're staying with Theodas."

"Correct."

"So she's staying in your house, sleeping just down the hall."

Tasha smirks. "Someone's jealous," she sings.

"I'm not jealous," I snap, in a way that totally makes me sound jealous. But come on. Rhys can't be alone with me, but he'll let a random girl stay in the same house as him?

"It was not my decision," he says, patting my hand. "Rest assured, Maria — Theodas simply wants to keep an eye on Karina and avoid complications."

"Sure," I grumble. "Whatever you say."

CHAPTER SIX

"I'm not jealous, for the record," I insist, rummaging through the pantry in the science lab. The spell ingredients are kept in little glass jars, the labels written by hand in chicken scratch. The more complex the spell bags get, the more important it is to have very accurate measurements of ingredients. I learned that the hard way last week, after nearly blowing up the entire lab. Luckily, Mathers is here to supervise me. He insists that I don't practice blood magic without him. "I'm not."

"I never said you were," Provost Mathers replies. "I was thinkin' it."

"Well, stop it. I have a right to be upset. My boyfriend is living with some other woman!"

"Along with myself, my nephew, and the chancellor. Additionally, Siraye is often stoppin' by. It isn't as though Miss Swan will be stayin' in Rhys' room."

"I know," I grumble. But I still don't like it.

"Are you concerned he'll cheat?"

"No, Rhys would never betray me." He might not want

to sleep with me, but he wouldn't cheat. He'd just...stay with me in a loveless relationship out of pure obligation.

"Are you concerned she'll come onto him?"

Karina didn't seem very interested the other night, but that doesn't mean much. She could easily get bored and decide to hit on my boyfriend. Not that he would do anything about it. But the thought of them together pisses me off.

"Maybe. I don't know. I just don't like it. And I told Rhys as much. You know what he said?"

"Yes, I was—"

"He looks me dead in the eyes and says, 'I already told Theodas we should seek alternate arrangements, and he refused,'" I mimic.

"Well, it's a good impression," Mathers says weakly.

I huff, finally finding the ingredient I was looking for, and turn to the black-top table. In front of me is a food processor, baggies of herbs that kind of resemble weed, and a jar of animal blood. Yes, it looks as sketchy as it sounds.

"Have you talked to Karina yet?" I ask him.

"The chancellor wants to have a deeper conversation, but neither of us have spoken with her much. The cleanup efforts are takin' longer than expected, especially with the ferry bein' out of service. Most of the things on our to-do list were solved with magic, but there's some damage that requires human construction workers to be safe and compliant." He hesitates. "I chatted with Miss Swan briefly this mornin'. She's quite...abrasive."

"As abrasive as an industrial sander."

"Yes, well, if she can't help with our efforts, we might need to come up with a different plan of attack."

That's what I was dreading he'd say.

I don't *have* a different plan of attack. I had one hope, and Karina single-handedly shattered it. It's not her fault, but now I'm back to square one: moping, whining, and training until my mind and body are numb.

Sometimes, I wonder if it even matters. The timekeepers are time travelers, right? What if they choose to erase me and try again? Why am I fighting so hard if the statistical probability of success is not in my favor?

"The timekeepers won't use time travel against us yet," Mathers says, as if he's reading my mind. "Time is delicate and complex, and you haven't pushed them into a corner yet. You'll have to destroy them all at once to ensure your victory."

"They're beastbloods. It's entirely possible they have powers other than time travel," I point out.

"I know. But at a certain point, we can't get lost in the 'what ifs.' We have to work based on what we know, and do our best to have contingencies."

"Now you're starting to sound like Dr. Jones."

"She's still on campus?"

"No, we're doing teletherapy." Once a week, no exceptions. As you can probably tell, we've hit a bit of a roadblock when it comes to my self-esteem. "I've never really had to come up with battle plans, Provost. I'm not sure what to do. Can't I just leave all the thinking to you and Theodas, and I'll just be the bait?"

"You could," he relents, "but I don't think that's really what you want."

I can't be trusted with these important responsibilities! Shouldn't the people with actual battle experience be the ones calling the shots? But I have a feeling Theodas and Siraye are just as clueless as I am about this mess. It's been hundreds of years since they've had to fight, and Theodas in particular was more of a foot soldier than a strategist. Siraye was a princess, then an elf queen. While she didn't fight, she did make political decisions.

But deep down, I know they're just helping me out. The timekeepers, along with Neil and Astaroth, are my responsibility.

I turn on the food processor to mix the herbs. It's much more efficient than a mortar and pestle. Measuring the contents, I prepare the spell bags. I like to keep a supply of flash bangs and silver nets on hand, because the ingredients are cheap and the spell is easy to make and cast.

Blood magic exhausts its users with nasty side-effects, like throwing up blood, which makes practicing difficult. With Mathers watching me to make sure I don't overextend myself, I feel safe. And that's something I never thought I'd say about a teacher before. But Provost Mathers is a good guy, to put it in simple terms, and I trust him. He's always helped me, even when it didn't benefit him to do so. Hell, right now, it's putting him *and* his nephew in danger.

Speaking of Declan, his girlfriend Ava bursts into the room just as I finish up the last spell bag. It's not very smart to startle someone creating a spell bag. Thankfully, I don't spill any of the ingredients.

Ava is a petite blonde, and even when she glares at me, she's kind of adorable. I just want to put her in my pocket. She's the child of Iacar, one of Rhys' elf guards from the past. Despite her delicate features and slightly pointed ears —not as long and pointed as Rhys' or Theodas'—Ava can be pretty intense. She's a top marksman at school, and she's one of the friendliest people I've met here. So when she comes barreling in, slamming the door shut so hard I'm surprised it doesn't break off the hinges, I'm a little scared.

And then I look at her face, and I'm downright terrified.

"Mar!" she barks. "*What* is the meaning of this?"

"Declan told you that Karina is staying in the same house?" I guess, taking a few steps back to put some distance between us.

Ava's frown deepens and her hands go to her hips. "Yes. I can't believe you're letting that vixen stay under the same roof as our boyfriends."

"She's hardly a vixen," Mathers protests weakly, but Ava completely ignores him.

"Do you know what she's doing right now?"

"Well, considering I'm not clairvoyant, I can't say that I do," I reply, washing my hands. I can already tell this isn't going to be solved with a simple conversation, and even if that were the case, Lord knows I wouldn't be the one to talk her down from the ledge. "Karina isn't going to seduce Declan or Rhys. Sure, it makes me uncomfortable that she's staying with them. But maybe we should give her the benefit of doubt and—"

"She's in a bikini, borrowed from Ophelia, doing laps in the pool," Ava complains, her voice growing shrill. Note to self: do not say any jealous thoughts aloud. It will come off as annoying any way you spin it. "Do you know what she looks like in a bikini, Mar?"

Nope, but I can certainly picture it.

"Declan isn't interested in anyone but you," Mathers assures her, but it's a moot point.

"That doesn't mean I want him looking at some other girl's six-pack!" Ava exclaims, her hands flailing as she speaks. "Mar, Ophelia and Karina are friends now. Do you understand the implications of that?"

"They're a bitchy duo?" I guess.

Ava tugs on my arm. "You're done here, right? Come put a stop to this."

"I don't really care—"

Ava nearly pulls my arm out of its socket, her arms muscular from using a bow as her weapon of choice. Mathers is helpless to stop Hurricane Ava from sweeping in and taking me away. We run downstairs to the indoor pool beside the gym, where sure enough, Karina and Ophelia are. Rhys is nowhere in sight, and Declan is in the pool at the opposite end. Wait a minute.

"Isn't Declan on the swim team?" I ask.

"Yeah."

"It looks like he's training and not paying attention to Karina." Though I don't know how he isn't. Ava must really have her claws in him. They've been dating for about a year now, and anyone can tell he's head over heels. Ava's more difficult to read, but with this display of jealousy, I'm certain the feelings between the couple are mutual. Sadly, I'm more confident in their relationship than my own.

When Karina sees us, she swims over and gets out of the water. It's like I'm watching her in slow motion, with sexy music playing in the background. The water, the black bikini, the wet hair pushed back…it's a lot.

Ever since this series began, I've been surrounded by attractive people. Rhys, Archer, Allegra, Ophelia…everyone I've met has been good-looking! It's not fair. Unless, maybe, I just have really low standards for everyone else and high standards for myself?

No, that can't be it. I'm pretty sure I'm just cursed. Even

if I had a glow-up overnight, I wouldn't know what to do with myself. Maybe I'd be as conceited as Karina is and look at myself all day.

"Hey, Mar," Karina greets. "Hi, Ava."

"Aren't you cold?" Ophelia asks, looking up at her from the water. In typical Ophelia fashion, she doesn't acknowledge me or Ava, even though Ava's her roommate.

I look unabashedly at Karina's stomach, which doesn't even have a trace of a scar. She's got abs, though. How did she maintain abs when she's been in a coma? That doesn't even make sense!

At least she isn't angry. Unless she's hiding it and giving an Oscar-worthy performance. She looks at me curiously, and I realize I'm still in a dirty lab coat speckled with blood. That's not suspicious at all.

"It's frigid in here," Karina says, circling me like a shark. Water beads down her body, over all her lean but defined muscles. I try, and fail, to keep from ogling. "Do you need something?"

"No." I turn to Ava. "I'm good. Are you?"

"Nope!" Ava marches over to Declan, who barely notices her until she's standing right in front of him. "We're going."

"What? But I just got here."

She hauls him out of the water. I thought he'd be angry, but he leaves with a stupid smile on his face, not even concerned with Karina. Unfortunately, this means I'm left to stand in front of her, looking stupider than ever. How is it that every time we interact, I make a fool of myself?

Karina shrugs. "Well, if you don't need me, I'm going to get back in the water. I'm freezing my tits off."

Ironic, given that's the one area she's lacking.

Jeez, that was mean. Why does she bring out such bitchiness in me?

"Are you doing okay?" I ask. "I mean, with the room change and all?"

She offers a small smile, like she knows exactly why I'm asking. "The room is fine. And Ophelia was kind enough to lend me some clothes until I can get my own."

"We're a similar size," Ophelia says, "though Karina is taller than me by a few inches."

"Everything fits, but I don't fill out your tops as well," she acknowledges. "In any case, Mar, I'm looking to get out of your hair soon. Have you come up with a plan yet?"

"No," I say honestly. "Look, if you give me a little more time, I'll come up with something. I can't rush into things and risk lives unnecessarily. But I need to be concealed from the timekeepers. Can't you search for your family here? I'm sure there's some way to get into contact with them."

"It will be faster if I do things my way. I'm not afraid to get my hands dirty," she says. "Though I doubt that will happen. After I've tended to my own business, I'm going to help you."

"Really?"

She nods, jerking a thumb at Ophelia. "She convinced me. Thank her."

I'd rather not, especially with how smug Ophelia looks right now. I guess "smug" is better than "disgusted" or "bitchy," which are her usual expressions when speaking with me.

"My family is my priority," she reiterates. When she steps closer, our height difference becomes more pronounced. I look up, watching the water droplets trace her smooth cheeks. "Even if you saved my life... That's just the way it is. And nothing you say is going to change my mind."

RHYS DOESN'T THINK IT'S A GOOD IDEA TO TRAIN together, since we're dating and all, so Archer is still helping me out. He's being a good sport about it, even if he's not getting extra credit for helping me anymore.

I would never say this aloud, but I'm not sure how much this training is impacting my swordsmanship skills. I barely see improvement, and I move like I have two left feet. The sword has gotten lighter and easier to swing given my supernatural strength boost, but in terms of coordination, I'm a zero.

Archer, contrary to his name, is a good swordsman. He's not the best teacher. After showing me the basics, it's hard for him to lower himself to my level for effective sparring. He's been using a sword his whole life, so it's second nature to him. Even with self-imposed handicaps, he beats me in less than a minute.

The future is not looking good for me.

After we go a few rounds in the ring, we hang up the wooden swords and launch into strength training. The intensity of the workout makes my muscles burn, but at least my back and shoulder injuries are mostly healed.

"I think we're done for the day," Archer says, looking at his phone. "Two hours and twelve minutes without breaks. You're doing good, Mar."

Lip service. "Let's get dinner. All this exercise is making me hungry."

"You're not having dinner with Rhys? I thought you

were in your honeymoon phase," he comments, his tone teasing. "Ophelia and Ava were talking about it."

"So?"

"So, at your birthday party, you were giving each other googly eyes all night. It was gross."

"Gee, tell me how you really feel."

"Don't shoot the messenger."

"I love Rhys, but I have no interest in spending every waking moment with him," I say. I don't have much interest in talking about my relationship with my ex, either, even if we're friends now. It's just weird.

"Are you sure he feels the same?"

No. I can't tell what's going on with Rhys. He plays the role of the perfect boyfriend, but I wonder if his heart is really in it. He says and does all the right things. Am I just overthinking it?

The state of our relationship is up in the air, but I'll be damned if I let Archer of all people mention it. And I'm not afraid to tell him as much.

"Can you not?" I demand. "You're the last person to make comments about my relationship. Besides, I already texted Rhys and told him I'd be missing dinner to train. And I know you don't want to go back to your dorm yet."

If Archer comes home before ten, Celeste will wait up for him and insist on coming over. They won't sleep in the same bed, but because Archer lives in a dorm with room-mates, Celeste gets his bed while he sleeps on the floor or the couch downstairs.

Celeste is the girlfriend Archer's dad chose for him. They're not in love—if anything, it's a hate-hate relation-ship. And not in the enemies-to-lovers way. I've seen the way Celeste talks to him, and it's pretty clear they only have one thing in common: their parents are forcing them into a relationship. I don't understand the shadowborn politics behind it, but despite them clearly disliking each other, they won't break off the sham of a relationship. The difference is, Archer might not want to officially break up with Celeste, but he doesn't want to pretend to date her, either.

Celeste wants to go through the motions. She thinks, inevitably, they'll have to get together. And when they do, she's worried about her reputation. If people think that Archer is being forced to marry her, which he will be after college, apparently, then Celeste loses face. So she insists on taking Archer along to functions, making him go on dates, hold her hand, and so on and so forth.

I'm not a totally apathetic person, so from her perspective, I kind of get it. But Archer has made it clear he can't stand this behavior, and Celeste has made it clear she cares about everyone else's opinion on the matter but his.

"My dad has been hounding me to pick out a ring for her," Archer laments. "Celeste, thank God, is too picky when it comes to rings. She's been working with a designer for the past month, and they haven't made a single decision. My dad just wants it over and done with."

"That's so romantic," I say sarcastically. "Is your dad marrying her, or are you?"

"I wouldn't wish that on my worst enemy."

"Is Celeste your worst enemy?"

"No, but she's been talking more about how many kids we need to have. She won't do surrogacy—I have a feeling her parents told her she couldn't. Neither of us are too happy about it."

"That's insane." Archer is a year ahead of me and graduates next year, but from the way he talks about it, he'll be taking off his cap and gown and putting on a wedding tux. And what if Celeste doesn't want to have kids or get pregnant? "Why don't you just find a fake fiancée instead?"

Archer snorts. "Are you volunteering?"

"Hell no."

"I thought so. No, I've considered it, but there are two problems with that. One, I don't have anyone to do that with—they would have to be of a similar social standing for my father to approve," he explains. "Two, as much as she annoys me, I couldn't do that to Celeste. Aside from me, her father has been quite clear she doesn't have many other options around our same age range."

I roll to my feet. "What about Allegra?"

"What *about* Allegra?"

Sometimes, I think he's just playing dumb. I grab my bag and begin walking to the cafeteria, with Archer trailing close behind. "Well, you two had sex last year, right?"

"And I haven't talked to her about it since," he concludes.

"I'm just saying. You dated her in the past—wasn't she your first girlfriend? And then you went out with me, who is kind of her sister. Are you sure that you're not into her on some subconscious level?"

"When you and I had our little lapse in judgement, I didn't know you were sisters. And you're *not*, by the way," Archer says. "You're not biologically related, and you don't look anything alike."

"I got it. And don't think I missed your little 'lapse in judgement' comment. You're lucky you got to kiss me. I'm great at it."

We walk into the cafeteria and grab boxes of pre-prepared food from the fridge, since the kitchens are closed for the night. I get a sandwich, and Archer, true to form, gets a salad. We're the only ones in the entire food hall, so we pick a table in the middle of the room.

"Look, all I'm saying is, there was no real conclusion to whatever you and Allegra had. Maybe you should talk it out," I suggest.

"While I appreciate the fact that we can psychoanalyze my love life, I find it hilarious that you're giving me advice on romance."

"Why?"

"Because you and Rhys are so awkward together."

My jaw drops. "We are *not*. You just said we were making googly eyes at my birthday party!"

He crunches his salad, and I find it very difficult not to jump over the table and choke him with his wedge of iceberg lettuce. "You were, but that doesn't mean much. I don't even understand you both as a couple. What do you have in common? Like, interest-wise. Don't take this as a come-on, but you and I have more in common than you and him. Tasha told me that most of your 'dates' consist of watching movies in the family room."

"We're taking things slow," I defend hotly.

"Please. If I didn't know any better, I'd think he works for you."

"That's not true at all!" Now, I'm full-on lying about it. And I know it—I'm not in denial. I don't want Archer, of all people, to call me out. God, how embarrassing!

"He basically waits on you hand and foot," Archer says, not knowing when to shut up. "And you still haven't had sex yet, right?"

I can't believe he's bringing this up. I might have

mentioned it offhand once, but why does he remember? "Can we not talk about my sex life right now?"

"You mean, lack of a sex life?" he asks, no punches pulled. "I know this isn't what you want to hear, but as your friend, I need to be honest: you and Rhys are like puzzle pieces from two different boxes. You don't fit."

My heart sinks, and I know that on some level, he's right. Rhys and I don't make sense on paper. He's smart and calm, a picture of maturity and finesse. He understands art and is more well-read than I am. Meanwhile, I'm just...*me*. Not smart or well-read or worldly. I'm certainly not mature.

There's an undeniable connection between us, and I love him, but what if that's not enough?

"How interesting," Rhys says, his voice dripping with sarcasm as he approaches our table. I didn't even hear him walk in. "You think you can give Maria advice on her own interests?"

Oh no.

Archer stands up, glaring at Rhys' intrusion. "I'm just trying to help her. Unlike you."

This is bad. Rhys looks seriously pissed — I've never seen him so angry. And okay, it's a *tiny* bit hot. But mostly, it's dangerous. For Archer, that is. "My relationship with Maria is none of your business."

Archer shrinks back a little. "Mar and I were more intimate than you are with her now."

An idiot could tell that's the wrong thing to say.

Rhys is so caring and warm toward me, it's easy to forget that he's not that way with everyone. I mean, sure, he's polite toward most people, but in a cold, detached way. He doesn't make an effort to speak to Ophelia, for instance, when she's around. The feeling is mutual, on that front.

With Ava and Declan, Rhys is attentive, but they're more his acquaintances than his friends.

Rhys grabs Archer by the shirt collar and hauls him up. And, okay, it's admittedly hotter than I expect—I'll have to tell Tasha I was wrong, after all. But I can't even enjoy it, because I'm pretty sure Rhys could kill Archer. Judging by his expression, things aren't looking great for my friend here.

I jolt to my feet.

"God, you have a death wish or something," I tell Archer, putting a hand on Rhys' shoulder. "Let him go, Rhys. He's not worth it."

"Why should I?" he asks, eerily calm.

"Former elf princes don't have diplomatic immunity here," I joke, trying to lighten the mood. It's a blow to my ego when neither of them even cracks a smile. "Besides, Archer didn't mean anything by it, right?"

"I meant it, a hundred percent," Archer replies, because he doesn't know what's good for him.

I don't *enjoy* what happens next, but I can't say it's a surprise. Rhys easily escapes my grasp, punching Archer square in the face. Archer expects the blow, but he's not fast enough to dodge. Instead, he barrels into Rhys, knocking him down.

"Keep your opinions to yourself," Rhys snarls, grabbing a fistful of Archer's shirt.

"Mar is my friend. I'm not going to let her waste her time on you. What can you do for her?" Archer demands. Great. The one time he sticks up for himself, it has to involve my boyfriend. "You've made her a miserable, insecure mess ever since you started dating!"

Hey. I'm a miserable, insecure mess all on my own—Rhys doesn't get the credit for that!

The boys continue to exchange blows while I dial Mathers to come over here and pull them apart. Lord knows I'm not strong enough to do it myself, and with all the fists flying around, I don't need to get caught in the crosshairs.

Provost Mathers picks up immediately. "Mar?"

"Why does your voice sound weird?"

"We have a situation."

I don't like that tone. "What kind of situation?"

"Karina Swan is goin' to the mainland."

"What? The ferry isn't even running yet."

"I know. She's swimmin' across the channel."

CHAPTER SEVEN

R hys and Archer are still going at it as I leave. I shout,
"Don't kill each other," though I doubt they even
hear me over their very macho growling and grunting.

Men, I swear… So much posturing.

The minute I leave, I bet they're going to be best friends.
Okay, I bet they're going to stop fighting. I can't think of
even an alternate universe where Rhys and Archer would
become BFFs.

I race down to the beach, sprinting so fast I trip over a
rock, like every stupid character in a slasher. Thankfully,
Jason Voorhees isn't chasing after me with a machete. In
this situation, I'm the Jason—I'm chasing a girl into the
water and hoping I can capture her and drag her back to
shore. Granted, I don't plan on killing her, but she's going to
get a very stern talking-to!

I deserve this. When I found out David was kidnapped
by Nic, I swam across the channel to the mainland for him.
At least I took a waterproof bag of stuff with me. Karina
doesn't have anything.

She's either stupid or desperate, but my guess is a little of both. No offense, but she doesn't strike me as a rocket scientist. I'm not, either, but at least I don't say "like" and "totally" in every other sentence.

Mathers looks out on the pier with a frown. I nearly knock him over when I approach, stopping myself right before I run off the dock.

"Mar, what are you —"

Shoving my phone and wallet in Mathers' hands, I dive into the water.

Karina pauses her stride, her dark figure illuminated by rays of moonlight peeking through clouds. She treads in place while waiting for me to catch up, not showing any sign of exhaustion. The same black bikini from earlier clings to her body, the wet material leaving little to the imagination through the clear water. Her hair pools around her, fanned out perfectly like she's a goddamn mermaid. Droplets of water race down her face, tracing her cheeks.

"Are you crazy?" I gasp for breath. When I begin treading beside her, all the exhaustion hits me at once. My limbs feel like lead, and I have to rise to my back to stay afloat. It's more difficult to yell at her this way, but I'd rather not drown.

"Certifiable, not that it's any of your business," she shoots back. "I told you I need to find my family, didn't I?"

"You couldn't wait until the ferry was fixed?"

"No. I'm worried about them." Despite the admission, there's not a trace of vulnerability in her voice. "I can't wait for you to decide what to do. That could take months at your current speed."

She's right, and I hate it. I wasn't able to stop the brawl between Rhys and Archer, I can't make David happy, and I can't figure out what I'm going to do about Neil and Astaroth. But I don't need Karina to point that out, especially when she's just an outsider. Does she think she could do better in my situation?

It's frustrating as hell to come up with a plan to defeat Neil, especially when the one thing holding me back is the limitation of my powers. I should be able to solve everything with time travel and blood magic, two powerhouses that not many other people possess. And yet I'm stuck here, frozen with fear that my powers will have lasting consequences on those around me.

What does Karina know about *that*?

"This whole situation is difficult to navigate," I explode, my frustration winning over logic. "It's not like I want to fuck around twiddling my thumbs. If I'm too hasty and make a wrong move, the people I love could die. I'm not going to rush into a plan just because it suits you."

"I didn't ask you to! In fact, I believe I asked you to wait for me," she replies, matching my energy.

"Who knows how long you're going to take! You don't even have powers, aside from the power to piss me off!" Okay, I recognize that was uncalled for. But I can't take it back now.

Karina's gaze hardens, to my relief. I'm not sure what I'd do if she was actually hurt by my words. "If it were your family, wouldn't you do the same?"

"Well..." Damn it, I don't have a comeback for that.

She's right, and I know it, but I hate admitting it. It's hard for me to admit my mistakes to anyone, let alone Karina Swan. Until I have a set plan in place to fight the timekeepers, Karina will be waiting around, hoping the people she cares about are okay. But if I just let her go like this, will she even come back? We're strangers, and she's made it clear that she doesn't think she owes me anything for saving her life.

I'm working on empathy with Dr. Jones in therapy. She hasn't said it outright, but basically, I can be pretty up my own ass when it comes to trauma. Everyone has their own shit to deal with, and it's not any more or less significant than my own. But when I see people like Karina, who look impenetrable, it's hard for me to empathize. It feels like nothing can hurt her.

I don't actually know Karina well enough to make that judgment, though. And I can't keep her here against her will, clearly. Maybe it would be better to just give in to her, even though everything inside me screams not to.

"Where's your house?" I ask finally.

"South Carolina," she says.

"We can take a bus there. It's not that far. But we should wait for a ferry, so we can actually bring a bag of clothes and toiletries," I suggest. "How did you plan on getting back to South Carolina in a bikini?"

"Look at me. I'm hot as hell. I could have hitchhiked."

"That's the start of a horror movie. Or *Dateline*."

"I'm not scared." And she doesn't sound it, either. It's false bravado, or she's genuinely stupid. But I won't press the issue. "I need to get home. My family could be waiting for me. So could the people who did this to me."

She doesn't have to elaborate—I know she means the people who tried to kill her. Why she would want to rush into a trap, I'll never know.

"All the more reason for me to come along," I say. She doesn't have powers, anyway. I don't want to play body-guard, and I'm probably not qualified. But no matter how much she bugs me, I'm not going to let her die. I just went to the trouble of saving her. "I'll bring you to your house, so can we please swim back to shore and stop arguing? I'm tired, and it's freezing."

"Hmph. Whatever." Karina puts her arms under me, cradling me to her chest as she begins to swim to shore.

"What are you doing?" I sputter, automatically wrapping my arms around her neck.

"I'm swimming back to shore, obviously."

"I'm not a dumbass."

"Really? Could've fooled me."

"Why are you…carrying me?"

She doesn't answer, instead rolling her eyes. When she's finally able to stand up in the water, she lifts me with ease. I don't like being princess carried by Rhys, and I certainly don't like when Karina does it. Her arms are muscular, so it's not very comfortable, and I can see every detail of her stupidly perfect face up close.

Maybe I was too quick to judge her. She makes a strong first impression, but right now, when she's being quiet, I can almost sense something deeper beneath her shiny plastic surface.

"You're trembling like a leaf," she says, setting me down in the grass. Her muscles glisten, and her skin glows in the dim light of the lamp. It's just not fair. "You should probably shower and go to bed. You look awful."

"Thanks," I say dryly.

"You're welcome."

It's like she's making it her personal mission to get under my skin. "I was being sarcastic."

"I know, and I was ignoring you. But now that you've gone and pointed it out, I suppose I should tell you some-

89

thing," Karina says, putting a hand on her hip. "Sarcasm isn't a replacement for a personality."

I take back everything even remotely nice I've ever thought about her. She sucks.

"You were reckless," Rhys says, holding a bag of frozen peas to his black eye. After a quick shower and change of clothes, I went to check on him at home. I didn't expect to be reprimanded, especially by a guy who got into a fight with my ex-whatever about *nothing*.

Let me tell you, having two hot guys fight over you is not nearly as fun as one would expect. In part because I missed practically the entire fight.

"I'm fine. See? All in one piece. And, unlike you, I came out unscathed," I say pointedly.

"Kinsey looks worse," Rhys grumbles.

"I'm sure he does," I soothe, rubbing his arm. Everyone else is upstairs, asleep, leaving us alone in the kitchen. The house is laid out like mine, and since Rhys practically runs both kitchens, everything is kept clean and labeled. "Have you ever considered that maybe whaling on Archer like that wasn't the best course of action?"

"It was the most appropriate response, Maria."

"That's very mature," I say. "Look, I'm not saying that I could've figured out a better way, but come on. You're not jealous, are you? It's not like I would ever go back to him, and I'm certain he doesn't want me."

"Do you agree with what he was saying? About us?" Rhys asks quietly.

He can tell when I'm lying, so I try to skirt around the

issue. "Archer doesn't know anything about romance. Look at his previous relationship history. He's not in any place to say anything."

"I did not inquire about his qualifications. I want to know what *you* think, Maria."

I should tell him now. Pour it all out. He's practically begging me to. But when I look into his eyes, I find myself unable to say anything. Because, selfishly, I know that if I talk about our problems, if I acknowledge them at all, it makes them real. And I don't want this thing between us to end, even if I'm second-guessing myself when Rhys is around. Being without him would be worse than being with him and feeling...like this.

"That's not important," I say. "Karina wants to leave Kingsmarch. And I can't blame her, even if she went about it in a troublesome way. But we got into an argument about it." I tell him all about diving into the water and swimming to her, only to have her carry me back. How infantilizing.

"You convinced her to stay," Rhys concludes. Leave it to him to see the bright side in all this.

"Somehow," I confirm.

Rhys pulls the bag of peas from his eye, wincing. "Is it swollen?"

"A bit, but it should go away quickly." Trueblood healing is faster than shadowborn healing. "It makes you look tough."

"You enjoy this?" he asks incredulously.

"Your totally uncalled-for fight with Archer? Not in the least," I say flatly. "But you two have some pent-up anger between you, God knows why."

"Yes, the gods know—the reason is you," he replies. "I thought perhaps you would have found it entertaining.

91

Tasha mentioned you had been reading an overabundance of romance novels lately."

"Stop talking to Tasha about me," I warn playfully, though I'm dead serious. I don't need them gossiping about me. My boyfriend and my best friend? A dangerous duo. "I might like love triangles in books, but I'm an adult now. I understand that books are different from real life. And besides, this whole macho, possessive thing is just not you."

"I will not talk about this anymore with your sister, but she already showed me some of the titles of the books you enjoy. Are you disappointed that I am not like the men in your...bodice rippers?"

I cringe, making a mental note to password-protect my Kindle and hide my paperbacks. "Please never say that phrase again. I like *you*, so I don't need you to change anything about yourself. Except, you know, doing your best to avoid conversations like this in the future. Because if I have to say one more cliché line to you about how I like you for who you are, I'm going to die of embarrassment. Is that what you want?"

He cracks a smile. "That would be one way to immortalize your name."

"As the first person to die of embarrassment? Yeah, that's a real achievement!"

"I will keep your words in mind. But it's getting late, and I should probably walk you back home."

I hesitate. I want more from him than an escort home. In the past, we talked a lot about ourselves and got to know each other on an intimate level. When I returned to the present, that stopped. Of course things had to change, given our circumstances, but now we're at a standstill.

I'm wondering if this was too good to be true. Are our

intimacy issues the beginning of the end? He wants a companion, someone who understands him. But maybe he doesn't want me beyond that.

And if I tell him all this, what do I expect? Will he feel obligated to have sex with me just because I ask? Whenever I've told him my insecurities in the past, he's been quick to reassure me. He says all the right things, or what *should* be the right things. But nothing makes me feel better.

In all the books I read, relationships are easy. Even forbidden romances have a clear villain, an antagonist as an obstacle to overcome. But I'm my own worst enemy.

Rhys puts the peas back into the freezer and opens the front door. "Shall we head out?"

"I think I need some time to cool down and think on my own," I say, because I'm clearly a coward. "But I'll text you when I get back, okay?"

I'm not lying, but the urge to deceive him stirs guilt in the pit of my stomach. And, like all my current issues, I need time to solve them.

It's funny, in a not-so-funny way. I'm supposed to be a time traveler, and yet, time is controlling me.

CHAPTER EIGHT

J ust my luck: the ferry is still broken. Or does this count as Karina's misfortune? It's hard to tell, because everyone I ask about her tells me she's doing amazing. Half the island is singing her praises, most of which are related to her appearance.

That's beside the point. The ferals did quite a bit of damage, and apparently the ferry needs parts shipped from Nevada. It won't be operational for another two or three days.

Karina hasn't made any other escape attempts, at least, but I do my best to stay out of her way. I don't know how to interact with her, and frankly, I don't feel like being interrogated by her about my plans. So I keep as busy as possible, which completely counters my need-to-think strategy. Between training with Archer and Mathers, I've volunteered to help with cleanup efforts around Kingsmarch. There's still debris across campus, so I'm given a plastic bag and one of those pointy metal spears to pick up trash. We don't want to pollute the ocean more than it already is.

My "good luck" streak is continuing, since I'm stuck with Ophelia as my cleanup buddy.

"How do you think this got here?" she asks, using her tongs to pick up a lacy black bra. She's also volunteered to help out, though I don't think she would have if she'd known we'd be put in the same group.

"Someone was having sex on the beach," I reply, because that's the most obvious answer.

"You sound jealous."

"I'm not jealous," I say defensively. "Jealous of what? Sand up my butt? Have *you* ever had sex on a beach, Ophelia? Because it's very unpleasant. Especially when your partner is Jeremy Frye, who doesn't stop even when you get stung by a jellyfish in the middle."

I still have a little scar on my ass. Unfortunately, that wasn't the last time I got frisky at summer camp, *or* the last time I was with Jeremy. Thank goodness my taste in men has improved.

"You're disgusting." Ophelia wrinkles her nose and drops the bra in her trash bag. "Sometimes, I still can't believe you're such a whore. Your face is so plain and unassuming."

"Thanks, that's sweet of you."

"When you were Mary Alice, at least it made sense."

I don't think I've ever explained my characters to Ophelia, but she probably heard about it from Archer. Instead of launching into an explanation or excuse, I stick to the truth: "You hated me as Mary Alice."

"I didn't hate you. You were just irritatingly nice," she clarifies. "But you're more annoying now than you were then."

This conversation is really boosting my ego. "Can we just get back to work now?"

"I'm just saying, most of your stories have to do with sex or bullies. I already know you're an unlikable slut; mix it up a little."

I know she's telling the truth, but the accusatory tone is completely unnecessary.

"This is the most you've ever talked to me," I point out. "How do you know most of my stories have to do with sex and bullying?"

"You talk to Archer about it. Don't you have any real hobbies, aside from getting laid? Or reading about fictional characters getting laid?"

"Why does everyone seem to know my book preferences nowadays!" I exclaim.

"It's called a book cover. Buy some next time you're thinking about reading something called *Tempting the Duke* in public and giggling like a pervert."

"I don't giggle like a pervert!" I throw my hands up in the air. "You are the last person I want to talk to about this."

"Why? Because I'm gay?" she challenges.

"Because we're not even friends."

Ophelia picks up a plastic bottle with her tongs. "So basically, I'm right—you don't have hobbies. Good to know."

"I have plenty of hobbies, but reading just happens to be one of them! Besides, most college students don't have a lot of time on their hands, or money. I used to work at the campus library, so the books were free. What are your hobbies, hotshot?"

"I have hobbies," she says.

"Being a bitch doesn't count."

"Pot, meet kettle."

Weirdly enough, this is the closest I've ever felt to being friends with Ophelia.

"I like riding my bike in the morning," she elaborates. "When the sun is just about to rise and there's still dew on the grass. It makes me feel like I'm in a movie, and I'm going to have a meet-cute with a gorgeous girl."

"You ride your bike every morning? You get up before sunrise?" Is that why she's so cranky?

Before she can reply—and I can tell from the look in her eye she has some biting remark about me—Lilly Hardwicke walks toward us. Watching her approach is like watching a tornado spin toward you. I'm locked in place, despite wanting to run the hell away.

Lilly is a demon shadowborn, and unfortunately, her sister was murdered right before I came to Southeastern. Not by me. Someone framed me, and I managed to prove my innocence...but she still blames me.

We probably wouldn't have gotten along anyway, but she went out of her way to make my life miserable. I haven't seen her much since—it helps that we don't live together anymore. I avoid her when I can.

Ophelia pales, and before Lilly can reach us, she drops her things and walks away. I thought Ophelia and Lilly were on good terms, but apparently not.

"Hi, Lilly," I greet, scooping Ophelia's tongs up from the sand. "Here to help clean?"

"Provost Mathers told me to tell you that your tutoring session is cancelled today," she says dryly.

"Thanks." I didn't expect her to actually pass along a message to me. Maybe she's changed.

She looks me up and down, her lips pursed. "This suits you. Picking up trash, I mean."

"Someone's gotta do it."

"I don't know what Provost Mathers, or anyone else, sees in you."

"Uh, potential?" I guess. "Spunk? Grit?"

She doesn't like any of my answers. "What did you do to your eyes?"

"Nothing," I say dumbly. It's not the best comeback; I always seem to think of those ten minutes after the fact. "Well, thanks for the message, I guess."

She doesn't take the hint to leave, so I turn away from her, starting back down the beach.

"You and that Swan girl belong together," she calls after me, needing to have the last word. Before I can turn around and ask her what she means, she's gone.

AFTER MY THIRD BURNT BANANA BREAD, I GIVE UP. IT'S time to call it quits and admit the cold, hard (or in this case, hot and crispy) truth: I'm a horrible baker.

I've never been good at it. My home ec teacher called Isabelle during my senior year of high school and told her to never allow me to use the oven at home, for fear I'd set the place on fire. If you ask me, she should have been the drama teacher instead.

"I don't think you should give him banana bread anyway," Tasha comments, whacking one of the loaves with a wooden spoon. "It sends the wrong message."

"Or the right message. Just poorly executed," Karina

adds, because of course, I can't mess up without her bearing witness to it.

It's bad enough that she's enthralled my little brother, who practically trips over his own two feet when she's around. Now, Tasha's taken a liking to her, too. Which makes Tasha friends with Ophelia *and* Karina. All she needs to do is add Lilly to her squad, and they can start an "I Hate Mar" club.

Karina and Tash are here to criticize, not to help. That much was made clear when they started giving each other mani-pedis, which, according to Karina, I desperately need. I believe her exact words were, "Nice nails would be a welcome distraction from your gross hands." As you can probably tell, we're getting along great.

The ferry is going to be up and running tomorrow, so before I leave, I want to do something for Rhys. He's always doing stuff for me, and if he won't let me return the favor sexually, I figure baking is the next best thing.

There's a lot between us left unsaid, mostly my fault, and I feel like I owe it to him somehow to act more like a traditional girlfriend would. You know, give him something he can enjoy. At this rate, all I'm going to be giving him is diarrhea.

"What would you do, then?" I ask both of them, ripping the oven mitts off and tossing them on the kitchen counter. "If you're such geniuses, help me out!"

"Let me tell you something, Mar: you can't just dance around the issue when it comes to dating. You have to be upfront," Karina says, as if she's in any place to give me advice. "Tell him outright that you want to have sex. No euphemisms, no bullshit, and no childish attempts to hint at it. He won't understand unless you properly communicate."

"What do you know?"

"Um, I have a boyfriend."

"You have a boyfriend?" It's hard to believe, because despite being pretty, she's a real piece of work. The same can't be said of me—I'm *not* pretty and I'm a real piece of work.

"Yes," Karina says, like it should be obvious. "He just doesn't know it yet."

Tasha laughs, but yet again, I don't think she's kidding.

"I'm not trying to get Rhys to sleep with me. I just want to do something nice for him," I insist.

"Sure. And 'denial' is just a river in Egypt." Karina blows on her freshly painted pink nails. "You can take my advice or leave it, but you know I'm right. Even if you refuse to admit it."

"You have plenty of other skills you could use to impress him," Tasha chimes in.

"Like what?"

"You can…" Her face scrunches. "You're good at…"

"You could get him a sexy coupon book," Karina suggests. "It's sort of lame, but you seem like the kind of person to enjoy that."

"Are all your compliments backhanded, or only the ones aimed at me?"

"I'm not being backhanded, I'm being honest. Something you're apparently not well versed in."

I let out a frustrated sigh. "I'll do something. I don't know what yet, but I'll figure it out. Now, are your nails too wet to help me clean up?"

"Yes," the girls say in unison.

Ugh.

This has been a full-day endeavor, and all I've learned is

that I suck at crafts. I can make spell bags with animal blood and herbs, but knitting a scarf? I almost poked my eye out.

"You're stressing way too much about this," Tasha says. "It's not his birthday or anything. He'll be happy with anything you give him."

"He looks at you like you're the best thing to happen since sliced bread," Karina adds, which isn't even true. Rhys is indifferent to sliced bread; he prefers baguettes. "If you can't bake, or knit, or draw, or cook..."

"Thank you for listing all my flaws; that's so helpful."

She gives me a stern look. "Well, what *are* you good at? Being self-deprecating and whiny?"

"I don't know! That's the problem. What would you do if you were in my shoes?"

"Cry, because your shoes are dead ugly," Karina says. "But my boyfriend and I don't have the same type of relationship you do. We've been at it like rabbits since day one."

Ew.

Tasha gets up and takes out a bottle of wine from the pantry. "We don't have glasses, but I think a little bit of relaxation is in order, ladies."

"I don't think that's the best idea," I say warily.

"Maybe it will get the creative juices flowing," Karina suggests, popping the cork. "You're too uptight."

"You never used to be," Tasha adds, but it's not a criticism. "Come on. Why don't we watch some romcoms and see what we can come up with?"

"Alright," I agree begrudgingly.

I don't know why we have so much wine on hand, but we go through three entire bottles. As soon as we finish one, Karina and Tasha produce another. Karina doesn't drink as much as Tasha and me, but she laughs and jokes right along-side us. We end up in my bed, reading passages from my romance novels aloud and writing down ideas. But we're too drunk to actually write by hand, so Tasha and I use the voice-to-text option on our phones. That's our third mistake. (The first was the wine, and the second was doing this in the presence of Karina Swan.)

I'm not sure exactly when we fall asleep, but after we open the third bottle of wine, everything is a blur. The next thing I know, I'm waking up in bed with Karina and Tash beside me, a tangle of limbs.

My head pounds as the morning light pours in, and I roll over with a moan. The knocking doesn't stop, and it takes a minute to realize it's real, not just inside my head. The door flings open and Ava storms inside, padding down the stairs with a look of sheer panic on her face. Ophelia is behind her wearing a stony expression.

"Mar, get up," Ava says urgently, shaking my arm.

I groan and sit up, my hair a rat's nest. Tasha and Karina stir beside me, pulling the covers over their heads and crawling into the darkness of the sheets.

"What?" I ask groggily. "How did you get inside?"

"David let us in," Ava says. "It's bad, Mar. It's *really* bad."

"Have ferals attacked the island?"

"No, it's worse than that," Ophelia warns.

"You're freaking me out," I tell her, sobering up a little bit as I blink the sleep from my eyes.

Ava hands me her phone, open to her school email. "You sent this out at four this morning."

I scan the contents of the email, and it immediately snaps me out of my sleepy fog. I knew I overdid it last night, but I figured it was a "pass out and get hungover" kind of thing.

"No," I murmur. Suddenly, I feel like vomiting. "Oh God, *no*."

I wrote a letter to Rhys. Or I spoke it; it's possible this was a text-to-speech mishap. Either way, I don't remember anything. And yet, the evidence is laid bare: the most embarrassing, cringy, humiliating chunk of prose I could have ever written is immortalized via email. Not even Ophelia makes a joke about it, which goes to show how awkward it is. There's nothing she could possibly say to make this worse.

"Why didn't you stop me?" I seethe, smacking the Tasha-sized lump beside me. "Oh my God."

Tasha peeks out from under the covers and looks at the phone in Ava's hand. She scans the screen, scrolling through the entire email before commenting. "Wow, that's bad. But it's not like Ava is going to show anyone, right? Don't freak out."

"I won't be showing anyone else," Ava confirms, "but you didn't just send it to me, Mar. You sent it to every single student."

CHAPTER NINE

Writing a pornographic letter to my boyfriend and sending it out to the entire student body wasn't on my bingo card for this year. Mostly because that is an insane thing to do, even when drunk.

"You know a lot of ways to describe genitalia. Maybe that's your hidden skill," Karina suggests, because she's just oh so helpful. "You have to admit, this is totally hilarious. I don't even know you that well, but I can tell that this shit would only happen to you. I mean, writing it is bad enough. Sending it out to the entire student body? You must be, like, super embarrassed right now."

"I'm glad one of us is finding humor in the situation," I sulk. "Wait. Actually, I'm not glad. If I'm miserable, you should be, too!"

"I've already paid my dues." She doesn't elaborate, and I don't think it would be polite to pry. Then again, I don't think it's very polite for her to laugh. Maybe in the future I'll be able to joke about it, but right now, the wound is too fresh.

The ferry started working again this morning, and I got on first thing with Karina in tow. I would have swum across the channel again if it meant running away from my problems. Packing took two minutes, and while I could've used a shower and a change of clothes, I couldn't risk running into Rhys. I'll need time, and maybe more alcohol, before I face him again.

I told Tash what was happening and promised to keep her updated, so it's not like I'm pulling a total disappearing act. But I'd really like to avoid talking to him, or anyone else for that matter, about this.

Karina says, "If you die of embarrassment, I can just toss your body overboard and make my way to South Carolina by myself."

I have no idea if she's joking.

I want to forget about the letter, but every time I close my eyes, I see it like a bad nightmare. Can I just sink into a hole and hide for a thousand years, please? Or, better yet, get into a time prison and lose myself in time and space? That would be fabulous!

"I wish I were an ostrich," I mutter.

Karina chuckles. "You can't just stick your head in the sand and forget this is happening."

"No. I want to be an ostrich, because an ostrich is a bird, and birds can't write emails."

I can't comprehend how my alcohol-addled brain came up with that smut! I don't even have plausible deniability — it was sent from my email address and signed by me. Attaching the letter to this book would get it banned, so I'm not going to show it to you. It starts off kind of romantic and cheesy, but it gets progressively worse as the paragraphs go on, ending in a naughty poem. I rhymed "pogo stick" with "throbbing d…"

"It's okay," Karina reassures me, patting my back. "I've been there, too."

"Really? You wrote your boyfriend a dirty letter before?"

"Oh, God no. Who the hell writes letters nowadays?" She wrinkles her nose. "I mean, I know what it's like to have the whole school mocking you. Of course, they were only making fun of me because of something beyond my control. They're mocking you as a direct result of your own drunk actions."

"Was that supposed to make me feel better? Because it didn't."

"That's not really my fault." She twirls a long strand of hair around her finger and leans over the rail, looking at the ocean below. I fight my instincts to push her overboard, shifting toward the shade of an overhang. The weather is beautiful, albeit hot. A perfect day to have my social life crashing down.

Leaving in such a rush wasn't the smartest plan, but I couldn't stand another minute on the island. People were already beginning to respond back to that email, and trust me, they weren't saying good things.

Not that I really care what strangers think. But I don't know if I'm up for facing Theodas, Provost Mathers, or even Archer after what I wrote. On another note, I feel like the letter was a total violation of Rhys' privacy. Now, our relationship is at the forefront of people's minds, and everyone knows my dirty thoughts. What if people assume we're already doing those kinds of wild things I wrote about? I can handle people thinking I'm a slut, but it's a different story with Rhys.

Not only are strangers evaluating my sex life and mental health, but my family probably saw that email, too. Even though they weren't directly on the mailing list, I imagine someone has shown them...which means that I've completely ruined Rhys' efforts to maintain a healthy distance in front of my family.

I steal a glance at Karina, who can't stop grinning. And why should she? She's getting exactly what she wanted: to go home.

Tash was right about one thing, though: Karina is very upfront with her emotions. I can respect that, but it's a bit uncomfortable at times, because I'm the total opposite. I'm used to play-acting, to pretending to be someone I'm not. It's actually a lot of effort for me to be honest and open with others. Words aren't easy to take back. Even with Archer, who I would consider a friend, there are times when I have to fight the instinct to lie. I've been doing it for so long, it's like I need deprogramming. I guess that's what Dr. Jones is for.

The ability to be honest is a privilege. Maybe Karina had a great support system growing up, or a lot of friends who allowed her to say whatever she wanted with no real consequences. She *has* mentioned being popular in high school; she probably had a whole crew of simpering students waiting on her hand and foot.

These fundamental differences in our pasts and personalities make it difficult for us to see eye-to-eye. The only reason we're even remotely getting along now, if you want to call it that, is because our interests align. She wants to go back home, and I want to get the hell off Kingsmarch.

The ferry finally docks, and we walk to the bus station down the street. Neither of us have a car, and I can't ask Rhys to borrow his. That would go against the whole "avoiding him" plan. So the bus is the next best option.

South Carolina isn't that far, anyway. It should take three hours, plus time for transfers. Unfortunately, there's not a direct bus to her small town.

Karina says we can sleep over at her house while she gets organized. She also promises that if her father is home, he'll cook us up a feast. I have no problem staying in South Carolina for a few days, if it means running from my problems.

The bus stop is an uncovered bench outside, with a faded map on the side of the ticket booth. I check which line we have to take before purchasing the tickets. Luckily, we don't have to wait on the benches in the sun for too long. The bus pulls up after a few minutes.

Once Karina and I settle in the back, she asks, "Have you heard from Rhys?"

"Not yet." I texted him a quick note that I would be leaving with Karina, but nothing more. We can have a long conversation when I get back, assuming I figure out what to say. I'm sure he'll know all the right things to tell me, which is pretty sad, now that I think about it. Rhys has been in far fewer relationships than I have. Actually, I'm pretty sure this is the *only* relationship he's been in.

I've had flings, so I should know better how to handle this, right? But so far, all I've done is act super insecure, jealous, childish, and...

Oh crap.

"If my little brother isn't at home, he might still be at Northeastern," Karina says. "I'll have to go there next, you know. He shouldn't be left on his own for too long. And not to mention, my friends are probably worried about me."

"Let's just focus on getting to your house first. Who knows, he might be there. If he's not, you can't freak out," I warn her sternly. "Imagining the worst-case scenario won't do any good."

Karina snorts. "Who are you, my therapist?"

The bus ride goes on, and I eventually fall asleep against the window. Unfortunately, I can't even escape the letter in my dreams. A humanoid envelope literally chases me, reading the contents of my email over and over again no matter where I hide.

The bus comes to an abrupt stop, rousing us both from sleep. With a relieved sigh, I look up. We're in the middle of a busy town, but something in my gut nags at me. I check my phone and open the maps app to see where we are exactly, and my stomach falls.

We're on the correct bus, sort of. The number is the same, but it can either go north or south from Georgia. We needed to go north, to South Carolina. We went south, to Florida.

"This is just a hypothetical, but if we ended up on the wrong bus, what would you do?" I ask Karina.

She squints at me. "Is this your not-so-cute way of telling me that we're on the wrong bus?"

"We wanted the northbound bus. We took the south-bound bus. I am so sorry," I apologize, because it's my own stupid mistake. It's a miracle that I picked the right bus number, but I probably should have checked with the driver before boarding.

Karina shrugs. "It's no big deal. Where are we?"

"According to my phone, Jacksonville, Florida."

"Jacksonville? That's not that far at all," she says, waving her hand. "You're so dramatic. Look, let's get off the bus, grab some food—on your dime—and get back on another bus heading north."

"You're really not mad?" I ask.

"No. It's an honest mistake," she says. "Besides, I have enough tools in my emotional toolbox to handle this maturely. Now, let's go."

Emotional toolbox? Seriously? She sounds like a cheesy self-help book. But at least she's not angry.

Karina drags me from the bus, leading the way outside toward the town center. The palmetto trees provide some shade from the blistering sun, and I'm ready to duck into a store for air conditioning. It's even hotter here than it is on Kingsmarch!

Despite plenty of food options, Karina zeroes in on a dilapidated diner. Once she knows what she wants, she goes for it—at least we're not wasting time debating on where to eat.

Checking my phone, I note two missed calls from Rhys, accompanied by a text: Stay safe. We'll talk when you get back.

The absence of his usual line-mouth emoji sends me into a dark spiral of overthinking. I should've just turned off notifications because now I'm going to be psychoanalyzing that for the next few days. I quickly check Reddit to see what this could mean, but none of the posts are reassuring.

As we approach the diner, I notice bold, inappropriate graffiti spray-painted on its outer wall. Karina is too ravenous to care about the aesthetics. We're seated almost immediately upon entering and given five-page menus. Karina picks out what she wants without hesitation, and I make a panic decision which I immediately regret when our food comes. I should have gotten a side order of pancakes. They smell great.

"So what did Rhys say?" Karina asks, cutting right through her short stack of chocolate-chip pancakes.

"I didn't talk to Rhys," I say, not technically a lie.

"I know he texted you. I looked at your phone screen over your shoulder."

"Can you refrain from doing that?"

She gives a noncommittal grunt and slurps her large Coke, no ice.

"Rhys just said we'll talk when I get back. It's no big deal." Or so I tell myself.

"Why did you write the letter in the first place?" she probes.

"I don't know. I was drunk. Why didn't you stop me?"

"It's funny that you think I would've stopped you, even if I hadn't been asleep at the time."

I throw my hands up in the air. "I don't know. Do we really need to have this conversation? Why do you care anyway? We're not friends or anything."

It's harsh, but Karina doesn't take offense. "I like Rhys. He seems like a good guy. And you're not so bad either, even if you're rude. And no, I'm not going to share my pancakes with you."

"I didn't ask you to."

"You didn't have to. It's written on your face."

Damn. They smell great. "And what do you mean, you like Rhys?"

"Men and women can be friends," she informs me, her tone condescending. "We live in the same house, and he talks to me. Alright, I overhear stuff, too. Even if that weren't the case, I'm not blind. You totally have issues."

"We don't have issues," I say defensively.

"You totally do. Add 'poor communication' to the top of that list. Look, I know we're not *friends*," Karina says in a matter-of-fact way, "but you're kind of like a speeding train headed right into a wall. It's not like I want you to crash. I can't look away, though."

We finish the rest of the meal in silence. When the check comes by, Karina is still eating, so I put some cash down and grab my bag.

"I'm going to the bathroom," I tell her. "Take your time. I left enough for the bill plus tip."

Her mouth is filled with food, so she gives me a thumbs-up.

I swing by the bathroom, washing my hands before slipping out the back door to call Isabelle. She answers almost immediately.

"Mar? Where are you?" she asks, panic edging into her voice.

"I'm in Florida right now. I took the wrong bus and ended up here," I explain. "We're getting back on the road soon, but I wanted to check in with you. I'll call you when we reach Karina's house."

"Honey, you really should have stayed. I know you wanted to get away from everything, but it really isn't that bad."

Confirmation she knows about the letter. Fabulous. "It's *horrifying*, Isabelle. You remember when that stupid bitch Allison Dolittle told everyone I had an STD? This is worse."

"I haven't read it," she says, to my utter relief. "Your sister gave me a hint about its contents. Remember, though: you're an adult, and you were drunk when you wrote that. Most of the recipients are strangers. They'll mind their own business, and if not, who cares? They aren't worth your time."

"I'm more concerned about my friends' opinions," I admit. "Just…don't read it, okay?"

"Everything will settle, I promise."

"Talk to you later." I hang up, stowing my phone back in my bag. But as soon as I turn around, I'm staring down the barrel of a gun.

Ever since Luke was killed by Neil's gun, I've been…not *afraid*, but I certainly don't like them. And having one pointed at my face freezes me up.

I don't register what the man is trying to tell me, and when he takes my bag from my arms, I don't fight him. He knocks the cold metal against my forehead and runs, but I'm too stunned to do anything.

Slowly, once he's out of sight, I walk back into the diner. Karina stands by the front door, her arms crossed. As I push the door open, she looks sharply at me.

"What took you so long?" she asks.

"I was just robbed," I say blankly.

"*What*? What are you talking about?"

"He took everything. My backpack, my supplies, my money, and my phone."

"You're joking."

"I'm afraid I'm not joking."

"You're saying that were stranded here with no money, no phone, and no way to get back to Georgia, much less South Carolina."

"Yes, that would be correct," I snap. "Thanks so much for laying out what I already know!"

"Well, that's just fucking great."

CHAPTER TEN

"You are the most useless time traveler I've ever met."

"Tell me something I don't know," I snap, my temper rising with the heat outside. God, if Georgia is hot in the summer, Jacksonville is miserable.

We're both on edge, but she doesn't have to be so condescending about it. And she certainly doesn't need to remind me of my mistakes. I'm well aware of my shortcomings.

"You can't use your powers unless you open a rift," Karina says, pointing up a finger. "You're scared to change anything and cause a paradox. You can't travel too close to a past version of yourself."

"Correct. Thanks for making me feel even more hopeless than I already do. Are we done now?"

"Not quite. You got robbed even though you can use blood magic and have trained in self-defense."

Her words sting more than I care to admit. She's right; I am useless. My inability to control my powers effectively has gotten us into this situation. But it's not like I can tell her why I froze up. I don't want to get into the whole Luke situation at the moment.

"Not as much hand-to-hand," I grumble.

She rolls her eyes so hard I'm shocked they don't fall out of her skull. "Okay. Okay, this is fixable."

"What approach do you recommend we take to do that?"

"Call someone from the school, tell them what happened, and—"

"I don't know anyone's phone number," I say flatly. "It's all stored in my cell phone."

"We can find a library and email—"

"Passwords are also in my phone."

Karina is seconds away from slapping me, but she manages to hold herself back. "Alright. We can get money another way."

"How?" I demand. "How are you possibly going to make money with nothing but the clothes on your back?"

We walk toward the boardwalk, both of us dejected. People crowd the beach, most of them teenagers and college students off for the summer. There's even a stage to the left, way down the boardwalk, with bands playing. The music isn't great, but then, I might just be in a horrible mood.

"We just need to make some quick cash," Karina says.

I glance around, desperate for an idea. My eyes land on a sign near the boardwalk that reads, "Win Cash Prizes—Competitions Today!" Maybe we can earn our way home by winning one of these contests…or at least get enough money to buy bus tickets.

"Hey," I call out to Karina, who's already halfway across the parking lot. "Maybe we can try our luck with these competitions. You know, make some cash."

She turns back and looks at me, her expression dubious. "Fine. You wait here. I'll go win us some money. Meet you at the big clock in a few hours, okay?"

"Wait, what?" I ask, taken aback. "You're going off alone? We could both—"

"Just stay put, Mar. I'll handle this." Karina rolls her eyes. "Trust me on this. I'm going to make some money, and let you just sit down and relax. Try to enjoy the beach."

"How exactly am I supposed to relax?"

"It's not really my problem." With that, she stalks off toward the boardwalk without another word, leaving me feeling patronized and seething with indignation.

This is just great. I can't leave without her, and I have no idea how I'm going to get money. I'm not going to steal, mostly because getting caught would be more costly than not. But I am clueless about how Karina will earn cash.

I walk along the crowded boardwalk, scanning the shops for any possible way to scrounge up enough cash. But none of the competitions look very promising. A wet T-shirt contest? *Please.* And beach volleyball? I'd probably sprain something, or get hit in the face with the ball.

"Maria."

I spin around, taking two staggering steps back. Maria is a common name, and I'm not unused to hearing it, but the voice sounded like it was right in my ear. I don't see anyone, though.

It could have just been someone passing by, talking about someone named Maria. But I quicken my pace anyway, unsure of where I'm headed until I hear it again, this time in front of me.

"Maria."

It's like a hiss of air.

Suddenly, I'm running like a crazy person into the first shop I see, tripping over my own two feet to get away. I push the door open and walk inside, only to be met with absolute darkness.

I can make out something down the hall—a mirror, though the reflection is hazy. Even when I get closer, able to reach out and touch it, my reflection is warped.

Wow, this is a scene straight from a nightmare. I'd like to wake up now, please!

"Maria." My reflection speaks to me, her mouth moving like a puppet's would, up and down without forming words. She reaches out to me, pressing a bloody palm to the mirror's surface. This can't be real. It's got to be some sort of weird hallucination brought on by stress and lack of sleep.

But then the reflection speaks again, its voice low. I don't sound like that, do I? "Don't be afraid, Maria. We're here to help you."

We?

"Just let us help you." A forked tongue darts from my reflection's lips, and at this point, I've seen enough. I book it out of the room, bursting out the door and straight into…

Well, *not* the boardwalk.

Not the white hallway, either.

This hallway is silver, like someone overdid it on the spray paint. Even the orchids on the table are silver. The walls are lined with doors, but each has a metal grate over top, like jail cells. Additionally, they're covered in chains. Any moment now, Pinhead is going to pop out and torture me, isn't he? Ugh, I should not have let Tasha convince me to watch *Hellraiser* with her!

Since none of the doors will open, and the door I came

from disappeared, I wander the hallway, looking for a way out. Walking feels endless, and everything looks the same no matter how far I go. There's no sense of time here. There's... nothing here, really. Just emptiness.

I can't wait around forever. In these hallways, time doesn't pass the same way it does in the mortal realm.

I grab one of the orchid vases and throw it against the wall. It shatters, thankfully, and I take one of the shards, cutting my palm open. Desperate times call for desperate measures. I know if I stay another minute in this hallway, I'm going to lose my mind.

Working purely on instinct, I stand in front of a bare piece of wall and begin smearing my blood on it.

"Maria."

I turn toward the voice. A snake slithers toward me— no, a *timekeeper*. It's metallic scales shimmer as it twists toward me, rolling as it surges forward. It's not speaking out loud, I realize; it's speaking directly into my mind.

"We've been waiting for you, Maria."

"The feeling isn't mutual," I assure it.

"Sooner or later, you will submit to us. You cannot escape your fate."

"Joke's on you. I'm great at running from my problems. I've got twenty years of practice, buddy." I finish my drawing—a doorway—and shove hard on the wall as the snake moves closer. The wall gives way, leaving me stumbling back to the boardwalk.

I land on my knees, out of breath and still bleeding. Several people look at me as they pass, but no one says a word.

On shaking legs, I stand and dust myself off. I walk to

the water and wash the blood from my hands, my thoughts muddled. What was that place? And how did the time-keeper know where to find me?

KARINA WAITS FOR ME AT A TABLE NEAR THE BIG CLOCK, her fingers tapping against the metal table.

"Hey," I call out, settling into the seat across from her. "Any success on your end?"

"You could say that," she says, sliding a wad of cash across the table. "I managed to make enough money for us to get on a bus to Savannah."

"Seriously?" I ask, unable to keep the surprise out of my voice. "How did you do that?"

"I entered the beach volleyball competition they were holding down at the boardwalk."

"Beach volleyball?" I scoff, feeling the sting of my own embarrassment and failure intensify. "You can't be serious."

"As a heart attack. But does it really matter?" she counters, raising an eyebrow. "Point is, we're not stranded anymore."

"Unbelievable," I mumble. Of course Karina would waltz into a competition and come out victorious. "Well, good job. I'm glad one of us managed to pull their weight."

"I know. I'm just, like, super athletic." She eyes me curiously. "What have you been up to?"

"It doesn't matter," I say, unable to even begin to explain. "Thanks for coming through. Now let's just get on that bus and put this godforsaken place behind us."

"Agreed," Karina says as we gather our things and head for the bus station.

A part of me is grateful for her resourcefulness, but another part can't help but feel a pang of jealousy. I got us into this mess, and I couldn't get us out. How pathetic is that?

"Hey, don't look so glum," she teases, nudging me with her elbow. "We all have our strengths and weaknesses. You may not be book smart or street smart, but you've got other talents."

"Like what?" I snap, irked by her flippant comment. Suddenly, all the stress and fear bubble over inside me. I'm hungry and tired and I can't moderate what I'm saying at all. "Being a mental nutcase who can't even make use of her time-travel powers? Getting robbed? Yeah, those are really useful skills."

"See, Mar, that's your problem. You have this whole guilty ego thing going on," Karina says, waving her hand in my face. "It's like you want to take on the world by yourself even though you have perfectly good people around to help you. It's not a weakness to rely on others."

"No, but it's weakness when you rely on others to the point where you're basically useless. I need to learn how to do things for myself and handle my own issues."

"That's really admirable, but you should probably say that about things that don't have such dire consequences. Like, for example, if you can't cook, which you definitely can't, you should take a cooking class or something."

"I would love to say something like that, but all of the choices that I've been making so far have dire consequences. I've been stuck in this hell of life and death decisions and I'm frankly terrified to move forward."

Why do I always have to look so pathetic in front of

Karina? I don't know if it's the heat or the hunger or my emotional state, but I feel sick.

Karina's smile falters, and she pats my back awkwardly. "Look, let's just get out of here, okay?"

I nod, embarrassed by my outbursts. "I'm ready to go."

CHAPTER ELEVEN

The automatic doors of the Marriott hotel swoosh open as Karina and I step into the lobby, a welcome contrast to the muggy Savannah heat outside. The smell of fresh flowers and air conditioning greets us like an oasis, the plush carpet feeling just right under my feet. It's a relief that the hotel is only two blocks from the bus station; otherwise, I think I might've just dropped dead on the sidewalk.

"Okay, what do we do now?" I ask, rubbing the back of my neck.

"We need to find a way to contact your friends at Southeastern and let them know where we are. They'll come get us."

"How do you plan on doing that?"

"Easy." She scans the room, her eyes locking on the young guy sitting at the front desk. "There, we'll just ask him for a computer."

"You think you can just walk up to him and ask? He's probably going to kick us out if he discovers we aren't staying here," I whisper.

"Please. He's not going to kick us out." Karina struts over to the front desk. I hang back, watching as she flashes the receptionist her best smile. The hotel employee, a young man with shaggy brown hair, visibly straightens up as she approaches.

"Hi there," Karina purrs, leaning in to rest her elbows on the counter. "I was wondering if you could help us out? My friend and I really need to use a computer for a sec. It's an emergency."

"Uh, well…" the guy stammers, clearly struggling to maintain eye contact as he surreptitiously scans her from head to toe. "I'm not really supposed to let guests use the staff computers."

"We're kind of in trouble, and we just need to contact our friends so they can come rescue us. Otherwise, we'll be stranded here," she says.

The receptionist seems to be weighing his options, but it's obvious that he's fighting a losing battle. "Alright. You can come behind the desk."

"Thanks, you're a lifesaver!" she exclaims. The poor guy practically melts on the spot.

As Karina sweet-talks her way into his good graces, I glance around the lobby, feeling suddenly exposed. The mood is tense, and I have this suspicion that someone—or something—is observing us. I stuff my hands in my pockets and try to suppress a shudder. But maybe I'm still freaked out about the silver hallway.

"Alright, Mar, you're up," Karina calls over her shoulder, motioning for me to join her at the computer.

"Here's the hotel's phone number, just in case any of your friends need to call you guys while you wait. And feel free to hang out in the lobby as long as you need," the young man says, handing me a business card.

"Thank you," I reply. "We appreciate it."

"Anytime," he says, his gaze lingering on Karina unabashedly.

My fingers fly over the keys as I type out a frantic email.

SUBJECT: MAR AND KARINA NEED HELP, ABSOLUTELY **urgent, please do not ignore**

Hey guys,

It's Mar from some random guy's email address. Karina and I are stranded in Savannah with no money, no phones, and no way to get home. Please call this number to reach us. We will be waiting in the hotel lobby.

Mar

"Done," I announce, stepping away from the computer. "Now what?"

"See? That wasn't so hard, was it? And look" — she gestures to the front desk guy, who's practically drooling over her — "we even made a new friend."

"Great," I deadpan, trying not to roll my eyes. "Just what we need right now: more distractions."

But leave it to Karina to find a lovesick guy anywhere she goes.

The phone rings, and I practically jump out of my skin. Karina gasps, surprised, which seems like a major overreaction. The receptionist answers with his usual professional greeting, and I strain to hear the conversation while trying not to look too eager.

"Of course, one moment please," he says, covering the receiver with his hand and turning to me. "It's for you."

I grab the phone, my heart pounding in my chest. "Hello?"

"Maria!" Rhys' voice comes through the line, and I let out a breath. "Are you alright?"

"Hey," I greet him, trying to keep my voice steady despite the sudden surge of emotion. "Um, we're at a Marriott in Savannah." I rattle off the address from the business card.

"Stay there," Rhys instructs firmly. "I am going to pack some essentials for you both, and then I will drive over. Return the phone to the hotel employee, and I will arrange a room for you."

"Thanks, Rhys." I sigh, swallowing down the lump in my throat. "See you soon."

I hand the phone back to the front desk guy, who begins tapping on his computer. He hangs up after a few minutes and looks up. "Your friend just booked a suite for you. We'll have it ready in about an hour. The cleaning staff still have to go and prep everything, but help yourselves to coffee or tea."

"Thank you," Karina chirps. "See? Everything is going to be fine. Rhys is on his way, and we're going to be in a hotel room soon. Think of the hot shower and warm bed waiting for you."

But an hour quickly turns into two, with the cleaning staff being way behind on their work. It's tourist season, so we're lucky we got a room at all.

"Mar, chill out. Rhys will be here soon," Karina says

dismissively, not even bothering to look at me as she continues to flirt shamelessly with the front desk guy.

I know she means well, but her nonchalance is starting to grate on my nerves. It's as if she doesn't understand the gravity of our situation, or maybe she just chooses to ignore it.

The silence of the lobby only amplifies my anxiety, making me feel vulnerable and exposed. I've never been one for waiting around.

"Alright, that's it. I need some air," I mutter to myself, unable to take another second of the lobby's oppressive silence. Karina doesn't even glance my way. Pushing open the glass doors, I step outside.

The night is cool, and I wrap my arms around myself and start walking down the empty sidewalk, trying to focus on the sound of my footsteps echoing against the pavement rather than on my racing thoughts.

I stop for a moment, leaning against a lamppost, its dim light flickering overhead. I need to get my shit together before Rhys comes. He didn't sound angry on the phone, but the last thing I want is for him to get here and for us to have a big fight about the letter...and about me running away again.

Still, I need to put on my big-girl pants and face it. Regardless of my drunken state, I can't change the fact that I sent that stupid, smutty email to half the school, addressed to Rhys. Thinking about it makes me cringe.

Just as I'm about to head back inside, I get that prickly feeling on the back of my neck—the one that tells me I'm being watched. I glance around, trying to see if there's anyone lurking in the shadows. But the only thing I spot is a flash of silver in the bushes nearby. It's too metallic, too unnatural. The hair on my arms stands on end, and my gut twists itself into knots.

Okay, so either I'm losing my mind, or something weird is going on. Both options suck, but they can be dealt with. They aren't unmanageable, right?

With a deep breath, I push off the lamppost and start walking back toward the hotel lobby. But just as I'm about to reach the doors, I glance over my shoulder one last time.

A silver snake darts from the bushes and lunges at me. Instinctively, I leap aside, barely avoiding its fangs. Unfortunately, I land on my ass.

"Shit!" I gasp, my heart pounding in my chest. The snake isn't a timekeeper—it's not silver, it's burgundy—but it's not normal. Mostly because it *talks* to me.

"You think you can escape me?" the snake hisses, slithering closer to me. "You are the final key, Maria Rochester. The girl who should not exist."

That voice.

It's not a timekeeper. When the timekeepers speak, their voices are tinny in my head. This one, though? It's a single voice, and the snake is actually speaking aloud. Moreover, it sounds very familiar.

"I gave you life. You should be happy to return the favor, girl. You are the timekeeper's daughter; you belong to them."

"I never thought I'd have to say this, but I refuse to lay magic snake eggs!" It just sounds painful, honestly. What if they're big? Like dinosaur eggs? Are snakes genetically related to the dinosaurs? Are there even dinosaurs in the Veil?

Rising to my feet, my heart thumps in my chest as I

weigh my options. I could run, but the snake is pretty fast. I could kill it, but I don't have a weapon. Or I could—

Someone screams from behind me. A blonde girl, her hair in complete disarray, runs toward me on the sidewalk brandishing a knife. There's a real-life jump-scare for you.

Why can't my life be more like *Outlander*? Instead, all I get is *Evil Dead*!

The fact that she's in a nightgown and slippers makes the whole thing even more unsettling. Where did she come from? She jumps on top of me, slamming me into the pavement.

"You make things too easy," she says with a laugh. The snake hisses beside me, but doesn't move to attack or stop her. Are they working together? "He said you'd be here. He said you needed this."

"I don't know who 'he' is, but I doubt very much he knows what I need," I say, my mind racing for an escape plan. But every opening seems to be blocked by either the snake or the crazed blonde girl. Her laughter echoes around me.

"Feisty, aren't you?" She grins wickedly, enjoying herself. "But it won't save you."

I bite into my arm, hard enough to draw blood. The blonde only laughs as I grab a flower with shaking hands, attempting to summon enough magic to launch an attack. My mind is too scrambled to come up with anything, unfortunately—that's the drawback of having no spell bags on me. God, why did I have to get robbed?

"Nice try," she drawls, digging her nails into my skin and forcing my arms to my side. "But you'll have to do better than that."

"Believe me, I'm working on it," I lie. I can't work on

anything when I can't move. And this bitch is freakishly strong—there's no way she's human. I need to end this, and fast.

"You should have just complied," the blonde says, running her blade across my cheek, drawing blood. "You shouldn't have made Lord Astaroth chase you."

Lord Astaroth? Crap, is she in his cult, too?

She licks the blood from the edge of the knife, her lips curling into a satisfied smile. "Ah, truly delicious."

"Can we stop with this blood drinking? None of us are vampires; this goes against so many health codes!" I exclaim.

"You can fight and fight," she says coldly, tightening her grip on my throat. "But it won't matter in the end. You were born for one purpose."

As I struggle for breath, my mind races for a solution. I can't let this be the end. I've come too far, fought too hard, to let some crazy cultist and a talking snake get the best of me.

Just as my vision starts to fade completely, the front door of the hotel slides open, and Karina charges out. The blonde's grip on my throat slackens for a moment, giving me a much-needed gulp of air. She lifts her head, fury contorting her features. With a snarl, she flings her knife at Karina.

Karina dodges out of the way without much effort. "Your aim sucks."

Probably not a good idea to taunt the blonde. She's too strong to be human, and she's with a talking snake, which makes her twice as dangerous. The timekeepers want me alive, but Karina? As their weakness, they probably want to kill her on sight.

Taking advantage of the distraction, I struggle to regain my breath, my lungs greedily inhaling oxygen. I don't have long before the blonde turns her attention back to me. Before I can even formulate a plan, the red snake darts toward Karina, its fangs bared, aiming straight for her throat.

As the snake lunges for her, she pulls a pen out from her back pocket and jams it right in the snake's eye. The movement is so quick, so fluid, it takes me a few seconds of staring at the twitching snake on the ground to understand exactly what just happened.

"I've learned that if you stab something in the eye deep enough, you can probably kill it," Karina informs me. She stomps on the snake's head for good measure, a crunch echoing through the empty parking lot. "That was a good pen, though."

The blonde on top of me snarls like an animal. "What have you done to him?"

"Hey, don't look at me! She's the one who killed it!" I shout.

The blonde drops a spell bag from her sleeve and wipes it on my face, my blood activating it. She smiles at me before disappearing, the weight lifting off my chest as smoke fills the air. She doesn't teleport, but the smoke screen gives her enough time to get away unseen before I can get up.

A flicker of disappointment passes over Karina's face, but it disappears as she offers me a hand. "Our room is ready, which is just as well, because you smell horrible."

"Really?" I ask, my voice shaking. "That's what you're worried about right now?"

"Chill, Mar," she says, turning to face me with an air of

confidence that makes me feel even smaller than I already do. "We won, didn't we?"

We? No. "We" didn't win. She did, all on her own.

"Sure," I mumble, averting my gaze from her piercing dark grey eyes. "But who knows when or where they'll strike next? How did they even find me with you around?"

"Who knows?" Karina shrugs.

"You know, it wouldn't kill you to show a little concern."

"Mar, you're alive and only slightly worse for wear," she points out, crossing her arms. "I'd say we're doing pretty well, all things considered."

"Thanks to you," I admit begrudgingly.

"You're welcome, by the way," she says. "Like it or not, we need to rely on each other right now. You can either sit around and pout about it, or you can deal with it."

"Fine," I agree, taking one last look at the lifeless snake before following her back inside. But the question remains: how the hell did they find me?

Chapter Twelve

The shower doesn't wash away my bad luck, no matter how hard I scrub. It does wash off the six hours of bus smell on me.

I linger in the shower until my fingertips start to wrinkle, delaying the inevitable uncomfortable conversation I have to have with Rhys. But the anticipation only makes my anxiety-fueled stomachache worse.

To summarize, today I have: sent a pornographic letter to my boyfriend, along with the rest of the school; escaped via bus, but took the wrong one, and ended up in Jacksonville, Florida; got robbed; saw a creepy reflection of myself in the mirror; and got beat up by a stranger and nearly choked to death. Talking about the letter with Rhys is a shitty way to end a shitty day. But you know what they say—the sun will come out tomorrow.

Oh my God, someone needs to stop me from quoting *Annie*.

This hotel room is not the ideal setting for an awkward

conversation. Rhys got a suite, which means Karina has her own room, but the walls are thin and offer little privacy.

When I'm finally ready and washed up, I walk into the living room where Rhys is setting up the pullout couch. There are two bedrooms separate from the living area, and Karina and I each get one. The beds are queen-sized, but Rhys won't share with me.

He hasn't mentioned the letter yet, and part of me thinks I'm an idiot for even bringing it up. If he's not going to mention it, shouldn't I just let it go? But the more mature part of me, which I didn't know existed until just now, thinks that if I continue to put off talking to him about this, we're both going end up miserable.

And I know I've been pretty insufferable about it, in the confines of my own thoughts. I just have to rip the Band-Aid off.

"Do you need help with that?" I ask, moving the cushions from the couch away so he can pull out the mattress.

"I am not quite sure how this works," he admits. Together, we get the rest of the cushions off and pull out the metal frame. There's a sheet already on, so all we have to do is arrange some blankets and pillows for him.

"You know, this mattress looks a little bit thin. There's a perfectly good bed in my room for both of us," I suggest. *Way to be subtle.* Of course, he ignores the hint.

"How is your arm?" he asks. "Do you need ice? The mark still looks red."

"I'm sure it'll be fine by tomorrow. The scrapes are shallow, and the bruise on my neck will fade, too, so you won't look like an abuser."

He looks horrified.

"People won't really think that," I tell him quickly. "It

was just...never mind. I wanted to talk to you, though. Before you go to bed and I lose my nerve. Can we go in my room for a little bit of privacy?"

"That is not the best idea right now," he says.

I take a deep breath preparing myself for, at best, a new chapter in our relationship. At worst, we'll break up and it will be super awkward tonight.

"Rhys, we need to talk about the email that I wrote. First, I owe you an apology. I was really drunk when I wrote that and I didn't mean to send it out to the entire school."

"You have nothing to apologize for," he says gently. Part of me wants him to yell at me and get angry at my violation of his trust and privacy. I don't really deserve his understanding. But of course, he'd never make me feel bad about this sort of mistake. He's perfect, and true to form, I'm going to ruin it.

"No, I do. As much as I want to say that I only wrote the letter because I was drinking a lot of wine with Tasha, that would be a lie," I babble. "I mean, I did drink a lot of wine, and sober, I would've never sent that letter. But it's not like it came out of nowhere. I wrote it, I think, because I am concerned about our relationship. God, this is really embarrassing. Please don't tell anyone this, but I...meant what I said in the letter. A lot of it was exaggerated, and yeah, the poem kind of sucked. But I *am* interested in doing that sort of thing with you. I can't gauge whether or not you feel the same."

Rhys' ears redden, but he doesn't say anything, so I continue.

"I know this is really uncomfortable, and as I ramble on, I wonder why I'm even admitting this to you. But I just don't understand what's happening between us right now. We've gotten past our time-travel issues, and the threat Neil posed, but now we're stuck in a rut. I'm not saying that we have to do anything, but we don't talk about our relationship. You're my boyfriend, but I have no idea if you want me the same way I want you.

"This probably is another me problem. I know I'm trying to work on my insecurities. With all my past flings, they were *only* about sex. I'm glad our relationship isn't like that. If you want to take things slow, we can take things slow. But I'm not emotionally intelligent enough to read between the lines—I have no idea what you want from me, or if you're holding back."

"To be quite honest, I am...nervous," he says cautiously.

Karina's bedroom door bursts open, and she waddles out with bleary eyes. We stop talking abruptly as she moves toward the fridge to get a cold bottle of water. But she doesn't go back to her room right away. She stands with her hand on the counter drinking the bottle of water in its entirety. Once she's finished, she throws the empty bottle in the recycling bin and puts her hands on her hips.

"The walls are really thin," she reminds us. "As cute as you two are, I really need my sleep."

Now, Rhys and I are both red as tomatoes when she goes back to her room.

"We'll continue this conversation another time," I say finally. "I just wanted to be honest with you."

He nods, and before I can turn away, he takes my face in his hands and kisses me. It's the kind of kiss that makes my brain short-circuit and my entire body feel warm. Talk about mixed signals. How can he kiss me like this one moment and push me away the next?

"We can continue this conversation in a more private setting," he promises, pulling back. "But for tonight, you should rest."

"Good night," I say absentmindedly.

But after that kiss, how can he expect me to sleep at all?

THE NIGHTMARES HAVEN'T COMPLETELY STOPPED, BUT they've lessened significantly. I don't get them every night anymore, and even on the nights I do, they're less intense. Despite that, they still bring tears to my eyes.

Max shows up tonight, which has become rare these days. I hate that I still dream about him, because when I'm awake, I'm not scared of him. And admittedly, I'm not as angry with him, either.

They say that the best revenge is moving on, and while I wouldn't classify it as revenge, moving on with my life and occupying myself with different things helps me stop obsessing over him. I haven't wondered where he is or what he's doing in a long time.

I'm not at the point where I can admit this aloud yet. It's like I'm betraying my younger self. I always justified the anger, telling myself that if no one gave a shit about me, I'd have to be selfish. I had to take care of my own emotional wellbeing, and part of that involved allowing myself to be angry and hurt by people who wronged me. So if I let go of this anger, am I giving up on myself?

When I wake up the next morning, I don't move right away. I let my tears dry and my emotions fade, and remember all the people in my life now who are with me. I have Isabelle, Tasha, and David back. Even if they aren't physically here, they're relatively safe at Kingsmarch. Safer than they'd be with me right now.

If it came down to it, I know Archer has my back. Ava and Declan, too. Hell, even Ophelia. We might not get along, but if I was really in a pinch, I don't think she'd stand idly by.

Provost Mathers, Theodas, and Siraye have helped me beyond measure. Rhys...

We may have our ups and downs, but Rhys would never abandon me. And even if we break up, I can't imagine loving someone as much as I love him.

I've relied on everyone so much throughout this ordeal, but now, I have to step up and become someone they can rely on, too. I don't want to be useless.

Taking deep breaths, I sneak off to the bathroom. The bad thing about having yellow eyes is that it is very obvious when you've been crying. Their light coloring emphasizes how bloodshot they look, and I press my cold, wet hands against my eyelids to get them back to normal.

My morning routine brings some normalcy to start off the day, and I can't believe Rhys actually packed my makeup bag. The concealer does wonders for me. I put on the necklace Rhys gave me before I went to the past—a small gold coin with elvish script on it—and tuck it beneath my shirt. Ready for whatever comes next, I open the bathroom door.

Rhys has already packed up the pullout bed and has trays of food arranged on the small dining table.

"Good morning," he greets. When I walk over, he gestures to a plate of food, which he's already prepared for me. Of course, it's all my favorites; he even got me a Belgian waffle.

"Thanks," I say, taking a seat. "Karina isn't up yet?"

"She took her food into her bedroom. Her night was restless."

"Maybe she's excited to be going home."

"That might be. But be gentle with her today. She seems off," he advises.

She always seems off, but I can hardly say that. "I'll keep that in mind."

Karina comes out after we finish, and Rhys is right—there's something off about her. I just can't put my finger on it.

We check out quickly and get into the car, blasting the air conditioning. I sit in the back while Karina sets up her GPS.

"The drive shouldn't be that far," she says, settling in.

I know I just woke up, but as Rhys turns out of the parking lot, I fall asleep against the window. I fade in and out, catching bits and pieces of conversation, but nothing that makes sense.

I wake up when we get to Karina's town. It's a posh, storybook town filled with gorgeous houses and a chic shopping area. Most of the houses are modest mansions situated on large plots of land with blooming gardens. I expect her house to be one of the biggest ones, based solely on her attitude. She gives off the impression that she comes from money.

But we drive past the big houses and get on a back street toward the woods. For a moment, I wonder if she lives somewhere like Foley-Hill, Neil's renovated plantation, with a large gate and a long driveway to seclude her mansion from the rest of the town. Instead, it's the opposite.

We travel on a winding dirt road in the woods until we

reach a small clearing. There's no pavement or driveway, and the yard is overrun with weeds and knee-high tall grass. In the middle of the clearing sits a brick-red trailer with a screen door hanging off the hinges. Dirt cakes the windows, and the concrete steps look like they could crumble any minute. Clearly, this place has seen better days.

Karina sports a huge grin. When she gets out of the car, she uses the railing on the porch to jump onto the roof. She pulls up one of the shingles and gets a key. Balancing perfectly, she jumps down and sticks the landing.

"I'm home!" she shouts, opening the door.

Inside isn't much better than outside. The carpet is stained so much I don't know what the original color was supposed to be. None of the furniture matches.

The kitchen, living room, and dining room are all one space, while there's a hallway on the other side with three doors and a narrow closet. There's no air conditioning, nor are their fans, so it's hotter inside than it is outside.

"I guess no one's here," Karina says. "I'm going into my room. Y'all can do whatever you want."

There's a hint of a drawl in her voice, so faint it's barely there. Is the valley-girl accent fake? Not like I'm one to talk about fake accents.

Rhys and I head out the back. It's actually much nicer in the yard with the shade. I head to a shed in the back and pull out a lawn mower. Might as well do a little yard work while we're here. Too bad there's not a spell for it.

"Do you know how to work that?" Rhys asks curiously.

"I mowed lawns one summer in my neighborhood. Made some good money, too, before Bernard Jacoby stole it," I say, wrinkling my nose at the memory. "He was a horrible kid. But you know what? He did apologize to me for it right before graduation."

"Did you forgive him?"

"Oh, no. But I probably should have." There were a lot of things I should have done.

I rev up the mower and quickly finish the back lawn, getting myself nice and sweaty. I hope Karina's shower is in working order, because I can't get back in the car smelling like this. The front yard doesn't take long, either, but once I'm through, I need to go back inside and wash my face.

Rhys follows me, searching the fridge for water. Unfortunately, when he opens it, the door creaks and nearly falls off.

"Oh, don't worry. It does that," Karina says, coming in. "My dad got it off the side of the road."

It looks like her parents got everything in the house off the side of the road.

Rhys leans down, peering at the photos on the fridge door. "Are these all you?"

"Yeah. My siblings aren't big on pictures."

Rhys takes a few down to show me. "Why are you wearing a crown in every photograph?"

"I won homecoming queen here," she explains, pointing to one photo. "Winter Formal Queen, Spring Fling Queen, and Prom Queen two times. We had a lot of dances."

"You won Prom Queen two times? How is that even possible?" I ask. "Were you held back?"

"No, I was just, like, super popular. My peers wrote me in. I would have won sophomore year, too, if Sandra McLaren hadn't gotten into a car accident and won via pity votes," Karina says bitterly. "No one likes to mention that she's the one who was drunk off her ass and drove into a barn. She killed a cow, you know. But no, everyone felt bad because she broke her stupid leg. Any votes she got were out of pity!"

"So, you're a walking, talking cliché?"

"In the best way." She smiles. "Now, let's grab lunch in town. All this sleuthing is making me hungry."

Well, I won't say no to food.

Karina's face pinches and she looks outside, pushing away the thin curtains. "Do you hear something?"

"No." I move cautiously toward the front of the house. "Am I supposed to?"

"Damn it!" she yells as the front door is blown in. That definitely isn't just the wind.

Outside, something moves between the trees. At first, I think my mind must be playing tricks on me, but a figure shuffles forward. It's pretty sunny, so it's actually more difficult for me to make out exactly who it is until they come closer. Unfortunately, even when they approach Rhys' car, I don't recognize them.

Karina scrambles to get the door back on, but as soon as she picks it up, a hand flings her away, slamming her straight into the wall.

"Maria," Nic Woolridge greets, crossing the threshold. He smiles, tossing a spell bag up and down in his hand. "Looks like you made some new friends."

CHAPTER THIRTEEN

N ic doesn't look like a glamorized version of a vampire
anymore. He's noticeably bulkier, though I'm not
sure if it's because he's been working out, or if it's because
the last time we met, he drank my blood.

Drinking the blood of a blood-magic user gives you
power. That's why Neil wants me to drink Astaroth's blood,
to "prepare" my body for laying snake eggs. Now that I
think about it, everything Karina explained about the timekeepers wanting to control the mortal realm makes sense.

Truebloods can only open rifts from the Veil to the
mortal realm. They can't close rifts in the mortal realm, and
their powers are weaker here. Shadowborn can open and
close rifts from either realm. Maybe, by being part human,
my mortal DNA will transfer to the new generation of timekeepers I'm supposed to birth, and they'll be able to control
the fates of mortals as well.

Ugh, the more I think about it, the worse it gets.

Nic, on the other hand, is a rogue agent. All I know is

that he wants my blood and he absolutely despises me. The feeling is mutual.

He walks into the house, stepping on the door that's crushing Karina, who is concerningly immobile.

Nic isn't alone, either. He uses blood magic for necromancy, but unlike the zombies he summoned when we fought in the cemetery, he comes with dead beastbloods trailing into the house. One carries the Divinities Sword in its mouth; I imagine the sword is still too heavy for Nic to handle. Even the beastblood zombie has a difficult time dragging it around.

They aren't feral—there's no black goo or smoke. Just guts and rot. Half of them don't fit inside the house, their hulking bodies lying in wait on the freshly cut lawn. There are at least fifty of them huddled in the clearing, and seven inside.

"Did you pack a sword?" I ask Rhys blandly.

"In the car," he answers.

Figures.

I have spell bags in my purse…across the room.

"This place is kind of a dump," Nic says, walking around. He looks at Karina, still motionless under the door. "Sorry I killed your friend. She was hot. Maybe I'll bring her back, after I'm finished with my favorite couple."

The undead beastbloods start to move, their eyes glazed and teeth bared. I can feel the power radiating from them, raw blood magic fueling their movements. It's like a wall of energy blocking us in.

Nic pulls out a gun from his waistband and points it at Rhys. "You know what I want, Maria."

"Is this the part where you tell me we can do this the easy way or the hard way?" I ask.

"No. This is the part where you give me your blood."

"I was really hoping you wouldn't say that."

"Maria, do not give him your blood," Rhys urges, but Nic clicks off the safety on the gun and takes a step forward.

"She has two choices. She gives me the blood, or I take it from her," Nic says. "What would you prefer?"

"How did you even find us?" I ask.

"I've been tracking you ever since you left Kingsmarch. The timekeepers might rely on their powers to find you, but I don't see what's so wrong with good old-fashioned stake-outs. I had some of my friends here watching the ferry for you," he says, gesturing to a dead bird perched on his shoulder. He's an eyepatch and peg leg away from becoming a pirate. "Now, go to the kitchen, get a knife, and start bleeding. Unless you want a boyfriend riddled with holes."

The griffin beside me gives my leg a hard nudge. I recognize the creature from a course I had to take on beastbloods last semester; it's a lion with wings and the head of an eagle. This one must be particularly old, because its decomposing flesh is falling off in small chunks, leaving a trail of gore behind it.

The griffin nudges me again, its beak piercing my leg. I wince in pain, but try to keep my composure as I walk to the kitchen.

"Maria, do not listen to him," Rhys warns. But how can I not?

Grabbing a knife, I think about what I can do with it. If I lunge at Nic, then what? He has a gun. He can pull the trigger faster than I'd be able to disarm him. And if Rhys gets shot...

"Why go after my blood?" I ask Nic, trying to keep my

voice level. "Why not go after Astaroth's? He's more powerful than I am."

"You think I can get ahold of Astaroth's blood?" Nic asks. "Neil would never allow it. And you don't have to put yourself down, Maria. You're plenty powerful—you just have no clue how to use your powers in a productive way. I don't think I've ever seen anyone as pathetic as you."

"Then clearly, you haven't met Molly Simmons," I reply, cautioning a glance behind me. Nic is focused on Rhys, watching for any sudden movements. He knows I'm not great in a fight, and with the beastbloods around us, he doesn't need to worry about me. Slowly, I reach for the bottles of herbs and spices on the counter. "Molly was another foster kid, like me. Except she was a traitor. She made fun of the rest of us, thought she was better than us. She put a dead roach in my lunch, poured hot water on my face while I slept, and accused me of plagiarizing her history essay."

"How does that make her more pathetic than you?"

"She apologized to me about it right before senior year. She told me she was sorry for everything, and said she only did those things because she was hurting. You know the saying, 'Hurt people hurt people'? That was basically her explanation," I explain, taking a knife and running it across my palm. The familiar sting of pain makes me grit my teeth, but I focus on the task at hand. "I was furious at her. It felt like she was making up excuses instead of actually being sorry. But now that I think about it, she was right. Hurt people *do* hurt people. I'm certainly like that at times, even though I should know better by now. And that's how you strike me, too, Nic. You hurt people because you're hurting. You're angry at Neil, and displacing that anger onto me."

"You think you've got me all figured out, Maria?" His voice is cold, hard.

"No. I don't have you figured out. And I don't really give a shit. I don't care about your sad past, your daddy issues. Keep your sob story to yourself," I say, sprinkling a little rosemary onto my bloody hand. I cut my other palm and turn around, walking slowly toward Nic. "You're the reason Luke is dead. And there is nothing you can ever do to make it right. That moment sealed your fate."

"You shouldn't take it so personally. It was all just a game—and you lost." He grabs my hand, holding the gun level with Rhys' eye as he bites into my bloody palm.

I shut my eyes, picturing the time my foster father threw a hot plate at me and burned my forearms. When I was a little girl, and I fell on the pavement, scorching my hands. Accidentally bumping against a hot skillet in a middle school cooking class.

Remembering that pain, my bloody palm shoots out and I grab for Nic's gun. The moment my blood makes contact with his skin, it begins to boil, as if my hand is composed of lava. Nic screams and flings me away, dropping the gun. Rhys dives for it while I grab a knife from the kitchen.

Nic, however, just stands there, laughing. My blood smears his mouth, and his eyes go wide as a grin spreads across his face.

"You're too late," he says. "I didn't need much. Just a little bit more for the final evolution."

His shirt begins to rip, the sound filling the room. The beastbloods back away on instinct, some even leaving the house as Nic levitates.

He howls as dark wings tear from the flesh on his back, so huge they take out the front windows. The metallic scales glint in the sunlight, and the total wingspan must be greater than twenty feet. They're definitely wings, but the texture reminds me more of a snake than a bird.

Wait, is that what Astaroth's blood is going to do to me?

Gross.

The beastbloods roar as Nic continues to rise, blowing a hole through the roof. Rhys pulls me away before I'm crushed by debris, rolling us toward the kitchen counter. I pull another knife from the drawer and we follow Nic outside.

The full sunlight makes it difficult for me to see anything but his shadow, a sinister dark figure in the sky.

With my bloody hands, I tear grass and dirt from the ground, focusing my energy on casting another bloody spell. Rhys, meanwhile, gets a fallen stick and transforms it into a sword.

The beastbloods aren't still anymore. Nic waves his hands like the conductor of a grotesque orchestra, and suddenly, the beastbloods attack all at once.

I need to concentrate to fling a good spell, but you know what makes it difficult to focus? A giant tiger lunging at you. Rhys' wooden sword doesn't do much good, and he dodges attacks as he creates more weapons from the sticks and rocks around us.

The beastbloods are fast and strong, managing to cut up my exposed legs and arms as I clumsily dodge their blows. There are too many of them, and Nic knows it.

He's controlling them. The smart thing to do would be to take him out first—but how would we even reach him? He's floating above the ground, well beyond my reach above the house. I can't even climb up to the roof to get him because of all these damn beastbloods. I'll die of exhaustion and heatstroke, if not by their claws.

Rhys' back presses against mine as we fight off the beastbloods, our makeshift weapons clashing against their sharp claws and teeth. We're outnumbered and outmatched, but...

There's no "but." We're fucked. Ironic, since we haven't actually gone that far!

Oh my God. You know, this is not how I wanted to die. Some people say they'd rather go down in a blaze of glory. I'd rather fall asleep when I'm ninety-something and just never wake up. But with my luck, I figured I'd die on a toilet.

This is going to be less embarrassing, but more painful.

A loud roar fills the air, but it's not from a beastblood. It's a...truck? Did someone actually come to help us?

No—it's not a truck.

Nic turns, but he has no chance of stopping the lawn mower as it slams down on his head. There are no final words from him, no dramatic send off. Just blood, gore, and brains scattering everywhere like a disgusting shower as Karina Swan presses the blades of the mower into his face.

The beastbloods drop to the ground, dead, as Nic's corpse slides off the roof and lands with a wet *splat* on the front steps.

Karina gingerly lets the mower down before sliding off the roof herself, once again gracefully landing on her feet, like a cat. She's the most disheveled I've ever seen her, her hair a tangled mess and her clothes covered in gore. I don't even want to examine the chunks of Nic sticking to her shirt.

I didn't see her get up after the door hit her, much less

get the lawn mower and crawl onto the roof. She can't be just a human, right?

"Insurance isn't going to cover this, is it?" she asks, pointing to the hole in the roof. "Damn it. My mom is going to, like, totally freak out. But on the upside, at least we have a lot of fertilizer."

CHAPTER FOURTEEN

I should be grateful Karina took care of Nic for me. It was certainly an interesting, and not quite dignified, way to go. And given how messy it was, I'm shocked Karina was able to clean everything up by nightfall. I would've helped, but I was too busy throwing up.

Zombies and ferals are gross, but I've gotten used to them, as much as it pains me to admit that. Who gets used to rotting corpses? Gross. Nic wasn't visibly decomposing, but seeing bits of him covering the lawn was way out of my comfort zone. Karina, on the other hand? Completely unfazed.

She didn't even let Nic have a big villain monologue. I guess he's already had those in previous installments, but I expected something more. A dramatic confrontation, lots of yelling. Instead, she took him by surprise. I think she took us all by surprise.

The shame I feel doesn't go away, even when we arrive back at Southeastern a few days later. Karina settled her affairs at home, put the tarp over the hole in her roof, packed her bags, and buried all the bodies in her yard. I should've dug some of the graves, but even after she took care of Nic's body, I couldn't stomach going back to the house.

When I told her that, she said, "But you were in the kitchen earlier."

"So?"

"This was the house where Daniel Reed killed his family. He baked his wife in the oven."

After looking it up and learning that Karina grew up in a murderer house, even though she assured me she's never seen a single ghost there, I begged Rhys to take me to a hotel. He was more than eager to get out of there himself.

Now that I'm back home, fresh from a shower, I thought I'd feel better. I don't know what's the matter with me these days.

I walk downstairs with the towel draped over my shoulders, my hair still wet from the shower. Isabelle stands at the kitchen counter, a steaming cup of tea in her hand. Buck curls by her feet, perfectly content until I step too close toward her. He lifts his head, giving me a lazy growl before dropping his head to his paws and closing his eyes.

"Oh, hi, honey. Do you want me to make you something? Are you hungry?"

I shake my head. "Where are David and Tasha?"

"David's in his room, and your sister has gone out with Ophelia and Ava for a little sunbathing on the beach. I think she likes living by the water," she says. "Is something wrong?"

I look around before answering, a habit I haven't quite

dropped yet. "Everything is going great. It should be going great, at least. The guy who was partially responsible for Luke's death, Nic, is dead now. He won't ever hurt us again. I should be over the moon about it."

"Oh, honey. Revenge never feels as good as we think it will. It only leads to closed doors and bottled-up emotions."

"It's not that. I'm glad he's dead," I blurt, wincing at my own admission. "I'm sorry. I know that's not a great attitude to have, but it's the truth. I hated Nic. He was awful, and now I have one less person to worry about. I won't be shedding any tears over it."

Isabelle nods understandingly, patting my hand. "If that's the case, then this should be a win in your book, right?"

"It should be. But I don't feel accomplished. Because I'm not the one who killed him. Karina did. Karina, who is human. Karina, who doesn't have any magic anymore. Unless she's lying. I don't know why I feel so bad about this."

I should be dancing down the sidewalk. Luke isn't completely avenged, but we're partially there. So what's with the pit in my stomach?

"Are you jealous because Karina got to kill Nic and not you?" Isabelle asks.

"No, that's not it either. It's not like I wanted to kill him. You know that with everyone, even Max...I didn't want to kill them. I just wanted them dead—regardless of how they got that way. I didn't want them to feel anything anymore, I didn't want to worry about them coming back to hurt me. Karina killing Nic is a blessing in disguise, but she's supposed to be weak, and I'm supposed to be strong. The fact that she killed him without powers makes me feel pathetic. And saying this all aloud makes me sound like I'm ungrateful for her help."

Isabelle pulls me in a hug, and I rest my head against her chest, listening to her heartbeat. "You are not pathetic. You've been through so much, and you've done a lot of it alone. I'm so sorry that I haven't been here for you. I know that Neil put a spell on me and that it was beyond my control, but not a night goes by that I don't think about how horrible you must've felt during this whole experience."

"No, it was my fault. Not yours. Never yours. You have always been there for me, even when I pushed you away. Even when I tried to make you give up on me, you didn't." I wouldn't be where I am if it weren't for her. Even though I am so far from perfect, all the little things that I've accomplished and that I like about myself are because of Isabelle's influence. And I don't think I've ever really told her that. I missed out on telling Luke how important he was to me, and I won't make the same mistake again. "You know I love you, even though it's super embarrassing to admit it out loud."

She laughs. "I love you, too, Mar. And I wish I could relieve your pain. Not just now, but from before. All the houses you stayed at, all the cruelty your peers showed you. I wish I could take those experiences and lock them in a box so you would never have to deal with the nightmares that haunt you at night. This feels strange to say to a time traveler, but there are some things in the past that can't be changed. All we can do is move forward."

"I'm trying, but it's an uphill battle. Sometimes, it feels like a losing battle." I withdraw from her arms, straightening. "Nic died, but there's still Neil and Astaroth to worry about. And I doubt they'll be easily taken out by a lawn-mower. I still have a lot of work to do, but when this is all over, I can't promise things will go back to normal. I'll still be a time traveler. And not the cool kind, like Marty McFly."

"I never liked Marty McFly anyway," she says. "I'm a Doctor Who fan all the way."

Talking to Isabelle was the right move. Even though I still have this gnawing feeling in my gut, I know that I'm not alone anymore.

After our conversation, I go upstairs and knock on David's bedroom door. He's going to find out about Nic sooner or later, and I'd rather the news come from me. I don't know how he'll react, but he deserves to know.

"Come in," he calls from the other side of the door.

I hesitate before entering. I've talked to David since he came back, but never one-on-one like this. I've never known what to say, and I'm deathly afraid he won't take the news well. It's fine if he's angry with me, but I have a feeling he's angry at himself, too. And none of this is his fault.

I push the door open and step into David's room. He's sitting at his desk, staring at his computer screen. He looks up when he hears me enter, and his eyes dart to my face.

"Mar, what's wrong?" he asks, his voice laced with concern. "Did you eat bad tuna from the cafeteria?"

"No."

"Really? You're making that face you do when you have to go to the bathroom, but someone's already in there."

"I'm not!" I check the mirror hanging off the back of the door. "I'm *not*. I...I came to talk to you."

Buck doesn't move from his place on David's bed, but I

swear the dog glares at me as I approach my brother. Shoving my hands into my pockets, I gather up my courage.

It's not easy talking to Isabelle or Tasha about these things, and it's even worse with David. At least Tash and Isabelle know I'm a bit of a fuck-up. David must, too, by now. But the kid used to look up to me, in some respects; I feel responsible toward him, like I need to set a good example.

"This is harder than I thought it'd be," I admit. "Lately, you've been…"

"Depressed," David supplies, completely calm. "I know. I'm sorry."

"No, no, you have nothing to be sorry for," I rush to say. "It's me who should be apologizing. I know being around me isn't easy for you—"

"Mar, you don't have to apologize," David says softly. "I know you've been going through a lot. And I know you've been trying your best. Things have been rough, but it's not because of you."

"Then what is it? What can I do to make it better?"

David leans back in his chair, regarding me with a thoughtful expression. "Honestly, Mar, I don't think there's anything you can do. It's just…life, you know? Sometimes things happen that we can't control."

I nod slowly, taking in his words. He's right, of course— but it doesn't make anything easier, on either of us.

"Listen, David," I say, taking a deep breath. "I need to tell you something. And I don't really know how you're going to take it.

His expression turns serious, and he nods. "Okay, what is it? You can tell me anything."

I hesitate, my mind racing with the right words to use. "It's about Nic," I say finally. "He's...he's dead."

David is quiet for a moment. His eyes widen as if he can't comprehend what I just said. "What? How? When?"

"At Karina's house, he ambushed us. I assumed he'd use magic to track me down, but apparently, he was just keeping an eye on Kingsmarch and waiting for me to leave. He followed us to Karina's house, and there was a fight." I don't want to get into too much detail. David's not a baby anymore, but he doesn't need to know about the lawnmower. "I just thought you should know, since he..."

"Kidnapped me," David supplied. "He kidnapped me and brought me to a cemetery."

"Yeah."

I can't read his expression, and for a moment, he doesn't say anything. Finally, he stands from his desk chair and throws his arms around me. I can't see his face, but there's no tremble in his voice. "I'm glad he's gone. I'm glad you don't have to worry about him anymore."

I feel a sense of relief wash over me as David hugs me. I didn't realize how much I needed to hear those words until he said them. It's like a weight has been lifted off my shoulders.

"Are you okay?" I ask, pulling away from him.

David nods. "It feels weird to say I'm glad he's dead, but...Mar, I *am*. He was horrible, and he hurt you. And I don't want you to be hurt anymore."

I nod, feeling a lump forming in my throat. "I won't be. I'm strong now."

"I might not be an elf, but you can't lie to me," he says, looking at me with those big brown eyes. "You don't think you're strong enough to take on Neil, but you are, Mar. So promise me you'll come back, okay?"

"I promise."

We stand there for a moment, just holding onto each other. It's a rare moment of vulnerability between us, and I savor it.

"It had a forty-two percent open rate," Declan says, showing me his computer screen. Like me, he's staying in the renovated basement of the dorm house with Rhys, Theodas, Karina, and Provost Mathers. He's a computer science engineering major, and his desk is big enough to fit four huge monitors on top. "And of that forty-two percent, half of them didn't even read it. They just deleted it."

"How much is forty-two percent?" I ask.

He and Ava exchange a look. She makes a cutting motion across her throat with her hand, and he answers, "Uh, it's not important. What *is* important is that less than half the student body has read your smutty fanfiction."

"Forty-two percent is a little over two thousand of Southeastern's student body," Ophelia supplies, playing with the Rubik's cube on the couch. "I took advanced statistics last year."

"But clearly, you didn't take etiquette," I reply, burying my face in my hands. "Are people talking about it around campus?"

"No," Ava assures, at the same time Ophelia says, "Yes."

"I thought it was pretty creative," Declan offers kindly. "Ava and I even talked about trying some of the—oof!"

Ava elbows him hard in the stomach. "Most people

probably think it was a joke or something. There's no context, and it's not like you're very well known outside of our circle of friends."

"Rhys isn't a student, so no one knows who he is, either," Declan adds. "And Ophelia's been spreading false rumors about it to scatter the masses. There's nothing to worry about."

Ophelia has been helping me? Has hell frozen over?

Provost Mathers knocks on the basement door before descending the creaking stairs with a platter of pizza rolls. "I thought you kids would be hungry."

"Hell yeah!" Declan exclaims. Before he can reach for one, Ava slaps his hand away.

"You're going to burn your mouth again," she says, shaking her head. "Thank you, Provost. Any news on Neil Abbott's whereabouts?"

"He has many properties scattered across the US, and our magic location spells are too weak to combat whatever shields he's got in place to hide his location," Mathers replies, setting the tray of rolls down on the coffee table. "I do have other news, though. There's goin' to be a summit at Northeastern to discuss the feral issue. Many leaders from the five schools have been invited to attend, along with interested students. I think it would be beneficial for you to go, Mar. It will coincide with Miss Swan's desire to return, as well."

"You're going instead of Uncle Theodas?" Ava asks.

Provost Mathers hesitates. "There are matters the chancellor must attend to here."

"So, you're worried he'll cause another scene?"

"Yes. He doesn't get along with certain members of prominent shadowborn families."

"The Churchills, basically." Ava turns to me. "They're some snobby fae family. One of the older daughters was among the first to die in a feral attack. They basically denounced her after she died and refused to fund any feral research until last year."

"My father hates the Churchills," Ophelia adds in. "He withdrew his funding when he learned Mr. Churchill started to donate money. I'm certain he's going to show up. He always stirs drama."

"This sounds like it's going to be a fun event," I say sarcastically. "Where do I sign up?"

"Despite the attitude of truebloods, it might be a good way to tap into external resources," Mathers suggests. "This event is a rare opportunity to meet influential figures in the magical world who could be valuable allies in our fight against Neil. Networkin' and such. I'm sure you're familiar with the concept."

I am, but I'm not good at it. "You really think a bunch of truebloods at a fancy conference are gonna care about helping me take down some demon scientist?"

"Maybe not all of them," Mathers admits, his drawl slow and measured. "But there's power in numbers. And there might be some attendees who've had their own run-ins with Neil or Astaroth. They might be just as eager to see them defeated as we are."

"Or they might be in league with him and try to drink my blood," I counter, feeling anxiety gnawing at my insides like a hungry beast.

"Archer and Ophelia will be in attendance, and I will be goin' if you need help."

"Alright," I say, finally making up my mind. "Thanks, Provost. I don't know how much it'll help, but I need to stick close to Karina, so I'll go. Who's going to be watching things here?"

"Theodas will personally see to it that Isabelle and your siblings are attended to," Mathers promises. "We need to leave in two days, so please pack your bag and start preparations."

I nod. "I'm going to head out, then."

"You're not going to stay for pizza rolls?" Declan asks.

"No, I've got someone I need to talk to before I leave." I head upstairs and walk back to my house. Isabelle has been keeping busy in one of the offices in the main building, running her nonprofit remotely. Tasha told me she was going for a swim with David today, which leaves the house empty. Perfect.

I enter through the back and check the first floor, just to make sure everyone is gone. When I don't see anyone, I go upstairs to Allegra's room.

Her door is open, but I knock anyway before entering. She sits by the window with a book, the light catching her eyes at the perfect angle, making them glitter. She looks up and crosses her arms when she hears me enter. "Mar?"

"Hey," I say, trying to sound as casual as possible. "Can we talk?"

"If I say no, will you leave?"

"No."

She keeps her arms crossed over her chest, like she's trying to protect herself from whatever conversation we're about to have. Her eyes flicker with a mix of caution and distrust as she watches me, clearly not thrilled by my presence in her room.

"Nic is dead, and I wanted to make sure you were okay. I never liked him, but he was like a brother to you, right?"

Allegra's face instantly pales at the mention of his name. "You're right. I did care about him. A lot. He was…complicated. But he meant something to me, and now he's gone. It's just…it's not fair, you know? Nic was always there for me when I needed someone. I realize now that he was just trying to manipulate me. Still…it isn't easy."

"Loss is never easy," I reply, remembering the various times I've experienced it myself.

"What am I even doing here, Mar? With everything that's happened…I feel so aimless. Like I don't know who I am anymore."

"Believe me, I get it," I reply. "But sometimes, in order to figure out who we are, we have to go through hell first. And if there's one thing I know, it's that you're resilient enough to face whatever comes your way."

"Mar," she begins hesitantly, "I'm uncertain about all this. I mean, I want to believe that we can move past our differences, but it's just…hard."

"Hey, I get it," I say, trying to sound as reassuring as possible. "It's not like we can just flip a switch and suddenly be best buddies. But I think it's worth giving it a shot, don't you?"

Allegra sighs, her shoulders slumping ever so slightly. "Yeah, I suppose you're right. It's just…I can't help but feel bitter sometimes. Like, why did all this happen to us? What did we do to deserve it?"

"Life's a bitch, isn't it?" I quip, offering her a crooked grin. "But seriously, we can't change the past. All we can do is try to make the best out of the present and hope for a better future. And maybe, just maybe, helping each other through this mess will make it a little easier."

She takes a deep breath, then slowly nods. "You're right.

And...thank you. For trying, I mean. I know it hasn't been easy for either of us, but I appreciate your persistence. Maybe we can find some common ground after all."

"Sounds like a plan to me," I reply, feeling a warmth in my chest that I haven't felt in a long time. It's not exactly a full-blown friendship yet, but it's a start—and that's more than I ever thought we'd have.

CHAPTER FIFTEEN

Starting our trip to Northeastern off with motion sickness has to be a bad sign, right? I spent most of the plane ride hugging the toilet, throwing my guts up. It got a little bit better when we got in the rental car, but now I'm severely dehydrated, and my head pounds.

Northeastern is just as I remember: a castle in the middle of the forest, exactly what I would picture a magic college to look like. We have to drive across a bridge to get to it.

As we drive up the winding road toward the castle, Karina's face grows more and more pinched. I thought she would be happier to be back here, but her mood is only worsening the closer we get to the buildings.

What's even more jarring is that she is wearing her own clothes. She brought them from her house, which I thought would be a comfort to her, considering she didn't have to wear Allegra's hand-me-downs anymore. But as it turns out, her hyper-feminine style makes her look like a Barbie. Her pleated pink skirt is short enough to be a belt, and her top is so tight, it clings to her chest and rides up her stomach. I suppose it's weather appropriate, given that even in New York, the temperature is climbing into the high 90s. But the pleated skirt, the cutesy top, the headband, and the kitten heels seem completely inappropriate for a girl who murdered someone with a lawnmower.

She's not disturbed by killing Nic. We haven't actually talked about it, but Rhys says he doesn't notice anything different about her.

He decided to stay on Kingsmarch with Theodas and the others. He promised he'd protect my family and help the other elves track Neil. Though we haven't found him yet, we're making progress little by little every day.

And as soon as we find him, I have to kill him. Somehow.

Mathers parks in the front lot, and the door slides open, letting Archer, Ophelia, Karina, Celeste, and myself slide out from the back. Provost Mathers and one other teacher, Professor Wentworth, sit in the front.

"Since the school is hostin' a summit, everyone has been assigned rooms. Mar," Provost Mathers says, turning to me, "you and Ophelia will be stayin' together. Karina will be stayin' in her old dormitory, and I believe Celeste, you have made other arrangements to stay off campus. Archer, have you done the same?"

"I'll be staying with my cousin," Archer replies.

Archer's uncle is the chancellor of Northeastern, and his cousin Ethan is a student here. It makes sense that he would have a place to stay.

"Well, if you log into the Wi-Fi network, you should be able to access your email from your phones. Room assignment details have been sent to your school email, so make sure you check it. We'll have a little bit of free time before dinner tonight in the cafeteria. Be sure to arrive by seven o'clock for the opening speech from Chancellor Kinsey. Are there any questions?"

"None from me," I reply.

Karina rolls her suitcase down the sidewalk, her voice absentminded as she says, "I'll see you all later." She glances around nervously, as if fearing someone might follow her. The campus is still quiet, with only a few students present and mostly adults walking around. Maybe she's worried she'll run into someone she knows.

Fortunately, Ophelia has a better sense of direction than I do, and she confidently leads us to the dorm. Seeing the school's apartment-style buildings is a stark contrast to the houses at Kingsmarch. These apartment buildings are much more cost efficient, I would imagine. More students can fit inside, which of course could lead to more friction. Given that the students can all use magic to some extent, I would imagine arguments could get slightly more violent.

Arriving at our designated room on the tenth floor, we find a bunk bed and two desks. It's clear that space will be a challenge. As Ophelia and I assess our close living arrangements, I can already sense the potential for rising tensions.

"You want the top bunk or the bottom bunk?" I ask her.

"If you snore, I'm going to smother you."

That wasn't an answer. "You seem more tense than usual. Nervous about seeing your dad again?"

Ophelia looks up from her phone, none too happy I guessed correctly. "How do you figure?"

"Every shadowborn seems to have daddy issues. I didn't think you'd be any different," I say.

Ophelia sighs, rubbing her temples. "I'm meeting my

father again this weekend. After all these years, I'm just...I don't know how to feel about it."

"Ah, family drama. My specialty. Why so nervous though?"

"Let's just say my dad isn't exactly my number-one fan," she explains in a rare bout of honesty. "He's always favored my older brother. My dad might be an ass, but I still want him to be proud of me."

"I won't pretend to know enough about your situation to give you advice," I begin, "but I'm going to check out the cafeteria and see if New Yorkers can really outdo the comfort food of the South. You want to join me?"

Food makes everything better. But Ophelia doesn't agree.

"No thanks," she mumbles, staring at her phone. "I think I'm just going to stay in tonight."

"Suit yourself," I say, grabbing my purse and heading out the door.

The campus is buzzing with students as I make my way toward the cafeteria. There's something about this place that feels magical, like Hogwarts, only with fewer broomsticks and more student loans. The castle-like main building stands tall in the distance, its spires reaching the clouds.

"Mar!" The voice startles me, and I turn to see Archer jogging up to me. His eyes light up when he spots me, like a kid on Christmas morning who just scored the last Tickle Me Elmo. "Hey, Mar, I'm glad I caught you."

"I thought you'd be catching up with your cousin still," I say. "Where's Ethan?"

"It doesn't matter. But I was hoping you'd join me for dinner with my dad."

"We're not in the meet-the-parents stage of our relationship. Mostly because we're not in a relationship," I remind him.

"I'm nervous to go alone. Would you mind joining us?" His pleading expression is a mix between a puppy begging for treats and a hostage trying to signal for help.

"Are you sure it's okay for me to come? I mean, won't I be intruding on family time?" I glance down at my outfit—a faded T-shirt and jean shorts that have seen better days. "Plus, I'm not exactly dressed for the occasion."

"Trust me, Mar," Archer insists, desperation in his eyes. "I need someone there. Anyone."

"Flattering." Is his relationship with his dad really as strained as he makes it sound? I know they don't see eye to eye about Celeste, but this seems to be way more than just a disagreement about an arranged marriage.

"I promise there will be free food and all the fries you can eat."

"Well, when you put it that way—how can I say no to free fries?" I sigh dramatically, giving in. "But just so you know, if your dad starts grilling me about my life choices, I reserve the right to respond appropriately."

"Deal," he says, chuckling nervously, leading the way. We walk together toward a sleek, black Rolls Royce that seems to be waiting just for us. The car is so polished, it looks like an expensive mirror reflecting our distorted images. The driver's door opens, and a man in a crisp uniform steps out, nodding politely at Archer before opening the back door for us.

"Really? A Rolls Royce?" I ask. The interior of the car is just as opulent as the exterior, with plush leather seats and that distinct new-car smell. "Are we going to a royal banquet or something?"

"My father likes to make an entrance."

Clearly.

"So where are we headed?" I ask, peering out the window.

"There's this restaurant downtown that my dad likes," Archer explains, nervously drumming his fingers on his lap. "It's called La Lumière—some fancy French place. He always insists on going there when he's in town visiting my uncle."

"Sounds...classy. I hope they don't have a dress code or anything," I say. "What does your dad do, anyway?"

"He owns a chain of high-class spa resorts across the country. He's very particular about his food as well, which is why we're going to this place."

"Ah, so now it makes sense—the fancy car, the dinner reservations. At least there will be good food, right?"

"Hopefully," Archer says, offering a weak smile.

As we pull up to the restaurant, the Rolls Royce slows to a stop in front of an elegant building with large, arched windows and ornate ironwork. The driver opens our door and helps us out, leaving us to face the intimidating entrance together.

We step inside La Lumière, and I'm immediately hit by the aroma of rich sauces and fresh-baked bread. The maître d' leads us to a reserved table in the back, where an imposing man with sleek gray hair and piercing blue eyes is waiting. This must be Archer's father.

"Ah, there you are," a stern voice cuts through the quiet atmosphere as we enter the room. Archer's father sits at the head of the table, his eyes scanning me from head to toe. He introduces himself with a curt nod, his voice cold and unwelcoming. "I'm Mr. Kinsey. Have a seat."

Despite the chill in the atmosphere, I try to keep my voice steady as I say, "Nice to meet you, Mr. Kinsey. I'm Mar Rochester."

"Mar," he repeats, as if tasting the name for the first time and finding it unpleasant. "Interesting."

"Interesting like a mystery novel, or interesting like a suspicious mole?" I ask, laughing awkwardly.

"Interesting like a girl my son plucked off the street," he replies, his gaze never leaving mine. Ouch. "Archer has told me nothing about you. You must not be a very significant person in his life."

I open my mouth to retort, but Archer's forced laughter fills the air, silencing me.

"Would you like some water, Mar?" Archer asks as he fidgets with his napkin. His eyes dart nervously between his father and me.

Archer is your friend, I remind myself. *It probably wouldn't be a good idea to piss his father off.*

"Sure," I reply, attempting to sound calm. "Thanks."

Archer's hands shake while he pours the water into our glasses. "Mar is a new student at Southeastern, Dad. She learned about magic after high school, and she's been adjusting really well."

"She doesn't concern me at all," he says. "I hear Celeste's parents are looking forward to the wedding. But you still haven't picked out a ring. Why?"

"We've talked about this, Dad," Archer replies, though his voice wavers slightly. "Celeste and I aren't ready to get married."

"But you will be soon, won't you? You're not bringing her here to tell me you've broken up with Celeste for trailer trash."

"I only lived in a trailer twice during my childhood," I say. "I'm not trash. I'm mold—I grow on people."

He ignores me, looking directly at his son. "I'd hate for you to screw this up like you've screwed up so many other things."

The conversation progresses, Mr. Kinsey's criticisms continuing to flow like a never-ending river of acid. "I still don't understand why you're pursuing that ridiculous major," he says, sneering at Archer. "You could be studying something useful, like finance or management. How do you expect to run the family business fooling around like you have been?"

"I'm double majoring. Business is my main major, but I've always found the Veil's ancient history fascinating," Archer tries to explain, but his father cuts him off.

"Of course you do. You always did prefer your head in the clouds. And this"—he waves dismissively toward me—"is the company you keep?"

"Archer has a lot of very high-quality friends," I say. "Well, he has Ophelia. And she's...Ophelia."

"Mar is great. She's funny and interesting," Archer defends, which is kind of sweet. But he can't even look his father in the eyes, instead staring at the very interesting plain white tablecloth.

"Your grades have been slipping, haven't they?" Mr. Kinsey accuses, staring down Archer like a hawk. "And I can only imagine what your physical training has been like if this is the state you're in."

"Actually, my grades are fine," Archer mutters. "And I've been working really hard at—"

"Hardly seems like it," Mr. Kinsey interrupts.

The waiter approaches the table, poised and professional, as he patiently awaits our order. Mr. Kinsey doesn't give Archer or me a chance to even glance at the menu before he takes over.

"Archer, you're having the grilled chicken with steamed vegetables," he declares, not even looking at my friend as he speaks. "You've been putting on weight; we wouldn't want that to get out of hand. And for you, young lady, the salad will do. A side salad."

"No need. I think we're done here," I say. "I didn't sit through that bullshit for a side salad."

"Excuse me?" he asks.

"You're a jerk, and we're done. Come on." I reach out and grab Archer's hand. "Let's get out of here."

Someone has to stand up to him, if fleeing the restaurant is what you want to call "standing up" to him. But Archer clearly isn't going to do it. I can't believe he's allowing me to drag him away, but thankfully, he's not resisting.

"Where do you think you're going?" Mr. Kinsey asks, amused, as if he doesn't think we're actually going to leave.

"We're going to get fries and burgers, and then we'll probably have unprotected sex on a bed of used hypodermic needles."

I've never been to this town before; I have no clue where I'm headed as Archer and I walk out the door. We go up the street, powerwalking until the restaurant is out of sight.

"Sorry," he apologizes, still dazed. "I didn't think he would be so...*tense* with company around. I really thought you'd get a free meal."

"Oh, you're still buying me dinner. I was serious about the burgers and fries," I say, looking around. "My replace-ment phone is still on its way, so can you look up where the nearest McDonald's is?"

"Sure," he relents. "You weren't serious about the sex part, right? Because I read your email, and—"

"And if you tell Rhys about what I said, he'll kill you, so you should keep quiet if you don't want another beating," I reply. "Now. McDonald's. Lead the way."

Archer takes the lead, and soon we are walking down the street looking for the familiar golden arches. A few minutes later, we find it, and walk inside the restaurant. The smell of fast food is mouthwatering, and my stomach growls in anticipation.

"Let's see...two cheeseburgers, large fries, and a Diet Coke." I rattle off my order, before turning to Archer. "What do you want?"

"Uh, I guess I'll have a salad," he mumbles, looking around the place as if it might be contaminated.

"Archer, we're at McDonald's, not some gourmet health food store. Live a little," I say. Reluctantly, he orders a burger and fries, too.

We find a booth near the window, and while we wait for our food, a heavy silence settles between us. I fiddle with a stray thread on my shorts before gathering up the courage to face him.

"I guess I owe you an apology," I admit. "I didn't expect to give you one in an empty McDonald's, but here we are."

"An apology?"

"Yeah. I'm not good at them, and I'm only going to do this once," I warn. "But I'm sorry for calling you a coward. After meeting your dad, it's like all the weird things you did suddenly make sense. I know I tore into you for freezing up when Allegra and I were being harassed. I was a total bitch about it, looking back. I'm sorry for being so harsh. You're not a bad person. You've been great, helping me train and hanging out with me, even though I'm not the most popular girl on campus. I'm *not* happy you're making me say all this mushy crap. Or that you punched my boyfriend in the face."

"Rhys hit me first," Archer said. "But thanks. You're a good person. Deep down. Very deep down."

"Hey!"

"Kidding."

I chuckle as we receive our food and find a booth to sit down in. We start to eat, the fries salty and hot, and the burger juicy and delicious. It's amazing how fast food can make you feel so much better after a terrible encounter, like the one we just had with Mr. Kinsey.

"You know that nobody deserves to be treated like that, right?" I express, making an effort to keep my voice composed. "I don't want to make assumptions, but in my experience, it's usually the parents who are the real problem, not the kids."

He looks at me with a mix of surprise and gratitude, and I suddenly feel embarrassed, like I've crossed a line by bringing up his dad. But instead of getting angry, he seems relieved. "Thanks, Mar. I'm…glad we're friends."

"There's no one else I'd rather be in this McDonald's with right now," I reply. "Especially since you're the one buying."

CHAPTER SIXTEEN

There's no such thing as being fashionably late for a summit. Instead, Mathers and I are fashionably early. By the time we arrive in the lecture hall, half the seats in the front are already taken.

I don't need to attend, but Mathers thinks it'll be good for me to show my face and learn more about the feral illness. With all these smarty-pants doctors and scientists around, I'm not so confident in my networking skills.

The lecture hall features twenty rows of wooden desks and benches on a slope toward the stage, which is at the lowest point in the room. Stained glass windows scatter pink and red light through gothic patterns of thorned roses, and a big chandelier hangs in the very center.

I can't help but squirm in my seat, feeling very much like a worm on a hook in the middle of shark-infested water. It's not that I think they'll devour me, but nonetheless, I'm being served up on a silver platter. At least Mr. Kinsey is seated at the opposite end of the room, so I'm out of his sight.

Provost Mathers is the only person in the room not dressed in business formal, wearing his usual suit with cowboy boots and a bolo tie. "You look paler than a ghost."

"They're not going to bring a real feral out to show us, right?" I whisper, tugging down my pencil skirt. I had to borrow Tasha's grey interview outfit, and despite it not fitting well, I'm glad I brought it. Everyone else is dressed in business formal clothing.

"No. The only thing you need to worry about is the overabundance of slideshows and charts. Now *that's* scary."

I force a laugh.

Chancellor Kinsey is the last to arrive. Archer's uncle doesn't look much like his brother, though the two share the same blond hair and blue eyes. Their faces and voices are completely different, highlighted by the chancellor's posh London accent. He's sharp in his suit and tie, his presence authoritative and calm as he steps behind the lectern.

"Welcome, esteemed guests," he begins, spreading his arms wide as if to embrace us all. "Thank you for attending this crucial summit on the feral crisis. It is imperative we come together to address this growing threat. Here to begin the presentations is Dr. Woods, who is our nation's expert in feral research. Her work and dedication to the cause has been paramount in our efforts. Please, give her a hand."

Dr. Woods takes the stage to a round of unenthusiastic applause. She's an older woman with graying hair pulled back into a no-nonsense bun and shaking, wrinkled hands.

"Good evening, everyone," she says, adjusting her glasses before launching into her presentation. "Today, we'll be discussing the biology, behavior, and potential annihilation strategies for ferals."

The first slide shows a chart I can't begin to decipher. I

thought charts were supposed to have bars or a line, but this has both in spades. How is anyone reading it? I look around, but no one is as confused as I am.

"As you all know, the feral situation has grown dire in the past few years. We've had some rogue experimenters who think they can do a better job than me and my team." The audience laughs. "However, my team is using the top equipment available and magitech not yet released to halt the spread of the illness and keep our bloodlines secure. With your generous donations, we've eliminated hundreds of ferals across the country.

"Your children have been fighting. Some have died. But we *are* close. With more time, and more donations, I believe we can find a cure for the feral illness and administer it to the population of beastbloods. Vaccinations are undergoing testing, and we're very hopeful to launch them next year after the completion of successful trials."

Her words are met with a smattering of applause, but there's something off about her presentation—like a vital piece of information is missing. She begins going over what the studies have found, but none of the numbers hold any significance to me. Though it's possible that I'm just stupid.

"Thank you, Dr. Woods, for your enlightening presentation," Chancellor Kinsey says when she finishes, returning to the stage. "We will now open the floor for questions."

"I have a question!" Karina stands in the back. She's difficult to miss, in a hot pink halter dress and impossibly high heels, launching her over six feet tall. It's inappropriate for this setting, but as per usual, she doesn't seem to notice or care. "Do you eat your meals in the bathroom? Because all that's coming out of your mouth right now is crap."

Oh no.

Dr. Woods shakes her head sternly as Karina approaches. "Miss Swan, I didn't expect to see you here."

"Is that why you thought you could present my parents' research as your own?" she accuses. There's a hard edge to her voice that I've never heard before, a venom reserved solely for Dr. Woods.

"Miss Swan," Chancellor Kinsey begins, his smile faltering, "Dr. Woods relies on researchers to help her with research. She never claimed to accomplish this on her own."

"She hasn't accomplished *anything* because she's dismissed my parents' research. She's fought their progress at every turn, and the one time she did act, she hurt my sister," Karina snarls. She towers over Dr. Woods, who doesn't seem cowed in the least. "She's not interested in helping cure the feral disease. She just wants to profit off it."

"Miss Swan," Dr. Woods begins, perfectly composed. That seems to make Karina even angrier. "I understand that you have strong feelings on the subject, but —"

"But nothing," Karina bellows. "When your pseudo-science fails, you blame my family instead of owning up to the fact that you're a snake oil saleswoman."

"Enough," Chancellor Kinsey snaps, standing between Karina and Dr. Woods with a raised hand, as if Karina could lunge at any moment. In all fairness, that does seem to be where the encounter is heading. "This is neither the time nor the place for such accusations, Miss Swan. We are here to discuss solutions, not point fingers."

Dr. Woods nods. "This summit is meant to be a place of collaboration and understanding, not a breeding ground for petty accusations and conspiracy theories."

"How is the fact that your so-called vaccine is fake a 'petty' accusation?" Karina explodes. "It won't do anything except line your pockets! You know the truth, but you're more interested in making a quick buck than actually helping people."

"Truth?" Dr. Woods counters, crossing her arms defensively. "Your parents' research was riddled with inconsistencies and ethical concerns. The scientific community has every right to question its validity."

Dr. Woods' dismissal only fuels Karina's rage, and she mouths off a string of choice words that would make a sailor blush. Unfortunately, she's playing right into Dr. Woods' hands, appearing immature.

"Can you believe her?" a haughty voice asks from somewhere behind me. "Thinking she's so high and mighty, like she knows better than the scientists working on this."

"Typical arrogance from someone like her," another person adds with disdain.

"Excuse me?" Karina's eyes flash dangerously as she overhears the offhand comments. "You got something to say? Say it to my face."

She's crossed the line from "bravery" into "stupidity." I want to stop her, but it's not really my place to interfere.

A blond man stands up and walks down the steps toward the stage. He looks somewhat familiar, but I'm sure we've never met. "Dr. Woods has been gracious enough to leave you out of this, but we all know that you brought the ferals here. You brought the horde upon us, and still, you deny it. The chancellor gave your parents jobs and allowed you and your siblings to attend school here, and this is the thanks he gets? You should have never been admitted."

The best thing to do would be to walk away. I've learned that things can only escalate from here, and once both sides come to a point where no one is willing to budge, things get dangerous. You lose your head, and all rational thought flies out the window. It's better to retreat and wait for a more opportune time to strike.

But Karina is like wildfire—once she gets started, there's nothing anyone can do but let her burn.

THE NEXT TWO DAYS OF THE SUMMIT GO WELL, COMPARED to the first. Mostly because Karina doesn't attend. She disappears entirely until we're set to depart, her mood at an all-time low since I've known her—and her heels at an all-time high.

I attempted to feel out some truebloods for potential alliances, but they were more concerned about themselves than me. After the confrontation between Dr. Woods and Karina, I got to thinking: maybe these truebloods aren't the most trustworthy allies after all.

Karina's accusations against Dr. Woods seemed personal and anger-fueled, which made them less credible, especially since Woods herself was unruffled. But I know that some adults do it on purpose—they get you good and angry in public and remain stoic, so you look like the crazy and emotional one. It feels horrible to be on the receiving end.

Karina is a lot of things, but she's not a liar. It could be that she's misunderstanding the situation. Or she's a hundred percent right, and we *should* be worried about Dr. Woods.

As we prepare to leave for the airport, I'm stuffing my luggage with an assortment of wrinkled clothes and free pens. Karina comes up the sidewalk, rolling her suitcase behind her.

"Y'all ready?" Provost Mathers asks. He looks way too excited for someone who just attended a soul-crushing conference about a magical disease that threatens all our lives.

"Ready," Karina mumbles, with none of her usual liveliness. She hands over her suitcase, which he loads into the trunk. Getting in the car, I end up squished in the back between Karina and Archer.

"Did you find your friends or family?" I ask her.

"Nope," she replies, which explains her mood. That, and her confrontation during the summit. "But I found out where Neil is."

I freeze. "What?"

"My friends signed up for some sort of experimental feral lab program in Tennessee. I also discovered some letters between Neil and a few Northeastern professors. I think they're working together in that lab. The building is registered under a false name, but the plot of land belongs to the Ruby Council," she explains. "Specifically, to the Abbott family."

"How did you find these letters?" Provost Mathers asks, getting into the driver's seat. "I don't imagine they were layin' around in the open."

"What do you think I've been doing these last two days? I've been snooping, while everyone was distracted by the summit. I have the printed evidence in my luggage."

Archer gives a low whistle. "That's some James Bond stuff right there."

I can't believe Karina was able to find all that out on her own. This could be the break we've been waiting for.

"You have the address of the lab?" I ask her.

"Yes," Karina says, exhausted. "I have everything I need. If you want, we can drive over there right now."

"Not the best idea, considerin' our numbers," Provost Mathers reminds her. "But this is good. It's a start."

"Are we really going to trust *her*?" Celeste asks, finally speaking up. "I've heard things about you, Karina. Things I think everyone in this car would be interested in hearing, too."

Karina's glare is so sharp it could spear right through the seat cushion. "I'm sure your trueblood overlords had very pleasant things to say about me after day one."

"Dr. Woods is a well-respected member of the community. She has a history of developing magitech and medicines, and she's the inventor of the memory-loss powder we use on humans," Celeste explains. "You'll forgive me if her word means more than yours."

"She's a quack," Karina says flatly. "My parents used to work for her. She's the type to start with theories first and bend the evidence to prove or disprove the ones that will make her the most money. But if you want to kiss her ass, be my guest."

"I'm not kissing anyone's ass," Celeste says, looking to Archer for support. "I'm just saying that I think we should be wary of your information."

"Why did you confront her?" I ask, genuinely curious. "Was there something specific you were looking for?"

Karina shakes her head. "I was pissed. She's clueless about the feral illness—thinking it can be cured by a vaccine? Really? Look, I'm not knocking vaccines. There are regulations and agencies that regulate them for humans. Here? Not so much. You can't tell me that you haven't noticed it, too. The truebloods are completely unorganized;

nothing is regulated, there are no laws ruling over all true-bloods and shadowborn, and the justice system is as corrupt as they come. Dr. Woods could shoot saline into our veins and call it a cure, and there would be no one to hold her accountable.

"But there's no vaccine. The feral illness isn't something you can cure with any type of potion, magic or otherwise. Even if there was a vaccine, Dr. Woods wouldn't be able to come up with it because she doesn't understand crap about anything."

Provost Mathers chimes in. "Connections. Dr. Woods comes from a long line of scientists and researchers. Nepotism is rampant in the supernatural community, and she's no exception."

Oh, so it's another case of someone incompetent being given control over people's lives.

"It looks like you got what you wanted after all," Karina tells me, looking none too pleased. "My friends are being held in the same facility as Neil."

"Which means you'll be helping me?" I ask.

"Which means I'll be getting my powers back."

"You could have gotten your powers back this whole time?" I explode. How could she have not mentioned this? If there was a way to get her powers back, wouldn't she have tried it?

"Yes. I can get my powers back. They've already returned, to some extent," she admits. "But there's a lot I'd be giving up, too."

I don't know what she means, but I can't imagine there's anything more worthy of sacrifice than saving the world. "Like what?"

She hesitates, then shakes her head. "Doesn't matter. We're in this together, Mar. There's no going back now."

CHAPTER SEVENTEEN

It's been less than twenty-four hours since I returned to Southeastern, and I'm already in the gym. I'm so dedicated to training... Actually, I'm just panicking. Now that we know where Neil is, we're much closer to a final confrontation. I need to use all my spare time fine-tuning my skills. Or, in my case, gaining skills.

I grunt as Archer's wooden sword connects with mine, sending a jolt through my arms. Sweat drips down my face, but I don't dare wipe it away; I need both hands to keep up with his relentless attacks.

"Focus, Mar," Archer says, his eyes locked onto mine. "You're stronger than you used to be, remember? I need you to access that strength and really push yourself."

"I *am* pushing myself," I insist.

"Not enough. Let's try that again."

I square my shoulders and raise my sword once more. Archer comes at me fast, and I barely have time to react before he lands another blow. This time, I stumble backward, losing my grip on my sword.

"See?" Archer says, leaning in close. "You're not using your strength to its full potential. When we start, you don't automatically get into a fighting stance."

"It doesn't come naturally to me," I admit.

"Why don't we take a break, then?" Archer sets his sword down and steps closer to me, his gaze softening. "You're doing great, Mar. You just need to believe in yourself more."

What a cliché.

"I believe in myself plenty," I lie.

Archer narrows his eyes, seeing through my facade. "Don't try to fool me. I know you're scared; we all are. But you can't let that fear control you. You have to use it as fuel to become stronger."

A how-to guide would be nice.

I take a seat on the bench and take a long drink of water. We've been training for two hours already, and I know my muscles will be sore tomorrow.

"Have you talked to Rhys yet?" Archer asks, handing me a towel.

"No. I need to, but I don't know if I should do it now or put it off 'til later. If we talk now, and things go badly, it will put me in a really weird headspace and I'm not sure I'll be able to focus on the task at hand. But if we delay our talk and one of us ends up dying, then that's not good either, for obvious reasons. I'm not trying to be pessimistic, but the closer we get to Neil, the more I feel the weight of my own mortality pressing down on me. I don't want to leave anyone behind, and I don't want to have regrets."

"What makes you so sure that you are going to be the one who dies?"

"If any of us have to die, I'd rather it be me. I started this mess, even though it wasn't my intention, and I can't drag anyone down with me," I admit. "Maybe it's selfish, but I can't imagine losing someone in this fight and being able to live with that."

He nods in understanding. "So what loose ends do you have to tie? Aside from Rhys, have you made peace with Allegra?"

"I talked to her, and I wouldn't say we're friends or that I made peace with her, but I wouldn't mind if things were left as they are." It's mostly Rhys that I'm worried about. Of course, David is a concern, too, but I think that he, Tasha, and Isabelle would be able to move on without me. Rhys would, too, but there's a lot unspoken between us, and the more that I think about it, the more I know we need to have a conversation.

He never had a chance to answer me back in the hotel. I want him to talk to me, not just for my own curiosity, but for his sake. I'm sure he has things that he needs to get off his chest, and I would be a horrible person if I denied him the chance to do that.

"What about you? What are your loose ends?" I ask Archer.

He runs a hand through his hair. "There are conversations that I would like to have before we head off. I just don't know where to even begin."

"Begin with the easiest and work your way up to the hardest."

"Surprisingly, I think you and I have tied up everything. We're friends, and I'm happy with the way things turned out. Ophelia, too. But things are more difficult with my father. I don't even know where that conversation would end, and personally, I don't think I owe him anything. I should feel the same way about Celeste, but things are tense between us. She saw her parents at the summit, and while I'm not sure what they said to her, it wasn't good."

"Is her dad like yours?" I ask.

"Both her parents are. She's more sensitive than ever; it's like walking on eggshells around her. I wish we could fight off our parents together, but she's not interested in fighting. She thinks it's useless...and maybe she's right."

"Archer!" The sharp voice of Mr. Kinsey pierces through our practice room. He stands in the doorway, wearing a pressed navy suit.

"Father, what are you doing here?" Archer stammers.

"Is this how you spend your time?" Mr. Kinsey sneers, looking down his nose at me. "Fraternizing with low-class bastards? Related to Neil Abbott, no less. Surely you can do better."

"Technically, I'm not related to Neil," I correct, but they ignore me.

"Mar's my friend," Archer protests weakly, but his father cuts him off with a wave of his hand.

"Enough of that. We have more pressing matters to attend to. The Ruby Council has requested that you hand over Katherine Swan to them for further investigation. She may be involved with the supernatural creatures we've been tracking."

Katherine? He means Karina, right? Why does everyone get her name wrong?

"Aren't you an angel? Why do you care what the Ruby Council wants?" I ask. And why the hell do they want Karina? Is it because of her outburst at the summit? Or...is someone higher up acting on Neil's orders? It wouldn't be the first time.

"Never mind my motives, girl. Archer—you will deliver Katherine Swan to the Council immediately," Mr. Kinsey commands.

"No way," I blurt. "We're not handing Karina over to anyone."

And I'm sure she'd fight us if we tried. I don't want to be hit by a lawn mower or stabbed through the eye with a pen, or whatever other sick killing method she has loaded in her back pocket. No, thank you.

"Mar, don't…" Archer starts, but I cut him off.

"Archer, you can't seriously be considering this."

Mr. Kinsey claps a hand on Archer's shoulder, squeezing hard. "Your loyalty lies with your family, not with these… trifling distractions."

"There have been a lot of moments in my life where I was given a choice, and I chose wrong. I chose to be selfish because it was easier for me. I've hurt a lot of people that way," I tell Archer.

The tension between us is palpable, as if we're on the edge of a precipice, waiting to see which side Archer will choose. Finally, he speaks quietly, his gaze locked with mine.

"Father, I need some time to think," he says.

"Very well," Mr. Kinsey snaps, storming out of the training room in a huff. The door slams shut behind him, leaving Archer and me alone with the aftershocks of the confrontation.

The last thing we need is more conflict, especially when we're already on thin ice with the Kinseys. But I can't just let Karina be handed over to the Ruby Council.

"Archer, please tell me you're not actually considering this," I say, my voice low and urgent.

"I don't know what to do," he says. "Even if I tell him no, what happens next? My father won't stop until he gets what he wants. And if he believes that delivering Karina to the Ruby Council will benefit him, he will do so without hesitation, regardless of our consent."

I take a deep breath, trying to calm the panic that's starting to bubble up inside me. "We can't let them take her. We don't know what they'll do to her."

"I know," Archer says, running his hands through his hair. "I just need some time to figure out what our next move is."

Archer's shoulders slump, his eyes downcast and filled with a particular sort of shame I know very well—the kind that flourishes on guilt and indecision.

"Archer," I say gently, reaching out to touch his arm. He stiffens, then looks up at me, his expression haunted.

"Mar, I need some time to think," he confesses, his voice strained. "I just…I can't deal with this right now."

"All right. I have my new phone already—it came while we were at Northeastern. Text me if you want to talk," I say.

Archer nods silently, then turns and walks out of the training room without another word.

RHYS IS WAITING FOR ME WHEN I GET BACK TO MY ROOM. I don't notice him at first—he doesn't make much noise. I throw my gym bag on the floor and peel my top off, throwing it in the laundry basket, before he clears his throat.

A very unattractive scream leaps from my throat, and I

stumble backward into the laundry room door. "Rhys? What the hell are you doing here?"

"Waiting for you," he says, his back turned. He sits at my desk with a book, though thankfully it's not one of mine. "You have been busy since returning. I wanted to see you as soon as I could."

"Normally, you avoid my room like the plague," I point out, pulling on a robe and tying the sash at my waist. "You can turn around."

"We need to discuss a few things. Your email, in particular." Uh oh. "Your...*candidness* caught me off guard."

"That's a nice way to put it."

"Maria, when we were at the hotel, you said that you do not always understand what I am thinking when it comes to our relationship," he begins, his voice measured and calm. "I want to assure you that I am committed to us and that I value our partnership."

That's good to know, but it's a pretty far cry from a passionate declaration of love.

Rhys is, as always, composed and reserved — the opposite of how I currently feel. "Relationships are complicated. Especially for someone like me. I apologize if my actions have caused you confusion or distress."

It's a nice sentiment, but I still can't tell what he means by it. I should have just written him a note: Do you like me? Check "Yes" or "No."

"But you don't want to sleep together?" I guess. "I know how desperate and sad I sound, but... Okay, so in the past, you know I've had a lot of flings. I'm not exactly girlfriend material here. Not to sound too self-deprecating, but I don't have much to offer. I can't cook, or clean, I'm not winning any beauty contests, my powers are more trouble than they're worth, and my fighting skills are subpar at best. Sex, though? That's one thing I'm not completely terrible at."

Rhys hesitates. "Maria, our relationship is not based on physical intimacy. I value you for who you are, not what you can offer me in bed."

I feel my cheeks heat up with shame. Of course, he's right. I know he's right. But it doesn't make the ache inside me go away.

"I'm sorry," I say, looking down at my feet. "It's pretty pitiful of me to say aloud. I know I shouldn't have brought it up. I don't want to pressure you into doing anything you don't want to do."

"Is that what you think?" he asks, sounding almost hurt. "You think I am holding back because I do not want you?"

"Well, yeah. You don't even seem to want to kiss me. How else can I interpret that?"

"There seems to be a misunderstanding between us. I may have…limited…" He stops mid-sentence, letting out an exasperated sigh. "This is difficult to say."

"Just spit it out."

"I will be forthright," he says, taking a deep breath. "I have never engaged in…intimate relations before."

"What? Wait, you mean you've never had sex?"

"Correct," Rhys confirms awkwardly.

That's what he's so awkward about?

"But I already know that!" I figured it out, given the time period he was raised in and the fact that he went to war at thirteen. When would he have had time for a relationship? Theodas also told me that Rhys never partook in the brothels with the other soldiers, being a young prince and all.

"You know?" he repeats, shock coloring his features.

"I'm bad at a lot of things, but even I can put two and two together in this case," I say.

"Then, you must understand that I am concerned my performance will not be...up to par with what you are accustomed to."

"I don't care. Plenty of people have awkward first times. I always figured I'd take the lead until you got the hang of it." Besides, I heard that actually having feelings for your significant other makes the act itself better. But it never even crossed my mind that his inexperience would be an issue for him.

Rhys is usually so calm and sure of himself, and he's great at everything he does. It's jarring to see him so down on himself about something that's pretty common. Everyone starts somewhere, right?

"We can just practice a lot," I suggest. "When you're ready, of course."

"Practice?"

"Sure! Like, you know, the more we do it, the better we'll get at it."

"Ah, I see," Rhys says, a hint of a smile crossing his lips. "Well then, I appreciate your understanding, Maria. And the offer to...practice."

A wave of relief washes over me as I realize we've finally laid everything bare, no more secrets or unspoken fears between us. Rhys seems to share my sentiment, his expression softening into a smile.

"Now that we've cleared that up, we should probably return to our usual routine," I tell him. "I believe it's your turn to be charmingly witty."

"I fear that attempting to match your level of charm would prove to be an exercise in futility," he says.

"Alright, you really need to learn how to change your tone when you're being sarcastic. Otherwise, I can't tell."

"I was being sincere."

"Sure." Now that our conversation has lightened up, I remember I'm smelly and half-naked under this robe. "I need to shower, but why don't we watch a movie? Not *Titanic* again. Are you busy right now?"

"I would very much enjoy a movie, just the two of us," he says.

"No *Titanic*," I clarify again.

"Because you once thought Leonardo DiCaprio and Leonardo DaVinci were the same person?" he teases.

"Alright," I say. "That's it. You got that information from Tasha, right? She's so going down. And—"

Before I can finish my sentence, Rhys silences me with a kiss.

CHAPTER EIGHTEEN

The cafeteria just got a new waffle machine, so Allegra and I get up at the crack of dawn to head over. She looks polished as usual in a long sundress, while I haven't changed out of my PJs.

"How was the summit?" Allegra asks, tucking a curl behind her ear. Her arms are bare, with no tattoos or scars left from Neil. One good thing came from her experiments with Nic: Allegra's condition stabilized. Previously ill due to Neil's experiments, Nic was able to cure her with blood magic.

"Boring. It was like watching paint dry," I grumble. "The truebloods didn't care about the feral disease—they were more interested in showing each other up. Karina caused a scene with Dr. Woods. Do you know her?"

"Callista Woods was previously an associate of my father's—I mean, Neil's," she corrects swiftly. "But Woods and Neil had a falling out. In the end, she was kicked off his research team. Neil always referred to her as an idiot."

"Well, after that incident, I went to dinner with Archer

and Mr. Kinsey." I grimace at the memory. "How did you deal with him when you and Archer dated?"

"Archer came over to my house at night, while everyone was asleep, and we fooled around under the cover of night." Allegra wrinkles her nose. "But we don't have to get into that. Even if we aren't related...that's just strange to talk about with you."

I thought it was, too, at first, but I'm over it. "Archer and I didn't do anything except kiss. I think you and I are in the clear. Besides, didn't you sleep with him again while I was gone?"

"It was a moment of weakness," she says.

She pushes through the doors of the main building and we enter the cafeteria, which is busier than I've seen it all summer. There's actually a line for the waffles, and rightfully so—they put the station right next to the soft-serve machines.

"Now that I'm better, I can eat whatever I want," Allegra says excitedly, looking at the toppings station. "I'm thinking double chocolate with caramel sauce and a cherry on top."

"Just because you're not bedridden doesn't mean you're immune to diabetes."

"Truebloods don't get diabetes."

"Are you a trueblood now?" I thought Nic cured her illness—not turned her into a trueblood.

"Not really," she admits, "but I'm not quite shadowborn, either. I'm somewhere in between."

"Did Nic make you practice blood magic, too? I know he used it to help stabilize you, but..."

"No, but I imagine he didn't want me to become powerful enough to disobey him." Hence why she lost a fight against him. "I have no interest in blood magic. Now that I'm healthy, I'm going to do everything I missed out on. Traveling, playing sports, eating delicious food. I might even go to California and smoke pot! Have you ever tried weed, Mar?"

"No, but I grew up thinking my biological father was a drug dealer, so I swore off illegal substances." Pot was only legalized recently, and it's still illegal in Georgia. "I'm happy for you, though. Really, I am."

"I can only do these things if you kill Neil, though," she adds. "I only get my inheritance if he dies. If you could hurry up, that would be lovely."

I cannot tell if she's kidding or not, but she's smiling, and it seems genuine. That's a good sign, right? She's okay with talking about me killing Neil, which is strangely the most normal I've seen her since she recovered.

We get our waffles and ice cream and scan the cafeteria for a seat. While it's nice to see students hanging around, making the school feel less like a ghost town, it's getting loud and crowded. I glance over to a nearby table, where Karina and Ophelia are eating breakfast together.

"Let's go join them," I suggest to Allegra, who doesn't protest as we gather our trays and make our way across the room.

Karina is too busy crafting a masterpiece to notice us at first. She put soft serve in a separate bowl and is currently handpicking pieces of Lucky Charms cereal to put on top.

"Uh, good morning," I greet. "What are you doing?"

"Making sure the ratios of cereal, ice cream, and waffle are perfect," Karina replies, not looking up.

"It's like watching an artisan create their magnum opus," Ophelia says seriously.

SAM GAO

More like watching a crazy person be validated by another crazy person.

Karina doesn't acknowledge Allegra or me again as we sit down. By the time I've wolfed down my breakfast, Karina is finished with her art.

"It's beautiful," she says with a sigh.

"It's melting," I point out. "And you have almost a full bowl of cereal left. Do you plan on eating that?"

"I usually have someone to eat it for me so it doesn't go to waste."

She might as well get "high maintenance" tattooed across her forehead.

"Now that we know where Neil is, what are you going to do about it?" Ophelia asks me.

"Isn't it obvious?" Karina cuts in. "We're going to drive to his lab and kick ass. And rescue my friends. I can show you their pictures to help you recognize them. I know battles can be chaotic, but I'd rather you not kill them by accident. Once the weapon I commissioned is ready, we can leave. The shop girl said she'd have it by next week."

"You want to storm Neil's lab next week?" I sputter. "That gives us no time to prepare!"

She blinks, genuinely confused. "What do you need to prepare?"

"We don't know how big the lab is or how many people might be inside," Allegra answers, thankfully being the voice of reason. "We have no way to determine the layout or how much manpower we'll require. We need to do at least a week or two of surveillance before jumping in."

"Time isn't on our side, no thanks to you," Karina says, looking at me pointedly.

"Sure, but storming his lab? That's like walking straight

into the lion's den," I argue. "This feels like the kind of plan that could get us all killed. It's not even a plan!"

"Sometimes you have to face the danger head-on. Besides, with the right weapon, we could take him by surprise."

"We have no idea what we're walking into."

"Neil, cultists, and timekeepers. They're all sitting ducks in a lab in the mortal realm. It's like they're *begging* us for a fight! We should strike them while they're weakened. If they retreat to the Veil, we have no advantage," Karina insists. "What would your plan be, Mar? Surveil them for a few weeks and then what? Scrape together your already dwindling resources and manpower to end up at my plan again?"

"Maybe I don't have a detailed plan right now," I admit, heat rising in my cheeks, "but at least I'm not so overconfident that I'm willing to just rush into danger without thinking things through."

"Overconfident? As opposed to what? Sitting around and doing nothing, like you've been doing for the past few weeks?"

"Y'all, let's just calm down and talk about this," Allegra interjects, putting a hand on my shoulder. Ophelia looks increasingly uneasy, her gaze shifting from side to side as if searching for an escape route.

"You don't have any better ideas, so why don't you just admit that mine is the best option?" Karina demands.

"Because it's not!" I retort, slamming my fist on the table. The sound echoes through the cafeteria, drawing the attention of several nearby students—including Lilly Hardwicke, who smirks as she saunters over to our table. Great. Can't she just leave me alone? We don't even live together anymore; she doesn't have to go out of her way to taunt me.

"What's the matter? Can't handle a little disagreement?" Lilly asks, standing at the head of the table.

"Leave me alone, Lilly," I snap. "This doesn't concern you."

"Actually, it does," she says, crossing her arms over her chest. "You're all delusional if you think this pathetic little group can actually make a difference against Neil Abbott. Why don't you let the Ruby Council deal with the mess you've made?"

"Because they're obviously corrupt and Neil was a huge influence on his peers, so we're not sure who we can trust?" I suggest. "That would be a huge part of why I wouldn't go running to them all willy nilly."

"Newsflash, sweetheart." Lilly sneers, leaning in closer so she can really get in my face. "The Ruby Council doesn't play games, and neither should you. You'd be wise to just hand Karina over and stay out of their way."

What the hell? Mr. Kinsey said the same thing yesterday. I know Lilly is connected to the Ruby Council through her own family, but why does she care what they do? It's not like she's the one working for them—it's one of her parents, I think.

"We're not handing Karina over to anybody," I say, even though I would love to get her out of my hair. "Why do they care about her, anyway?"

"It's not my place to ask questions. But getting her off the island and locked up somewhere is in the best interest of everyone," Lilly replies. "Think about it, Mar. Who benefits the most from all these ferals running amok? Someone who can control them—like Karina."

I'm about to say that Karina can't control ferals, but I don't know that for sure. When she woke up, she seemed to be able to cure them. But she said she doesn't have powers...even if all evidence might point to the contrary. It's not like I can check—she could have lied. Hell, she could be lying to us about everything.

That doesn't mean I can just hand her over to the Ruby Council.

"Karina is not the enemy," I say. "Even if she's kind of annoying."

"That's fair," Karina chimes in.

The ever-mature Lilly tips my tray over onto my lap, spilling the remnants of syrup and ice cream on my clothes. I shoot to my feet with a curse, hating the sticky liquid running down my bare legs. Gross.

"Are you serious?" I groan. "What is your problem?"

"All you've done is bring trouble to campus," Lilly says, shoving hard against my chest. I stumble back, clenching my fists. "You don't belong here. You never did."

"Wow," Karina muses, staring at us with unmasked interest. "Are you just going to take that, Mar?"

Nice of her to step in and help out. *Not.*

Lilly shoves me again, and I slip in the puddle of ice cream and land on my butt. Ugh, this is a horrible way to start the day. I might just have to get another waffle and eat my feelings.

"Seriously? Grow up," I snap, rising to my feet. Why did I have to get chocolate ice cream? There's definitely an embarrassing brown stain on my butt now. "This is low and childish, even for you."

"Like you have any room to talk," she replies. "You're harboring a criminal. Then again, you are a criminal."

Karina does nothing to help, not that I expect her to. She just sits there, eating her ice cream waffle and looking mildly amused. Until Lilly turns her attention over.

"You'd rather stick with this girl than your own kind?" Lilly asks me, though she doesn't use the word "girl." I'm not going to repeat it here, but she says a slur that rhymes with "sink." So she's a bigot, on top of being a bitch—what a surprise.

Things only get worse from here. Not for me—for Lilly and Karina. Well, a little for me. I'm wearing white sneakers, and now they've gone and splashed blood on them.

THE LAST TIME I WAS CALLED TO THE PRINCIPAL'S OFFICE, it was because I put shaving cream in Tiana Ford's gym locker. It ruined her jacket, backpack, and textbooks. In my defense, she started it by stealing my clothes and hanging them on the flagpole.

After the "altercation" in the cafeteria, I'm called into the chancellor's office along with Karina. I've never been called into the principal's office knowing I wasn't the one in trouble. I don't get to change out of my dirty clothes first, so I have to stand while Karina sits perched in the chair across from Theodas and Provost Mathers, perfectly calm.

"Do you know why we called you here, Miss Swan?" Provost Mathers asks her.

"Not really," Karina says, completely full of it.

"Miss Hardwicke's jaw is fractured. She might need to get it wired shut."

"Well, I *did* tell her to shut her whore mouth, or I'd shut it for her. And I don't like to lie," Karina muses. "So I guess…I'm here because I followed through on a promise?"

"Miss Swan."

"Okay, so it wasn't technically a promise," she relents.

Theodas turns around in his chair to face the window, but I swear I catch his shoulders shaking with laughter. Provost Mathers, on the other hand, is unamused. "Miss Swan, this is *very* serious."

"I know. She's a shadowborn, and she can't take a little slap from a human? That's totally embarrassing for her. You should, like, reevaluate her admission here or something."

"You punched her with a closed fist," I interject. "I think. It was a little too fast for me to catch."

One moment, Lilly was standing around looking smug. The next, she was on the floor, blood mixing with the chocolate ice cream she'd spilled.

"A punch, a slap, it's all the same," Karina writes off.

"As I've experienced both, multiple times," I say, "I can assure you that they are not one in the same."

"The real question here is, did she deserve it? And the answer is yes."

"Well, that's a good point—" Theodas begins.

"Not it's not," Provost Mathers says firmly. "Mr. Hardwicke is goin' to be very angry if we don't do somethin' in defense of his daughter."

"Even if she had it coming?"

"Chancellor, you cannot tell Mr. Hardwicke that his daughter 'had it comin'.'"

"I don't mind telling him," Karina volunteers. "Besides, I'm not a student at this school. You can't expel or suspend me."

"She has a point—"

"Chancellor, please," Provost Mathers says, rubbing his temple. "Here's what we're goin' to do. We're goin' to give you a demerit. And you're banned from the cafeteria for a week."

"What does a demerit do?" Karina asks.

"Nothing, but it sounds threatening," Theodas says.

"I can live with that."

"So she's just going to get off scot-free," I reiterate.

Karina's temper flares. "What's your problem with me? I defended you!"

"You defended yourself! And, admittedly, rightfully so," I relent. "But you can't just get into fights with people. Especially not people who want to hand you to the Ruby Council, who want to do God knows what with you! It's reckless. And do not look at me right now with that smug grin, Theodas."

"This is my office! I can grin however smugly I want!"

"Alright, I didn't want to have to do this," Karina says, standing up. "You leave me no choice."

"What?"

"I'm not crazy enough to think I can do this alone," she says, "but we have to work together, you and me. Which means overcoming our differences."

I scoff. "How do you propose we do that?"

"We're going to fight, and I'm gonna beat the shit out of you," she says flatly. "And then we're going to be best friends."

"Wait, what?"

She says, as if it adds any credibility to her plan, "I saw it in an anime."

CHAPTER NINETEEN

My nose gushes blood all over the front of my shirt. Rhys holds a washcloth to it to staunch the bleeding, though he doesn't look as indignant as I thought he'd be after witnessing me hobble inside after the fight with Karina.

"Here," Rhys says softly, cleaning my face with a wet rag. "This should help."

"Thanks," I mutter. He sits beside me in my cramped downstairs bathroom, a first aid kit balanced on the sink. After taking care of my nose, he hands me a cold compress for my rapidly swelling eye and places my ankle in his lap. It's double its normal size, which can't be a good sign.

"Do you need me to defend your honor?" he asks seriously.

"Very funny," I grumble.

"I can, if you wish. Just ask, and I will go to her room right now and request a duel."

"Please. She'd kick your ass, too!" I got in two hits, maybe, before she pummeled me on the front grass of the main building. I thought it was going to be sparring, like what Archer and I do. Not a total beatdown. I can't even lie and say it was a draw. Karina is fast and vicious. She's got no qualms about jabbing a thumb in your eye or pulling your hair.

"Perhaps," he admits. "But it seems your altercation may have been beneficial in its own way, even if it did result in these injuries."

"Yes, but we can never tell Karina that." I'd rather get beaten up again than admit she was right.

I don't think we're best friends now, but fighting allowed us both to release some pent-up frustrations we've had with each other since day one. I guess, in this particular case, violence solved the problem.

I flex my hand, my knuckles quickly beginning to bruise. Punching her in the stomach did more damage to my body than to hers—it was like hitting a concrete wall. At least I got her once in the face.

Rhys gently massages my ankle, his fingers expertly probing the tender spot. "You might have sprained it."

"Of course." I lost my footing when she backflipped, landing a kick to my chest.

"Have you considered asking her to train you?"

"I'm not a masochist, so no, I haven't."

"It is something to consider," he says.

"I'd rather steal honeycomb from a nest of angry wasps."

"Most wasps do not make honey."

"Oh, you get what I mean!"

Rhys chuckles. "I do. But sometimes, the things we fear the most are the things we need to face head-on."

"You sound like a self-help book."

"Karina lent me one," he admits. "In other words, she

forced me to buy them for her and allowed me to read one after she finished. But it was quite interesting, after all. It's called *The Cure to Sadness: How to Stop Enjoying Anger and Embrace Happiness.*"

Wow, that sounds like the last thing I want to read!

I wince as Rhys tightens the wrap around my ankle. "You really think she'd teach me if I asked?"

"Of course. There is no harm in asking," he assures me. "But it may require some humility on your part."

I roll my eyes. "I'll consider it."

"The worst she can say is no."

THE NEXT DAY, I DECIDE TO PAY KARINA A VISIT. AS I round the corner, I can hear laughter coming from the backyard. Two trash cans are set up on their sides, and Karina is dribbling a soccer ball with my brother chasing after her. Rhys and Provost Mathers, in his full cowboy regalia, guard each trash can goal. Buck wags his tail, rolling around in the grass with his tongue flopping out. As soon as he senses my presence, he barks and trots toward the shade. Ungrateful much? I just walked Buck this morning! Isabelle said it would help foster our relationship. Instead, the stupid dog still hates me.

Rhys waves when he sees me, which earns him a soccer ball in the chest. He winces, but is otherwise unharmed.

"Are you okay?" I call, jogging over.

"Fine. The last time she hit me, she aimed for my throat," Rhys says, casting a wary glance at Karina.

She shrugs, like it doesn't have anything to do with her. "I like winning."

"Care to join us for a game, Mar?" Provost Mathers looks at me with pleading eyes.

"Uh, no. I wanted to talk to Karina," I say. "I was wondering if you would consider helping me."

"With your wardrobe? Oh my God, I have been dying for you to ask me!" she says, clapping her hands together. "We'll start with a purge."

"No! What's wrong with my clothes?"

"Do you really want me to answer that?"

"I need your help with *training*. Like, hand-to-hand combat," I say.

Karina blinks at me as if I've suddenly sprouted a second head. She crosses her arms and looks me up and down, clearly unimpressed by what she sees. "You want me to teach you how to fight?"

"Ye-yes," I stammer, feeling even more foolish than before. "You beat me pretty badly when we fought. I thought you would be the best person to learn from. I haven't been making much progress on my own, or with Archer."

"Absolutely not." Karina's response is so blunt it cuts through the air like a knife.

"Wait, what?" Of all the responses I expected, this was definitely not one of them.

"I'm not going to be your Mr. Miyagi stereotype," she declares.

"Wha—?" I splutter indignantly, taken aback by her refusal. A thousand counterarguments spring to mind, but Karina's steely gaze silences them all. Why did I think this would be easy? "I don't care that you're Asian! You're a good fighter—that's why I'm asking you! What, do you think you're going to sprout a beard and speak in proverbs if you agree? I mean, do you even know any proverbs?"

"Isn't Mr. Miyagi Japanese?" David points out. "And you're Chinese."

"That's true. I should've said Pai Mei, but I didn't know if your sister saw *Kill Bill*," Karina relents, speaking to David in a far kinder tone than she does to me.

Rhys raises his hand, looking very self-satisfied. "I saw that movie!"

"Not the point," I cut in.

"Karina, you are a very skilled fighter," Rhys says, turning to her. Maybe my schmoozing skills rubbed off on him. "Even Theodas, an old warrior, acknowledges your prowess on the battlefield. You would not be a mentor to Maria; you would be leading our operation."

"Leading?" she asks, intrigued.

"You possess great strength and leadership qualities. Your assistance could significantly bolster our chances of rescuing our friends. We would be grateful for your guidance."

Karina contemplates her choices, but with a glance at David, she heaves a sigh. "Fine, I'll train you. But you have to follow my methods and do exactly as I say."

"Your methods?" I'm scared to ask.

She nods. "I told you, I was cheer captain in high school."

"Seriously?" I can't help but laugh, trying to imagine Karina teaching us to fight using cheerleading tactics. "You're going to teach us to battle monsters with pompoms and high kicks?"

She responds by kicking me in the face.

It's not hard enough to actually hurt, but my pride is severely wounded.

"What the fuck?" I exclaim, my hand flying to my nose.

"Everyone underestimates how useful flexibility is in a fight," she tells me. "I'll whip you into shape in no time. But I'm only doing this once, so your allies are going to join us. The format will be like the cheer camp I ran during summers in high school. We trained for five days straight before the season started. It was intense, but it paid off; we made it to states two years in a row."

"Really?" David asks, impressed.

"Yup," Karina confirms. "We would've won, too, if Laura Whiteman hadn't decided to go rogue during our routine. She snapped her ankle, and we lost points for it."

"Yes. The fact that you lost is definitely the most important thing in that scenario," I say blandly.

"You don't know Laura Whiteman. Total skankoid. I'm glad she broke her stupid ankle; I just wish she'd done it at home."

"I look forward to seeing your progress," Rhys says solemnly, patting me on the back.

"Oh, don't worry," Karina says. "You'll be joining us."

"Pardon me?"

"We'll start tomorrow," she decides. "Wear something you're not afraid to throw up on."

THE ARMORY IS IN THE OLD BUILDING, A MILE HIKE from the main campus on the far side of the island. Provost Mathers asked me to take inventory and see if there were any usable weapons. If we're going to be fighting Neil, we need all the ammo—or in this case, swords—we can get.

I asked if we could use ammo, by the way. It might come as a shock, given how bad I am with guns, but I'm willing to bear with it if it means getting rid of Neil. Unfortunately, Mathers denied my request. In magic fights, bullets are rarely used because a counter-spell could cause the bullets to bounce back at you. And swords, he said, are more effective with beastblood hides.

Rhys comes with me. He hasn't said it, but I think he's more conscious of the fact that this fight with Neil could be the end. We hold hands as we traverse the woods, despite the sticky heat and rampant bugs. Somehow, his skin manages to stay dry and somewhat cool to the touch.

"Do you think we'll find anything useful?" I ask. "Mathers said this place is old. Anything we find probably needs to be sharpened. Or saged."

"Saged? You think the weapons will be haunted?"

I love that he's starting to get more references now. Our movie marathons have done him well. I wish elves made movies, so there could be a more even exchange, but Rhys assures me that he enjoys watching Hollywood films with me. Given that we're making an effort to be more open with each other—no matter how embarrassing the subject may be—I'm inclined to take his word for it.

"What are you thinking about?" he asks. God, when he smiles at me, it's like everything in the world is better.

Ugh, I'm such a loser. "Let's go on a trip somewhere, after this is all over. Just you and me."

That piques his curiosity. "Where would you like to go?"

"Anywhere. Without big bugs," I add. "And the weather has to be nice—not too hot."

"That is certainly doable."

"We'll eat a lot of ice cream," I promise. "And we can go to cafés and try a lot of good food. You can charm the pants off some bakery owner and get their recipes to try at home. Maybe I'll take up a domestic skill, too, like…making vegan cleaning products or something."

"You have it all figured out," he murmurs. "What brought on these thoughts?"

"I'm just trying to be positive. I know we could die. One of us, both of us," I ramble, "all of us. Or we could both live. And I'd rather prepare for *that* scenario than…you know."

Rhys squeezes my hand. "We will both survive," he says firmly. "And then I will take you on a long, relaxing trip. I promise."

"Don't make promises you can't keep."

"Never." His absolute certainty might be rubbing off on me, too, because for the first time since this all began, I'm starting to have hope that things will actually work out. Fuck if I know how, but I think they will.

We finally arrive at the old building, a stone structure with a patchy roof and a metal door. I expect the inside to be just as decrepit, but it's not as bad as I thought it would be. The first room is the armory.

There's no power, so the first thing we do is open the windows for airflow and light. Rows of swords and other bladed weapons line the shelves on the walls and a metal rack in the middle, cutting the room in half. We start making our way down one aisle, inspecting the weapons. Most of them are rusted and dull, but a few are in decent condition. I pick up a long sword and swing it experimentally. It's heavy, but not too heavy. I think I could handle it in a fight.

"You know, there's one good thing about raiding Neil's lab," I say. "I bet it's air-conditioned."

"And clean," he adds, skirting around a rusted blade sticking out dangerously.

We begin in one corner, sorting through the various blades without cutting off any fingers. There are some usable swords, but most of the weapons are so rusted or dull, they would be useless in a fight.

Useless to someone like me, anyway. Who knows? Maybe Karina could make something here work. She killed a timekeeper with a pen.

"If all else fails, I could always use my irresistible charm," I mutter.

"That may work on me, but I doubt Neil is sophisticated enough to appreciate your magnetism."

"I love how you complimented us both with that sentence."

"I aim to please." He holds out a curved knife, handle toward me. "This might come in handy."

I take the knife from him and examine it closely. The blade is thin and sharp, with a slight curve to it. It's definitely not a sword, but it could be useful. "I like it. It's not too heavy."

"It will work well for quick movements and close combat," he says, nodding. "A secondary weapon to compliment your sword."

"Blood magic will be my primary mode of defense. Or offense. Whichever means I avoid dying while simultaneously taking down the enemy."

"You will be a force to be reckoned with."

"Let's just hope it's enough for the timekeepers." Which reminds me—I never told him about what happened at the boardwalk in Jacksonville. I can't just write it off—I know my mind wasn't playing tricks on me. The timekeepers did something, who knows what. "Hey, so there's something I forgot to mention…"

"That is a worrying way to begin a conversation," he informs me. "But please, go on."

I quickly explain what happened, which sounds weirder out loud when I recount it. "They spoke to me using 'we' and the voice was, like, inside my head. But the snake from the hotel was different—definitely not a timekeeper. And it spoke using 'I' and 'my'. I don't know if that's significant, but it freaked me out."

Rhys listens to me, despite my horrible storytelling skills. "Perhaps they are connected to you through a psychic link. When you went to the Veil on a hunt, you said you were bitten by snakes. Subsequently, your eye color changed. And Astaroth's blood must have had some effect on you as well."

"Then do you think they can see me, regardless of whether or not Karina is around?"

"They might not be completely blind to your actions," Rhys considers, "but they have yet to launch a full attack. Perhaps they can project images into your mind, but not physically hurt you."

"If they can look into my mind, they can hurt me. They were aware of my surroundings at the boardwalk, enough to make me walk into a dark storefront and look into a mirror. What if they decide to make me walk off a plank next?"

"Are you a pirate?"

"No, I'm just concerned!"

He tries, and fails, to suppress a smile. "The incident at the hotel sounds unconnected to the incident at the boardwalk. I would venture to guess that the hotel attack was purely launched by Astaroth. You said the voice sounded familiar, correct? And the woman was a cultist."

"You're right." The red snake's voice did sound like Astaroth. "In which case, do you think Karina killed him when she stabbed him with a pen?"

"Unfortunately, no. I believe the snake was merely a vessel he created with blood magic. He is...powerful, Maria. Honestly, it is concerning."

Damn. I was hoping he'd say something a little more comforting. But at least he's being honest.

We spend the remainder of our time moving the usable weapons to the hallway. Rhys finds a wheelbarrow outside, so we load the weapons in that and begin our trek back to the main building to drop everything off. It's late evening, so we dump it in Theodas' locked storage room and head back to my house.

We're one step closer to being prepared for whatever comes our way, at least. And tomorrow, we start training. I don't know how much help cheerleading training will be, but Karina clearly isn't a "wax on, wax off" kind of girl. She's too impatient, and way too sadistic.

As I unlock the back door, Rhys turns to me with a serious expression. "I meant what I said earlier about taking you on a trip. Anywhere you want."

"I could be cheesy and tell you that it doesn't matter where we go, as long as we're together," I begin, "but I would really rather go somewhere without large insects and lots of people. Somewhere quiet, where we can just be a normal couple and not have to worry about cultists or demons or mad scientists attacking us. And are you coming inside?"

"Would you like me to?" he asks hesitantly.

"Yes, as long as you promise that you are going to relax. We have a big day tomorrow, if Karina is to be trusted." I guide him inside and head directly downstairs. "So no cooking, no cleaning, just cuddling and couch-potatoing. Got it?"

"*You* aren't going to make dinner, right?"

"Why do you look so scared? I'm not that bad. And there's pre-prepared food in the freezer!"

He breathes a sigh of relief, and I try not to be offended.

"Ouch. You wait here, I'll get some snacks," I promise.

I make my way upstairs and into the kitchen, humming to myself. I'm just about to open the pantry when I hear a voice behind me.

"Mar? I thought I heard voices," Isabelle says, padding downstairs in her slippers. "We just ate, but there are leftovers."

"Thanks, but I think we're going to start off with something light." I grab a few water bottles and a bag of popcorn. "What are you up to?"

"Tasha and David are watching a movie with Allegra in her room, and I'm catching up on *The Bachelorette*," she says. It's always been her guilty pleasure. "Is Rhys here?"

"Yeah, he's downstairs. We're going to hang out and— what are you doing?"

Isabelle slips me a handful of foil squares from her robe. "You can never be too prepared."

"Oh my God."

"Honey, don't be embarrassed. I just want to make sure you're being careful," she assures me.

"There are ten here."

"There are more in the first-floor bathroom, right behind the tampons."

"Oh my God," I repeat.

"I don't know much about elf physiology," she admits, "but I've read some of the romance books you enjoy. You really should put a password on your Kindle if you're going to leave it in the living room. Anyway, the supernatural creatures in those books seem to be — "

"Please, I am *begging* you not to finish that sentence. Or this conversation," I plead, on the verge of spontaneously combusting.

She waves a hand. "There is nothing to be embarrassed about when it comes to protection, Mar! All I'm saying is, you aren't ready for a baby right now. I know your hormones are raging and your emotions are high, but honey, you can't even take care of a houseplant. At least wait until you finish college."

"I'm going to go downstairs now," I tell her, "and I assure you, nothing is going to happen."

"Well, when 'nothing' happens, make sure you put it on correctly! We have bananas you could practice on. Or there are some great YouTube tutorials — "

"La la la, I can't hear you!" I run downstairs, slamming the door shut behind me as I toss the condoms in the laundry bin.

"Is everything alright?" Rhys asks, alarmed. "You look pale."

"Everything is fine."

"You are lying."

"Isabelle gave me condoms," I choke out, beet red.

"Oh. There is no need to be embarrassed," he lies, very unconvincingly. "She is not watching television on the first floor, is she?"

"No, she's in her room, thinking about how we're down

here alone with our raging hormones and lack of a chaperone." I groan, setting the food down on my desk.

"Perhaps I should take my leave, then."

"You don't have to. It's awkward, but I guess she's showing her approval. In the most embarrassing, roundabout way possible," I explain.

Rhys nods in understanding, a small smile playing at the corners of his lips. "I suppose it is a good thing that she cares enough to make sure we are being safe."

"Yeah, I guess so."

Rhys clears his throat. "So, what did you want to do tonight? Watch a movie?"

I nod, grateful for the change in topic. "That sounds good. What's next on our list? *The Princess Bride*? Have you seen it?"

"No. But Theodas has a poster in his room," Rhys says with a chuckle. "Shall we open the popcorn and begin?"

"As you wish."

CHAPTER TWENTY

I sabelle used to wake me up in the mornings by opening the curtains and pulling the sheets off me. Max once woke me up by shoving a sewing needle under my fingernail. And of course, Nic has used an air horn on me.

Karina's method is what I would expect from her: brutal and efficient. She kicks my bedroom door open. And someone—God knows who—thought it would be a good idea to give her a megaphone.

"Wake up!" she shouts, ripping the curtains open.

I rub my eyes with a yawn. "What time is it?"

"Time to train. Get up and come upstairs to eat!" she yells. "Are you both clothed?"

She doesn't wait for an answer, ripping the sheets off the bed and blasting the air horn again. Clamping my hands over my ears, I try to kick her, but she only laughs.

"We start in thirty minutes. Get up, get dressed, eat, and let's *go*!" She sounds the air horn one last time before leaving.

Groaning, I roll over. "This was your idea."

"I realize," Rhys replies, speaking into my pillow. Maybe he's trying to smother himself.

We somehow manage to get up and get ready, though we're both sluggish after staying up last night. Rhys returns to his house to change, while I throw on a sports bra and shorts. Karina never explained the specifics of what we would be doing, but I figure it's going to be grueling and outside, so I slather on sunscreen and pack a bottle for Rhys. His coloring is pale; he'll probably roast in the sun.

Tasha waits for me in the kitchen with a protein shake and a granola bar, already in her workout gear. "Mornin', Mar. I heard you were up to no good last night. Rhys slept over?"

"Can we not? I already had a talk with Isabelle." I lower my voice. "She gave me, like, ten condoms."

"Sweet. How was it?"

"Nothing happened!" Certainly not after my talk with Isabelle! I don't think I'd be able to make eye contact afterward. She knows my...colorful history. But this time, it's different. Rhys isn't just a lapse in judgement, drunken or otherwise. "Are you training with us?"

"I thought it'd be nice to get some exercise. And we haven't had much quality time together."

She's so full of it! "Are you coming to laugh at me?"

"That's just a bonus," she admits. "Come on, let's get going. Karina said she planned a bunch of fun activities for us."

Karina's version of "fun" and mine probably don't align.

We get to the athletic field behind the main building, which is fenced off but gives any passersby a good view of what we'll be doing. Karina stands in the middle of the field with her hair in a high ponytail, lathering on sunscreen with the rest of the students gathered. Declan rubs lotion on Ava's shoulders, while Archer and Celeste are reluctantly helping each other. Ophelia lays out yoga mats, and Rhys, Theodas, and Provost Mathers stand to the side in a shady tent with a fan. Rhys is, however, in workout wear.

"I don't think I've ever seen you in shorts," I comment, approaching their little oasis.

"They are not my clothing of choice," he admits.

"His legs are smoother than yours," Tasha says unnecessarily.

"That's not true!" I just shaved!

"Some elves just aren't that hairy," Theodas explains. "Also, good morning, you two. Excited for today? We've got first aid kits, coolers, and a cooling station inside."

"I'm very interested to see these fightin' techniques," Provost Mathers admits. "Miss Swan mentioned these aren't ancient Chinese techniques, but just run-of-the-mill things her parents taught her. Let's hope it's worth it."

"She's underselling it." I turn to Tasha. "Don't push yourself. If you need a break, please take one, okay?"

She salutes me. "Yes, ma'am."

"Alright, everyone!" Karina shouts into the megaphone. Seriously, who gave that to her? I need to "talk" with them. "Gather 'round."

I join the group of students, most of whom I recognize. Not everyone is in my immediate friend group, but the school isn't big. I must have seen these students in my classes last semester.

"We're going to begin with stretching. Everyone to a mat! We're going to start with my daily splits routine."

To my surprise, the routine isn't too intense. I don't have anything close to a split, and some of the positions are uncomfortable, but they aren't outlandish. Most of the students here can't do a split either, though Ava comes close. Stretching actually feels good, and by the time our bodies are warmed up, Karina leads us to the shade behind the main building so we're not directly in the sun.

"Now, we're going to start with some sparring," she declares. Something tells me she enjoys bossing us around. "This is usually how I started cheer camps. We'll go one at a time, and everyone else should pay attention. Now, you might feel like you're being put on the spot. You might get stage fright, or feel like you're going to be judged for your performance. I just want to assure you that this is *totally* the case. This isn't a judgment-free zone. We're going to spar, and then everyone is going to pick you apart. Now, who's up first? Can I get a volunteer? Archer, maybe?"

Archer looks around, but no one else volunteers. Instead, we begin to sit in the grass while Karina has Ophelia block off an area with cones.

"Now, attack me. Don't hold back," Karina warns. "I want you to come at me like you're trying to kill me. You have five minutes to break one of my bones."

"What? But this is just a practice match," Archer says.

"And *go*!"

Archer grabs at her, but his heart clearly isn't in it. Karina dodges, spinning and ducking every punch with minimal effort. The way she moves is mesmerizing, like she's dancing; every motion is fluid but intentional. There's never a point where she's not in control. Archer looks slow and clumsy in comparison, though it could be because he's used to sword-fighting as opposed to hand-to-hand. Still, he hasn't landed a single blow on her.

It makes me wonder if she *let* me hit her during our fight.

When the five minutes are up, the pair stop abruptly. Sweat dots Archer's brow, but Karina isn't even out of breath.

"Alright. Give me reasons why that sucked. Anyone?" She scans the group, but no one raises their hand. "Obviously he didn't land a blow. Do you know why?"

"You're too fast?" someone suggests.

"Wrong. Archer here suffers from a problem most students at these magic schools seem to have. When you spar, you hold back, which stunts your growth. He didn't even attempt to gouge my eyes out," she says, jerking a thumb at him. "And hello, I'm wearing earrings. Why didn't you try to rip them out? You just tried to punch me and grab me, without any proper grappling techniques."

"I'm not going to seriously injure you," he sputters.

"Right. But that means you aren't training properly. You should be looking to actually hurt me, because when a real fight breaks out, you need to let your instincts take over. By holding back when you're training, you repress that killer instinct that will save your life in a dangerous situation."

I hate to admit it, but she's making sense.

One by one, she calls us up to fight. With each match, the students get braver, but only a few manage to land a hit —and nothing seems to affect Karina at all. Even Ophelia joins in, managing to punch Karina in the jaw. But ultimately, Karina ends up the winner.

When it's Rhys' turn, I half expect him to hold back, since Karina is a woman and all. He doesn't, but all his efforts earn him is a headlock. I'm not much better, ending up face down in the dirt with Karina sitting on my back.

Lunch in the cafeteria is a much-needed break for everyone, though for once, I get a sandwich with no fries or chips and an electrolyte drink. I even leave the tomatoes and lettuce on the sandwich, instead of picking them off. What is happening to me?

The workout wasn't intense, since we all took turns sparring in the shade, but my will to continue is thoroughly zapped.

Karina sparred the entire time, and while she doesn't look fresh as a daisy anymore, she's the type of person who glows instead of dripping sweat, giving me yet another reason to resent her.

"Why the long face?" she asks, settling down beside me with a tray of salad.

"I thought we would be hitting the dumbbells," I tell her honestly.

"That sounds like it would hurt."

"You know what I mean, smartass."

"You've been working out with Archer for a while now. You feel like you're stunted, right? Like you aren't making any progress? Maybe that's because lifting weights isn't what you need," she says patiently. "In a perfect world, I'd push you harder and we'd have more time to turn you into the Hulk. But we have five days, and then we're going to strike Neil's lab. I can't make you a superhero overnight, but if we train your technique and mentality, we can make more progress."

I get what she's saying, but I'm still not 100% on board with this. Nonetheless, she *is* trying to help. I just hope it will be enough.

THE NEXT TWO DAYS OF BOOTCAMP ARE BLISTERINGLY hot, so Karina turns the sprinklers on and makes us fight in the water. More students join our little group, and even Theodas jumps in. Though, due to Provost Mathers' pleading, Theodas is only allowed to fight Rhys. Having the chancellor of a school spar with the students is inappropriate, and according to Mathers, they can't have another PR disaster. The cultists on the cruise ship were bad enough publicity within the supernatural realm, apparently.

Karina is a lot of things—blunt and insensitive, to name a few—but she actually takes good care of us, forcing regular breaks and bringing in refreshments for us to keep hydrated. It's not easy work, believe me, but it's not unfair or even torturous. Yet.

On the third day, in the morning, Karina announces that we will have a break while she conducts one-on-one private training with each of us. I'm slotted for the afternoon, so I spend the morning relaxing.

Until I see the faces of people who come out of her one-on-one sessions in the gym.

Over lunch, I meet with Ava, who confirms my suspicions.

"It was like being tortured mentally," Ava recalls. "I don't think I'll be able to look her in the eye again!"

Declan nods in agreement. "I have bruises in places that no one should have bruises. She has no sense of mercy."

"You must be exaggerating," I say, though I'm not entirely confident that they are.

"Just make sure you don't eat too much," Ava says, looking at my lunch tray. "You wouldn't want to get sick."

Well, that's just great. I'm not mentally prepared for what's coming next, so I trudge my feet as I walk to the private room in the gym.

But when I open the door, Karina, and Tasha are waiting for me on the bench.

"I thought these were one-on-ones," I say cautiously. "Are you guys ganging up on me or something?"

"Or something," Karina agrees, closing the door behind me. "You're a little bit different, Mar. In a good way, though. I gathered some information about you, and I learned that you have killed before. You killed a cultist, your roommate?"

That's not a fun memory. I'm not ashamed, and I don't regret it, but I didn't enjoy it or anything. Even if Penny was annoying. It seems like forever ago now. "Yeah. I stabbed her in the neck because she was trying to kill me."

"Archer tells me that you pulled the knife out of him and used it to stop her. No hesitation, no punches pulled, no remorse. I really respect that," she says, sounding like she means it. "You did what you needed to do to survive. But I don't see any of that fire in you right now."

"I don't really understand what you mean." I didn't *think* when I stabbed Penny. I just did it. It was her or me—and I chose myself. Of course, I ended up releasing Astaroth from the time prison because of it, so who knows if I made the correct choice?

"I'm going to be honest with you," Karina says.

"You're always honest."

"I don't know what happened. I don't really care. Something made you go from being decisive to insecure and indecisive."

That feels like a personal attack, and even though I know she's right, my voice comes out defensive and high-pitched. "I can't afford to be reckless. If I make a mistake, people I care about will pay for it. Neil was very adamant that I understand that."

I don't know how she's getting me to admit this, since this is a topic I usually discuss with my therapist, but it just comes out. Like diarrhea.

"Your problem isn't your technique or your powers, Mar. It's all mental. That's why I brought Tasha here—to help you go back to your bullshit. To help you remember who you are."

I don't see how that's going to help. The girl I was... I was *weak* in the beginning.

Tasha steps forward with a smile on her face. "You remember that time Jeremy told everyone that you were sleeping with Mr. Decker? And then they stole a frog from Mr. Tucker's supply room and glued it to your locker?"

"How can I forget? The smell never came out of my backpack."

"And what did you do?"

"With the backpack? I threw it out." What a waste of money.

"No," she says impatiently. "With Jeremy."

"I painted 'Frog Fucker' on his car. Not my proudest moment."

"Really? Because your expression says the opposite," Tasha teases. "Or that time those girls poured lighter fluid on you, do you remember what you did to them?"

"I poured a bucket of ashes on them." Decidedly not as

intense as lighter fluid, but hey, ashes were far more easily accessible. And apparently they hurt when you get them in your eyes.

"You were never able to let anything go. One way or another, you always got back at the people who pissed you off, which I've always respected," Tasha admits. This is news to me.

Tasha was well-liked in school — not popular, exactly, but she had a solid friend group and never got bullied. Unfortunately, while I was getting beat-up at school, she was dealing with shit at home. And unlike me, she couldn't afford to piss off her foster families.

"Even when you were being ridiculous about it," she continues, "and sometimes a little bit obsessive. It didn't matter what they did. You didn't care, and you weren't scared; you just knew you had to stand up for yourself. No matter what character you were, at your core, you were always Maria."

"I guess," I say. "But Neil changed everything. Magic changed everything. And Luke... I can't, Tash. Really."

"You're allowed to be afraid. Neil is, from what I've been hearing, a pretty scary guy. But you don't need to worry about me, or Isabelle, or David. We're not the ones who are going to be fighting out there, Mar. You are."

"I'm not strong enough, even with this training camp. I know I won't be strong enough to face him. Maybe we're all just fooling ourselves He's...untouchable."

"No one is untouchable," Karina interrupts. "Not Neil, or Astaroth, or the timekeepers."

"That's easy for you to say. You're strong," I tell her. "But Neil and Astaroth are way more powerful than you realize. They're stronger than Nic, and their powers are off the charts. The timekeepers can control time itself. No matter how hard we try, we might end up getting slaughtered upon arrival."

"Seriously?" Karina bursts into laughter, confusing both Tash and me. I don't know what's so hilarious. "Let me tell you something: I don't care how powerful you think Neil and his band of misfits are. This isn't about who has the ability to time travel or who can use blood magic. Magic isn't the be-all and end-all. It's a tool. You're the one using it. It is what you make of it."

"That's very nice and all. I'm sure you'd do a much better job in my shoes—"

"Not at all. When I fight, I don't rely on my powers alone. I bring everything I am to the battlefield, every single time. Otherwise, why even bother? If I wanted to see who was the strongest between us, we could lift weights or have an arm-wrestling competition. This upcoming battle isn't a test to see who between you and Astaroth is better at using blood magic. You're fighting him to kill him. And *you* have the advantage."

"Me? How do I have the advantage?"

Karina rolls her eyes impatiently. "When he was in the time prison, all he did was practice blood magic, with nothing and no one but himself. You, on the other hand? You were growing up, learning how to survive in a world that didn't give a shit about you. You took beatings, got revenge on classmates, found people you would give the world to protect. All your experiences, everything that makes you who you are, are weapons you can use against your enemies."

"How is that?" I ask dumbly.

"Think about it. When the time is right, you'll know."

CHAPTER TWENTY-ONE

My mile time hasn't improved. I can't lift more weights or do any more pull-ups than I could before Karina's training camp. But I've done one thing today that I was never able to do before: punch Archer directly in the face.

Not that I've wanted to, or that I'm proud of it. Well, I *am* proud of it, but not because I have any ill will toward Archer.

But it's pretty incredible what a few tweaks can do. After the whole "be yourself" crap Karina fed me during our one-on-one, she pointed out a few weaknesses that I need to work on. My main issue is being so in my head and not trusting my instincts enough. In my defense, my instincts haven't always been trustworthy, especially when it comes to fighting.

Instead of following the rigid rules that Archer set out for me, and even the guidance that Rhys used to bark at me when we would train, everything comes much more naturally to me. It's not all about punching and kicking. Karina's fighting style focuses solely on winning, using whatever methods possible.

I'm not afraid to admit I was wrong about this—and, possibly, about Karina herself. She's actually really knowledgeable when it comes to fighting. I could never tell her that to her face. If her ego gets any bigger, this whole island will sink from the sheer weight of it.

After the match with Archer, Karina has us switch partners. She somehow manages to look glamorous in the ninety-degree heat, her long legs and toned arms tanned from being outside these past few days. It's attracted the attention of most guys here, who look at her like she's a goddess or something. Hard not to, considering how effortlessly this all seems to come to her.

"Mar, you're going to be paired with Celeste." Karina gestures for me to walk over to station one, a coned-off section where we can spar. There are six stations on the athletic field and six pairs of fighters. Everyone else who is not fighting gets to critique, and Karina walks around pointing out any improvements to be made.

I haven't fought Celeste yet, and despite landing a punch on Archer, I'm not totally confident in how I'll fare against Celeste. Not that I think she's better than me, even though she might be. But I think she holds a lot more animosity toward me than I do toward her.

I'm not her biggest fan, considering every interaction we've ever had has involved some sort of painful confrontation, be it emotional or physical. And I know that the way she treats Archer isn't the nicest. The underlying problem, though, might not be her personality or even that we're incompatible as people. After the way I witnessed Archer's father behaving toward him, it made me wonder how

Celeste's parents treat her. It's possible that they treat her worse, and frankly, I wouldn't be surprised. While it's no excuse, it does make me feel a little bad for her.

Obviously, I know what it's like growing up with parents who aren't...*ideal*. And I haven't handled it well, so it would be hypocritical of me to judge others based on that. And I'm kind of trying to not be a hypocrite anymore.

When Celeste steps in front of me, there's more fire in her eyes than I anticipated. It's true that our past interactions haven't been good, but I didn't think she hated me to this extent unless I'm just misreading things.

"Ready when you are," I say, trying to keep my tone cheerful. She answers by kicking me in the stomach. Ouch.

We circle each other warily, both of us searching for an opening. Celeste lunges first, her fist aimed squarely at my face. But I'm quicker than I used to be, and I manage to dodge her attack with ease.

Celeste glares at me, her frustration evident. She launches another flurry of attacks, but I've learned well from Karina—there's a sentence I never thought I'd say. I duck, weave, and counter as best I can. And for once in my life, I actually feel competent in a fight.

"Wow, someone's been practicing," Celeste snaps, her breath coming in short puffs.

"Yep," I say, grinning. "And it looks like it's paying off."

In that moment, I see an opening. Celeste's guard is down, just for a second, and I take my chance. I sweep her legs with my foot and my fist connects with her stomach, sending her curling on the ground.

"Did you just—" she chokes out, her eyes wide with disbelief.

"Looks like it," I reply, lending her a hand.

Celeste's face turns a deep shade of red, her nostrils flaring in anger as she storms off the field and into the building. I can't help but think what a drama queen she is. But something inside me tells me to follow her, to make sure I didn't seriously hurt her.

"Hey." I call out after her, jogging to catch up. "Are you okay?"

She whirls around to face me, her eyes full of fire. "Why would you think I could possibly be okay right now? A loser like you just beat me."

"I think once you've graduated high school, you can't call people 'losers' anymore. It sounds childish. Besides, technically you're the one who lost."

"No!" Celeste snarls, and she actually looks genuinely hurt. "God! Why do you have to ruin everything? You're like King Midas, except everything you touch turns to shit!"

"Ha! Joke's on you! If you just made a reference, I have no idea what you're talking about!"

"Good Lord, you are an idiot!" she yells, then promptly bursts into tears. It's very difficult to have a rational conversation when the other person is crying. I'm caught between comforting her and running away. "You cannot fathom what it's like. Archer and I were fine, and then you showed up and convinced him not to be with you, and everything went to crap! And then you brought the timekeepers on our heads and that cheerleader bimbo! She is the most annoying, idiotic person I've ever met!"

"So," I say, "do you hate her more than you hate me?"

"Shut up!" she hisses.

"Before this, I would have wholeheartedly agreed with you. But maybe she's smarter and more...whatever the opposite of shallow is, than you give her credit for. Is it deep? Does that sound right to you?"

If looks could kill, I'd be dead five times over.

"You think you know everything, don't you?" she snarls, her voice trembling with anger. "You just waltz in here, acting like you're so much better than everyone else!"

"Whoa, hold on," I say, raising my hands defensively. "That's not what I said at all."

"Isn't it?" Celeste takes a menacing step toward me, her eyes blazing. "You should hand Karina over to the Ruby Council already. It will make things better for everyone."

"Look." I grit my teeth, forcing myself to remain calm. "I'm doing my best to manage these insane situations, just like everyone else here."

"Your best?" She scoffs, crossing her arms over her chest. "You're just making everything harder for everyone else. You brought this business with Neil upon all of us."

She can't be serious. But when I look into her eyes, I don't think that she's kidding or even exaggerating. She's totally convinced that all the bad stuff that's been happening lately is because of me.

I can admit that all this is connected to me, and I have changed Archer's priorities by enlisting his help with this. But she is delusional if she thinks that everything was fine before I came along. Even without me, Neil was doing his shady business in the background. Once again, everything is his fault.

A few months ago, I might have just agreed with her or tried to get out of this conversation because she's shadow-born, and she's much more powerful than me. But now the tables have turned. Sort of. I know that I'm not outstand-ingly more powerful than her. But shadowborn don't respond to acting meek or having healthy conflict-resolution tactics. They respond to power and violence. I don't really want to use violence again, so I'll just give empathy a try.

"That's tough, isn't it?" I tell her. "Look, I get that you don't like me, and trust me, the feeling is mutual, but the door's over there. You don't have to be involved with this; you can just walk away."

"As long as Archer is involved, I can't walk away."

"So your plan is to suffocate him? That's a really good strategy for when you're eventually married. It's nice to know how little you care about his feelings."

"You don't know anything."

"I know that you and Archer don't get along. I know that you don't love each other, and that he would rather break your engagement off. But you won't let it go. Or, rather, neither you nor your parents will let it go."

"What do you think is going to happen if I break this off? Do you think we're just going to find other people and skip into the sunset? If I don't marry Archer, my dad is going to marry me off to some old geezer. And Archer's father will do the same. At least I'm a more age-appropriate choice. And you know what? This isn't even about happiness or love. This is about duty and responsibility, something you know nothing about."

"I've never been forced into marriage, but I have been pressured into a lot of other things," I say. "This is pointless. Whatever you're trying to do, it's not going to work."

For a moment, Celeste looks like she might argue further. But then she just sighs, her shoulders slumping as she turns away.

"Whatever," she mutters, the fire in her eyes gone. "Just...leave me alone."

"Fine," I agree, backing off. "But at some point, you have to understand that a third option might exist, even if you can't see it now."

As I turn to leave, I can't help but wonder if there's any hope for the two of us ever finding common ground. But for now, I have my own battles to fight, and I can't afford to waste any more energy on someone who refuses to see the truth. With a heavy heart, I slip out of the building, leaving Celeste to face her demons alone.

CELESTE DOESN'T COME BACK TO TRAIN WITH US, AND I don't see her for the rest of Karina's bootcamp. Archer doesn't say anything about it, and pressing him on the matter is a bad idea, so I let it go. I must have really hit a nerve.

I don't regret what I said, though I could have delivered my message more effectively. But what's done is done, and at the end of the final day, I'm too busy roasting marshmallows to worry about Celeste.

We decided to end the bootcamp with a bonfire, complete with marshmallows, alcohol, and pop music. Apparently, no one can resist a bonfire, so the majority of students still on campus, along with a few faculty members, show up.

I search the snack table for another bag of marshmallows since someone spilled the first bag in the sand. Archer doesn't even like junk food, but he's decided to make an exception tonight. I even opened a beer for him, which I'm proud to say is his very first. It was a little sad that he didn't know how to open the twist top, but he'll get the hang of it.

Yes, I realize I am not the best influence.

Karina, meanwhile, truly is Little Miss Popular. She's too busy to hang out with me, surrounded by a group of male students who fall over their feet trying to get close to her. It helps that she's wearing a bikini top. She's got them all practically drooling—an unofficial Karina Swan fan club in the making. Even if the conversation isn't exactly pleasant.

"My dad always told me to aim for the eyes," Karina says, flipping her hair over her shoulder. "People have, like, a really hard time fighting after you cut their eyes out. You don't need to extract them, but cutting them open is super painful. And kind of gross. Have you ever tried biting someone's eye out? The texture is totally weird."

The guys in her harem either aren't paying attention, or they just don't care about the grotesque stuff coming out of her mouth. They're all lovestruck. I'm not sure how she has that effect on them, but it's creepy as hell.

I return to my group with the bag of marshmallows, plopping down in a chair between Rhys and Theodas. Tearing the bag open, I give a marshmallow to each of them and pass the bag around. Rhys made wooden spears with his powers, so we all have long enough sticks for roasting at a safe distance.

"You're just in time," Tasha says, gesturing to Archer and Allegra beside her. "Allegra was about to tell us how she and Archer first met."

"I just finished telling everyone about your valiant efforts in the past," Theodas quips, giving me a lopsided grin.

I would hardly describe my efforts as "valiant," so I'm

slightly concerned, but I decide to let it go for my own mental health. "How did you meet Archer?"

Allegra smiles. "I was thirteen, and Neil took me to a conference at the Kinsey house. The other kids weren't very welcoming, so I decided to take a walk on my own. As I traversed the gardens, I saw him sitting in a tree, eating an apple. He looked so casually cool, so effortless; I was... pretty much smitten. I found out later that he had actually gotten stuck up there, and later that night, his parents had to call the fire department to get him down."

"Wow. As Karina would say, that's super embarrassing for you," I tell Archer.

He blushes. "I was thirteen. Cut me some slack."

"You met her while you were stuck in a tree, and when we first met, you flashed me," I remind him. "You're not good at meet-cutes, are you?"

"He's meet-cursed," Allegra adds, sending both Tash and me into a fit of giggles. Archer doesn't look as amused.

Theodas' brow creases. "I was naked when I met you, too, Mar. Maybe you're the one who's meet-cursed."

"Maybe you shouldn't be walking around a forest naked!" I retort. "Weren't you scared of bug bites? I saw those freaky insects you have in the Veil!"

"You were always so dramatic," he says with a laugh. But I'm not exaggerating—those bugs were bigger than my head!

Rhys pats my hand. "Our first interaction was normal, comparatively."

"From my perspective, our first meeting involved waking up handcuffed to a bed." Everyone looks at me with a mix of amusement and horror, and I clarify, "Because of the cultists on the ship. Not in a weird way—*stop looking at us like that*, Tash! I told you it wasn't like that! And it's not like I could even see you in the dark, Rhys. Mr. 'I-Must-Hide-My-Face-Because-I'm-Ugly.'"

"We agreed that was a lie," he says.

"Yes, a stupid one. And come to think of it, the second time we met, you didn't have a sympathetic bone in your body! You told me I better not throw up on you! After I was beaten up by Nic at Foley-Hill!"

"I had to be cold toward you. I could not pursue you and risk the timeline, despite my yearning," Rhys insists. "You told me I was cold in a sexy way!"

He was, but I can't just admit that aloud, especially not in front of my snickering sister.

"I think I'm going to be sick," Archer mutters.

"Shut up," I say, at the same time Rhys tells Archer to be quiet.

"Aw, you two are so cute," Tasha teases. "Which means it's my sisterly duty to share an embarrassing story about Mar."

The sad thing is, I've had so many embarrassing moments, I don't know which she's going to choose. "No one wants to hear it, Tash."

"I want to," Archer says, probably as payback for my earlier comments. Damn.

"I do, too," Ophelia chimes in, passing cups of red liquid around. "Someone just brought jungle juice. It's insanely good."

I take a cup from her. "What's in it?"

"Alcohol. Now tell the story, Tasha. Everyone wants to know," Ophelia says.

"Let me set the scene," Tasha says, in full storytelling mode. "We're fourteen, and Mar is being relentlessly harassed by this snotty kid who lives across the street from the group home—Scott Downing. Now, looking back, I'm pretty sure Scott had a crush on Mar."

"He told the entire school I rubbed a frog against my privates and had a crotch wart," I remind her.

Archer hesitates. "Well, did you—"

"NO!" I shout. "And the kids at school started calling me Warty!"

"Should I find him and defend your honor?" Rhys asks, half serious.

Ophelia snorts. "She doesn't have honor to defend."

"Hey!" I exclaim. "The marshmallows should be the only things we're roasting tonight!"

Tasha waves a hand. "It doesn't matter. Anyway, Scott was horrible, so Mar decided to get revenge on him. And you know Mar—once she hates someone, she hates them will every fiber of her being. It's one of the things I love best about her. We shared a room, and she would whisper his name through gritted teeth while she slept.

"She waited three months, and when school let out, she bought a bunch of Halloween decorations online and snuck over to his house to hang them outside his bedroom window. It was pretty brilliant...except for the fact that the tree she climbed to reach his window had a nest of bees in it. She ended up falling out of the tree screaming, waking the whole neighborhood. One of the decorations was a ghost, and the fabric fell over her head, so she stumbled out into the street and got hit by a car! In the end, she gets a broken arm, bruised ribs, and a *ton* of bee stings! I had to feed her applesauce in the hospital and wait on her hand and foot. I even had to help her in the bathroom! Boy am I glad she's got shadowborn super-healing now."

Everyone except Rhys and Allegra bursts into laughter. But somehow, Allegra looking at me with pity in her eyes is worse than Ophelia cackling and pointing at me. It was a ridiculous situation, and looking back on it now, it seems almost funny—in a painful, cringeworthy sort of way.

Rhys assembles a s'more for me and says, "It was a noble effort, Maria."

"Scott never bothered me again after that." Not that it mattered, because James Hartford took over in that department, giving me a swirly at camp. "I think we've all had enough embarrassing stories for one night."

"Cheers to surviving Karina's bootcamp," Archer jokes, raising his cup of jungle juice in a toast.

"Cheers!" we all echo, clinking our cups together before taking a sip. The juice is sweet and tangy, with a subtle hint of something I can't quite place. I can't even taste the alcohol. The smooth, velvety texture is almost luxurious, making it all too easy to drink.

"Wow, this is good," I remark, taking another sip. "Who made it? Ophelia?"

"Nope. Some of the students brought it. It was on the table, near the cooler of beer," Ophelia explains.

As I continue to sip at the punch, I can't help but notice that something feels...off. My head starts to spin ever so slightly, and my vision seems to blur at the edges. I didn't eat a real dinner, so the alcohol must be hitting me faster than I anticipated.

"Hey, Mar, you okay?" Tasha asks, her brow furrowing with concern.

"Yeah, just... feeling a little weird," I admit. "I think I drank too much and ate too little."

"Maybe take a walk by the water? Get some fresh air?" Rhys suggests, worry evident in his eyes.

"Good idea," I agree, standing up a little shakily. "Be back in a few."

"Do you want me to accompany you?"

"No, I'm fine," I say quickly.

The ocean breeze does little to alleviate my symptoms. If anything, they seem to intensify—my heart races, pounding in my ears like a drumbeat gone rogue. A wave of nausea washes over me, and I struggle to keep it at bay.

The moment my foot hits the wet sand, I know something's wrong. My head feels like it's spinning faster than a carnival ride, and my vision blurs like I'm looking through a smeared window. This isn't your run-of-the-mill tipsy dizziness.

What the hell was in that jungle juice?

My heart races like a jackrabbit on a caffeine high. I try to focus on my breathing, but every inhale feels like I'm sucking air through a straw.

The next thing I know, my legs give out from under me and I collapse onto the sand. As people near the bonfire start to scream, I realize that I'm not alone—several others have been overtaken by the same strange sensation. Some pass out on the spot, while others stumble in confusion, unable to keep their balance.

Whatever was in that punch has caused mass hysteria on the beach. And as for me? Thankfully, I don't pass out. Instead, I vomit up all the s'mores in my stomach.

CHAPTER TWENTY-TWO

Throwing up makes me feel better. As soon as I regain my bearings, I stumble toward my friends. Allegra is throwing up, while Archer and Ava look green. Ophelia is motionless in the sand. Tasha, thankfully, is awake and alert.

"What the hell is going on?" she demands, reaching toward me. "Mar, are you alright?"

"You look ill," Rhys says worriedly, coming around to my other side. "You should sit down."

"I'm fine," I reply, waving their concerns away. "Dizzy, but fine. Someone needs to call a medic. Or twelve."

"I'm on it," Theodas assures me, dialing a number on his phone.

"It was the stupid jungle juice," I mutter, attempting to stand. The world spins, and it's only through sheer stubbornness (and maybe a little help from Rhys) that I manage to stay upright.

The medics are there within minutes, setting up a small tent and working to triage students. I force Tasha to get checked out first, even though she only had a sip of the jungle juice. When the medics clear her, I force her to go home and get to bed. She doesn't need to be around to see — or smell — this. Some of the students are still violently vomiting, while others are unconscious and being revived by student volunteers.

"Maria," Rhys urges. "Come, you must be looked at."

Rhys steers me inside the small blue tent, where I sit on a folding bench. The medic's hands are cold and efficient as she checks my pulse and shines a penlight into my eyes. I try to keep a brave face, but the lingering pain in my chest makes it hard to breathe.

"Your throat is irritated from throwing up, but you should be fine after some rest," she says. "Just take a hot shower to wash off any remaining salt and sand, and get some sleep."

"Sounds like a plan," I agree, struggling to keep the exhaustion from my voice. "Can I leave now, or do I need to fill out an incident report?"

"Go on," the nurse says, waving me away. "But if anything feels off, come right back."

"Thanks." I stand, and Rhys is right there, offering his hand for support.

"We will find out who did this. Theodas is looking into the matter," he says darkly, wrapping an arm around my waist as we make our way out of the makeshift medical area. We pass by other students who also look worse for wear — pale faces, glassy eyes, and trembling hands.

"Hey, don't get too worked up," I say. The salty breeze tugs at my damp hair as Rhys and I walk away from the chaotic scene at the beach. My legs feel like jelly, and I'm pretty sure there's more sand in my shoes than on the shore itself. "It was probably just some idiot's idea of a prank. Besides, I wasn't the only one who drank it."

"Prank or not, someone could have died." Rhys' tone is icy, and I can practically feel the anger radiating off him.

As we walk, I can't shake the feeling that someone — or something — is watching us. It's probably just my overactive imagination playing tricks on me, but I glance over my shoulder every few seconds, searching for hidden threats lurking in the shadows.

We finally reach my house, and I let out a sigh of relief as Rhys helps me up the steps and through the back door.

"Come in," I say, pushing the door open wider, suddenly not quite ready to let Rhys go just yet. "You've got sand all over you, too. Do you want to stay and shower?"

Rhys freezes in his tracks and turns as red as a tomato. "I beg your pardon?"

"You can use the one upstairs," I clarify, raising an eyebrow at his reaction. "What did you think I meant? And why are you blushing?"

"Ah, it is nothing," he replies quickly.

Everything clicks into place, and I can't help but grin. "Oh my God. You thought I meant together, didn't you?"

"Of course not. That would be indecent."

Now it's my turn to call him out on his BS. "You're lying!"

"I am not," he denies vehemently. "I merely struggle with English at times."

I open the door to the basement, laughing and pulling on his wrist. "Come on."

"Apologies, Maria. It was not my intention to assume —"

he begins to ramble, but I cut him off with a dismissive wave of my hand.

"Let's just shower already. I'm exhausted, and I want to get some sleep," I tell him, leading the way down the stairs.

The shower is cramped, but we make do. The steam helps my throat a little, but it's not enough to get rid of the raw, scratchy quality entirely. After we finish washing off, Rhys makes me herbal tea and blow dries my hair while I drink it. It's early morning by the time we get to bed, settled against one another under the covers.

"Thanks for making sure I was okay," I tell him. "I don't know what I'd do without you."

He kisses the top of my head, wrapping his arms around me. "You will never have to find out."

RHYS IS A HOT SLEEPER—LITERALLY, HE'S LIKE A freakin' furnace. It wouldn't be so bad if we didn't live in Georgia and it wasn't the middle of summer. I must be turning into a total sap, though, because my annoyance quickly dissipates once I see his peaceful expression. He's still asleep, and I don't blame him; it was a late night, and despite not passing out, he still drank whatever drugs were in that jungle juice. Me, on the other hand? My internal alarm wakes me up at nine, clocking me in at four hours of sleep. Unable to drift off again, I extract myself from Rhys and get up. My stomach grumbles as I trudge to the bathroom and wash up, trying to reclaim some semblance of normalcy before heading to the cafeteria. I can't cook, but I can grab breakfast for the both of us.

I pick up my phone from the nightstand, ready to go in

my pajamas. As if sensing my intentions, Rhys stirs, his hand moving to my arm before I can leave.

"Where are you going?" he murmurs. He blinks, looking a bit disoriented for a split second before focusing on me.

"Breakfast."

"Not *making* breakfast, right?"

"I am perfectly capable of making breakfast if I wanted to, thank you kindly."

"You could prepare cereal," he agrees. "Stay. We can eat later."

I let him pull me back under the covers, despite the heat. What can I say? He's persuasive. And, on a completely unrelated note, he's a great kisser.

"Alright, alright," I concede with a laugh. "You win. No breakfast run for now."

Not when we have to face Neil. Karina's bootcamp is over, and as long as everyone recovers from the jungle juice incident, we'll be preparing to leave for Neil's lab in the next few days. I don't know what's going to happen, and I can't dwell on it. I just want to savor these sweet moments while I can.

So I let Rhys hold me, leaning against his chest and listening to the strong beat of his heart.

"Have you thought about what you're going to do?" I ask him. "After this, I mean. Now that you're no longer bound to Neil, or anyone else for that matter…"

"Theodas is arranging papers for me so I may enroll in classes," Rhys replies. "Not here—perhaps at a different college, online. After that, I will get a job."

Wow. I know I'm the one who asked the question, but I didn't think he'd actually have an answer.

"You don't have to work. You could just laze around all day. Buy a yacht," I point out.

"Do I seem like the type of person to do that?"

"No. I'm saying you could."

"There are many things I could do. That does not mean I will do them." He brushes the hair from my cheek. "Besides, I think staying away from boats is a good idea. Neither of us have had much luck on them."

"Cultists tried to kill me. That's beyond 'bad luck,'" I say. "What happened to you on the ship?"

Rhys closes his eyes, his lashes long and thick. "We met again, but you did not recognize me. We were strangers in your mind."

I barely saw him on the ship. Actually, I didn't see him at all—he hid his face from me the only time we met. But he probably saw me around; that couldn't have been easy. He'd already been waiting for me for three years at that point. And then, to meet me again, only to have me not recognize him…

"I fell ill every night the first week," he admits. "Boats are very unnatural, Maria. I would not go on a cruise ship again."

"But you'll go on a plane, right?"

"You might have to give me a tranquilizer."

"Well, better to know that now."

"I will still go wherever you want to," Rhys promises.

"I want to get breakfast." As if on cue, my stomach growls.

"Very well." He sighs dramatically, releasing me. But before I can even sit up, there's the sound of footsteps on the stairs and Tasha appears in the doorway.

"Hey, Mar," she says.

"What's up, Tasha?" I quickly get out of bed, pulling my clothes down and trying to look innocent. She's caught me in much more compromising positions before, so it shouldn't matter—especially since Rhys and I weren't doing anything. "Are you feeling okay?"

"I'm fine," she says, eyeing me suspiciously. "I didn't interrupt an afternoon delight, did I?"

"It's still morning," I say.

"What is an 'afternoon delight'?" Rhys asks.

Ignoring him, Tasha asks, "Have you heard from Karina? I've been trying to get ahold of her all morning, but no luck."

"Uh, no," I say, suddenly feeling guilty for not checking in on her earlier. "I haven't heard from her, either. Did something happen?"

Tasha shrugs, looking concerned. "I don't know. She wasn't at breakfast, and no one seems to have seen her since last night."

"Maybe she just decided to sleep in? Did you check with Theodas?"

"Of course."

Then it hits me—the jungle juice drugging. Could it have been a distraction? We were all on the beach, but there was no guarantee the juice would hit us all at the same time. What would be the point in drugging us? It seems too serious to just be a prank.

I didn't see Karina in the medical tent last night. Frankly, I wasn't thinking about her at all. She had a bunch of guys looking out for her, and she's made it perfectly clear that she can handle herself. But even the incredible Karina Swan is fallible to a spiked drink.

"Hey, Rhys," I say, struggling to keep my voice steady.

"I think we should go look for Karina. Something doesn't feel right."

"She would not vanish without a word. You are correct —we can check the cafeteria."

We quickly throw on some clothes and head out into the bustling cafeteria, scanning for any sign of Karina. Tasha goes to Archer's dorm and wakes him so they can cover more ground in the search.

But there's no Karina—not even at the cereal station, grabbing two bowls because according to her, she needs the "ratio" of marshmallows to cereal in her Lucky Charms to be just right.

"Maybe someone else has seen her?" Rhys suggests as we walk back out to the hallway of the main building.

"Maybe," I agree halfheartedly.

I start asking around in the halls, checking every room in the main building for students or teachers, my voice taking on a slightly panicked edge as each person I approach shakes their head. No one has seen Karina since last night.

Not only is she gone, but the protection her presence brings disappears with her. What if the timekeepers can see me now? What if Neil comes and attacks me? Then again, they sent a cultist and a timekeeper after me at the Marriott. Maybe they're using the same manual techniques as Nic had, relying on surveillance and not magic to locate me. It doesn't take a genius to guess where I am, but with Karina around, I felt...safer from them, somehow.

"Maria, calm down," Rhys says gently, placing a hand on my shoulder. "We will find her."

"Will we?" I ask. "Because at this rate, I'm thinking she might've been kidnapped."

"Jumping to conclusions serves no one. We will find her, and if we cannot, I have some ideas on where she might have gone."

"Fine," I grumble, trying to ignore the sinking feeling in my chest.

We continue our search, but as time goes on and Karina remains nowhere to be found, my anxiety amplifies. I send a text to Archer and Ophelia, asking to meet them on the beach. When we arrive, I see Ava and Declan have also joined in the search.

"Any luck?" Ava asks, still looking a little green around the gills.

Archer shakes his head. "Nothing yet, but we'll keep looking."

"Same here," Ophelia chimes in, her voice tense. "No luck on my end either."

"Damn it," I curse under my breath, frustrated by our lack of progress. With all of us looking for her, something has to be wrong. She might be the "blind spot," but she can't just disappear into thin air.

"You don't think someone…took her, do you?" Ava asks.

"Anything's possible," Archer says grimly. "But who would want to kidnap Karina?"

"A lot of guys like her. Maybe they kidnapped her and took her to their love cave or something," Declan suggests.

"I don't think so. That's extremely far-fetched, and clearly you've been watching way too much true crime documentaries," Ophelia says. "Besides, she already has a boyfriend. What about Lilly Hardwicke?"

"She mentioned handing Karina over to the Ruby Council." So did Mr. Kinsey. What if they really did it? I don't remember seeing Lilly at the party, but she could have stopped by.

It doesn't matter much now, I suppose. We need to recover Karina, and fast.

"If Karina was taken by the Ruby Council," Archer begins, "do you think she's in the Veil?"

"Well," I say grimly, "there's only one way to find out."

CHAPTER TWENTY-THREE

Going to the Veil is never a pleasant experience, but this time, we're going prepared. As prepared as we can be, considering we're up against a government agency of literal demons. Now that I think about it, why are we even doing this? Karina has repeatedly shown she can handle herself. I have a feeling that when we rescue her, she'll probably say something along the lines of, "I could've saved myself without your help." Do I really want to subject myself to that?

I know, of course, that the right answer is yes. Because even if she's insufferable and gets on my nerves, and she's probably the vainest person I've ever met, and she uses "like" and "totally" too often, she's...

Wait, where was I going with that? Oh, right. She's my friend. Well, acquaintance. And she probably got kidnapped because of me.

I don't know what the Ruby Council wants with her, but I imagine it traces back to me. Why else would she be on their radar? If they wanted to kill her, they'd send an assassin. They kidnapped her instead, so I imagine that whatever they want to do, torture will be involved.

Which leads me to hope that she's being held at the Ruby Council building in the Veil, and not stashed away somewhere else. Otherwise, this is going to be a massive waste of time. While Theodas and Provost Mathers investigate from Kingsmarch, Archer, Rhys, and I are heading to the Veil.

As soon as Archer comes back with the swords... I don't know what's taking him so long—I only sent him to the armory.

"Everything will be alright," Rhys says, as I pace the lawn of the main building where we agreed to meet Archer.

"I know. I'm fine, seriously," I reply, though not very convincingly. "When is Archer going to get here? He said he'd meet us at three."

"It is 2:45."

"Do you think someone on the Ruby Council is working with Neil?" David asks. He sits beneath a huge oak tree, petting Buck. The stupid dog even lets Rhys scratch behind his ears, his tongue lolling out as he lowers his head. Me, on the other hand? Once the petting stops, he gives me a suspicious look. I didn't even know dogs could do that.

"It is a possibility," Rhys says.

A strong possibility. David's right: someone on the council could very well be in cahoots with Neil. He's worked for the Ruby Council for longer than I've been alive. Who knows what connections he has? And even if that's not the case, it doesn't change the fact that the council wants Karina.

Finally, Archer comes jogging up the walkway with two

swords strapped to his belt. Slightly out of breath, he hands one of them to Rhys. "Sorry I'm late."

"This is the best you could find?" Rhys asks, looking at the blade in his hand.

Archer's face turns red. "Are you seriously criticizing me right now?"

"Are they fighting over you again?" David asks me.

"No. They're just having a sword measuring contest, which is silly, considering someone is in danger and we need to help her," I reply pointedly. "David, you and Buck stay put. We'll be back soon; I don't want Isabelle worrying about us. You distract her, okay?"

"Aye aye, Captain." David gives me a little salute. "Tell Karina when you find her that she promised to teach me the Nutcracker."

"I had no idea you were interested in ballet," Rhys says. "We can always watch some —"

"Not ballet. It's a fighting move," David interrupts. "She said she'd teach me. She also said that once I learn it, no one will ever mess with me again. On account of me crushing their nuts."

I need to have a conversation with Karina about boundaries and teaching my brother martial-arts moves.

I ruffle David's hair, until Buck growls at me. "See you later."

"We're having paella tonight," he replies.

Archer unsheathes the sword, lifting it over his head and creating a rift by slicing the air. Rhys pulls at the edges of the rift until the shimmering, mirror-like surface can be seen.

"Wait!" Allegra sprints across the field, waving her arms wildly. When she reaches us, she bends over, placing her hands on her knees and gasping for breath. "I heard from Tasha. I'm coming with you. I know the Ruby Council building better than any of you, and now that I'm not sick anymore, I can accompany you."

I would argue with her, but she has a point. She's recovered from her illness, and she knows the building because of Neil's work there. Moreover, it's not my responsibility to protect her. I trust Allegra to know her own limits—she's an adult. For the most part.

"Fine," I agree. "If things get messy, you take care of yourself. Got it?"

"All right," Allegra says, exhaling a sigh of relief. It's clear she didn't expect me to agree so quickly.

We all enter the rift, a gentle breeze blowing back my hair as I pass through. We emerge in the middle of a forest, on a road riddled with potholes running through the endless trees. On the other side of the road, a rusty bus stop sign squeaks in the wind.

We approach and wait by the rotting wooden benches. Everything in the Veil is like this: old, colorless, and falling apart. This place gives me the creeps. There's a certain bleakness, a colorlessness that pervades everything.

It isn't long before a bus arrives, stopping right next to us. We board the bus, and Archer informs the driver, a wrinkled old man, of our destination. Soon, we're en route to the city where the Ruby Council building is.

"Why did you decide to come with us?" I ask Allegra, holding on to the seat in front of me for stability. There are no seat belts on the bus, and who knows how far the nearest hospital is.

"Are you serious, Mar? Of course I'm going to help. I may not be Karina's biggest fan, but I wouldn't abandon you, especially when I know I can be of assistance," Allegra replies. "Do you not trust me?"

"That's not it. I'm just concerned."

"I'm fine, I promise. And I know that if danger arises, you'll have my back, just as I'll have yours."

Really? After everything that's happened, I didn't expect her to say something like that. It almost feels like we've gone back in time, to before she found out about my relationship to Neil. Part of me wonders if it's all a trick.

But maybe I'm just being cynical. Allegra was misguided in the past, understandably so, but she never actually hurt me. And she gave up working with Nic the moment she realized it put David in trouble.

The bus jolts and jerks along the road, the suspension groaning. The windows rattle in their frames, and dust swirls in the air. I lean back in my seat, feeling the weariness of the past few days settling into my bones.

Archer sits across from me, sword resting across his lap. He's silent, lost in thought, and I wonder what's going through his mind. I'm about to ask him when the bus suddenly slams to a stop, throwing us all forward in our seats. The driver curses loudly, and I hear the sound of a car horn blaring outside.

"What the hell?" Archer jumps to his feet, gripping his sword tightly.

I follow suit, and we all rush to the front of the bus. Outside, I see a bunch of cars and emergency vehicles parked outside of the Ruby Council building. They're on the sidewalk, though there are hardly any people in the city. People—trueblood demons—rush out of the glass doors, running from something inside.

"What's going on?" Allegra asks, her eyes wide as she takes in the scene.

"I don't know, but we need to find out," I say, already moving toward the door.

Archer nods and follows me, his sword at the ready. We push past the driver, who is struggling to open the door, and jump out onto the sidewalk. It should go against all my instincts to run *into* the chaos, but here I am.

We push our way through the crowd of demons, making our way toward the entrance of the building. Screams fill the air as we step inside.

The lobby is a mess of overturned furniture and scattered papers, with truebloods tripping over themselves to get away from something in the hallway. Or some*one*.

"So I'm guessing this has to do with Karina," Allegra remarks.

"I doubt this is their usual Tuesday." I follow the screams to the hallway, where a body flies toward me. It would have toppled me, if Rhys hadn't stepped in at the last second and pulled me against the wall.

"Careful," he warns.

In the middle of the mess is Karina Swan, covered in blood. She spins around, gripping an office chair and flinging it at a demon in a suit. The wheels hit the man's face with a sickening crunch, and he crumples to the ground, unmoving.

"Hey, Mar!" she calls out, waving at me. Simultaneously, an assailant charges at her, but she repels them with a powerful kick, slamming them into a wall.

One of the most astonishing things about Karina is her grace. Her movements are powerful and precise, yet most of them could still be executed by a regular human. I'm still not sure if she has magic, but it's evident she's gaining the upper hand due to her sheer skill. Even demons with supernatural strength can't seem to keep up with her.

Recognizing that I'd only be in the way, I hang back with Rhys, Archer, and Allegra. I don't need another head injury. More demons in suits, presumably Ruby Council security, join the fray. None of them stand a chance. Eventually, silence descends once Karina defeats the last of them. The building is almost empty now, and I have no desire to stick around and see what kind of supernatural SWAT team might arrive next.

Karina wipes her face with her sleeve, smearing blood over her cheeks. "After I realized y'all weren't coming, I decided to escape on my own. What took you so long?"

I decide against telling her that we hadn't noticed she was gone. "Come on. Let's get out of here before anyone else comes."

"You got it."

We all race down the halls, led by Allegra. She takes us through the back door. We find ourselves in a dark alleyway, with garbage cans and crates scattered around. The smell of rot lingers in the air and there's a chill that I can feel seeping into my bones.

"Come on, we need to get out of here before more truebloods arrive," Archer says urgently, already swinging his sword down to create another rift in the air. I can't help but feel foolish for having been worried about Karina when she clearly has everything under control.

It's not the most ideal place to open a portal, and we don't know what's on the other side, but Archer passes through without hesitation. Rhys and I follow, with Allegra and Karina close behind.

The moment we cross the threshold, we're enveloped by the familiar warmth of Georgia sunshine. A sprawling field of tall grass surrounds us, swaying gently in the breeze. It's a stark contrast to the bleak, grey world we've just left behind, and I sigh in relief. There's no place like home...or at least, as close to it as we can get.

"Nice landing spot, Archer," I say. "Very scenic."

He grins sheepishly. "Well, I figured we could use a change of pace."

"True, but how're we supposed to get back to civilization?" Karina asks, looking around with a skeptical expression. "We're in the middle of nowhere."

"Leave that to me," Allegra chimes in, already pulling out her phone. "All I need is a signal, and we can request a ride."

We wander around in the tall grass, searching for a path through the dense trees. We're lucky we come across a road and cell service, despite being in an obviously rural part of Georgia. Allegra manages to get a driver, but it will be an hour until they pick us up.

The air is thick with tension, and even the grass seems to be holding its breath as we stand in the field, waiting.

Karina plops down in the grass. "My skirt is ruined anyway. Do you think I could bill the Ruby Council for dry cleaning?"

"Probably not," Rhys says empathetically.

"How did you get kidnapped?" I ask her.

She looks at me for a moment, as if deciding whether or not to tell me. Finally, she shakes her head. "You aren't going to like it."

"Why?"

"Because it was Celeste."

Celeste?

I know she's been MIA for the past few days, and she was mad at me, but why would she have turned Karina over? It seems like a strange way to get back at me.

"Wait, what?" Archer interjects, clearly offended. "No, that can't be right. Celeste wouldn't do something like that."

"She did. She mixed the jungle juice, and she got a few guys to give me an extra dose." Karina shrugs, like it's no big deal. "She betrayed you. Not that she was even on your side to begin with."

"Maybe there's another explanation," Archer tries weakly.

"You can explain it all you want, but facts are facts."

His jaw clenches, and for a moment, I think he might explode in anger. But instead, he turns on his heel and stalks off without a word.

"Archer," Allegra calls after him, concern etched into her delicate features. "Wait!"

She hesitates for a second before following him, leaving Rhys, Karina, and me standing awkwardly in the field. I rub my temples, feeling a headache coming on.

Great. Just when I thought things couldn't get any more complicated. Why would Celeste do this? What's her endgame? Is she a danger to my family—should I not have left her on the island with them?

If she's working with Neil, then we're in trouble. While we haven't discussed a lot of details in front of her, it wouldn't be hard for her to figure out our plans and leak them to Neil.

Karina, on the other hand, doesn't seem concerned at all. She looks up at me and says, "So do either of you have something to eat? Like a chocolate bar? I'm starving."

CHAPTER TWENTY-FOUR

T he last thing I want to do when I get back from the Veil is confront Celeste, but better me than Archer. I'm not sure why he's so upset about the whole thing—he never loved Celeste, or even *liked* her, for that matter. But I won't try to untangle the complicated relationship he seems to have with her; it's not my place.

Instead, all I can do is talk to her about it. So once we get a ride back to campus—which takes two hours, because we landed in the middle of Georgia—I head straight to her dorm. I don't even get lost this time.

When I knock on the door, she answers right away, as if she's been expecting me. She's in a matching pink pajama set that makes her strawberry blonde hair look rose gold, and her eyes are slightly red and puffy. Has she been crying?

"What do you want?" she asks.

"Karina says you kidnapped her," I reply, cutting to the chase. There's no need to dance around the subject, since

I'm positive what Karina claims is true. She has no reason to lie. "Why?"

"She escaped?" Celeste doesn't sound surprised, but there's an unmistakable anger in her tone. "How?"

"How do you think? The Ruby Council building is a slaughterhouse now." And it's partially your fault. "Why do you care? You aren't a demon shadowborn."

"Demons and angels, huh? You know, before the first rift opened, they didn't have that distinction in the Veil. And truebloods are very long-lived. My father, Mr. Kinsey, and many other so-called 'angels' were on good terms with demons like Neil Abbott," Celeste explains, leaning against the doorframe. "If you take a step back, is what the time-keepers are doing really so horrible? It's survival of the fittest."

"Are you serious right now?"

"Dead."

"Just like all the demons in the Veil, then. Karina killed countless security guards while trying to escape, Celeste," I retort. "Do you think 'survival of the fittest' applies there?"

"It doesn't matter. All I meant was the timekeepers might have a point—but that's not why I turned Karina over. I struck a deal with Mr. Kinsey."

Archer's father? "Why?"

"Are you really this dumb?"

"Yes!" I blurt.

"It was an easy exchange. Karina for my freedom. I don't have to marry Archer, and I can still claim my inheritance. I figured Karina would escape," Celeste says, but I know she's lying. About the last part, anyway. She didn't care what happened to Karina, or the rest of us—she was just looking after herself. "You're the one who told me a third option existed. This was it."

"Okay, maybe I did say that. But I didn't mean you should drug us and kidnap Karina!"

Celeste's eyes narrow. "Don't be so dramatic. I'm not the murderer here—she is. If anything, you should be asking yourself why you're allied with a mortal monster. It's unnatural for her to have powers."

"It's not natural for anyone to have powers, but here we are!" I exclaim.

"Please. You and I both know there's something wrong with Karina Swan," she says. "But you need her, so you're using her. Why can't I use her, too?"

"I might be using her," I admit, "but I wouldn't do something that I know would hurt her. There's a line that shouldn't be crossed, and—"

"And what? You think you're so much better? You think you're any different? If our roles were reversed, what would you have done?" she demands. "It's not like you're completely innocent yourself. What about all those times you lied to protect your own interests?"

"Lying is not the same as drugging people. I hurt Archer's feelings, true. And Allegra's. And maybe Mathers'. But I didn't kidnap anyone."

"Ah, but you did put them in danger, didn't you?" Celeste says. "And now they're all trapped in this mess with you, whether they want to be or not."

"Shut up," I growl, clenching my fists at my sides. "Stop comparing us—this is about what you did, not what I've done."

"Maybe," Celeste concedes, her eyes narrowing as she takes a step closer. "But I'm not the one who's going to lose everything they care about because of their own stupidity and arrogance. You think you can save everyone, but in the end, all you'll do is destroy them."

NOTHING HAPPENS TO CELESTE IN THE END. SHE DOESN'T turn herself in or apologize, though I know she isn't sorry. Most of the witnesses at the party were drunk, and the only person with a credible account against Celeste doesn't care to pursue justice. Instead, she sunbathes on the beach wearing the smallest bikini I've ever seen. Seriously, it's a strip of fabric and two little triangles.

"Hey, pass the sunblock." Karina snaps her fingers in my face. "I need to reapply."

I toss her the bottle of sunscreen, which she catches with ease and squirts into her hand. I'm dying to ask her about why she doesn't walk over to Celeste's dorm and beat the shit out of her—I'd be pissed if I were in her shoes—but Karina doesn't bring it up.

We're going to Tennessee in the morning, and instead of being a nervous wreck like I am, Karina decides to spend the day relaxing.

"You need to chill out," she tells me.

"I didn't say anything!"

"I know—it was written on your face. Duh. I'm not, like, illiterate." She balances her sunglasses on top of her head, meeting my eyes. "Celeste is who she is. You can't change that."

"You'd just let her get away with it?"

"She'll get hers. I'm not concerned."

How?

Justice is rarely ever served. That's why you have to take matters into your own hands.

I'm not sure what I'd do to Celeste, but I certainly can't let her walk away unscathed. Not after what she did. And Karina, the one person most affected by this, doesn't care.

"Karina's right," Tasha tells me, sitting up from her towel. "There's no use worrying. You're going to be fine, so just try to calm down and read your book. The boys should be here with lunch soon."

"I am fine," I insist, though no one's buying it at this point. We've been on the beach for two hours, and I've barely finished a chapter of my book. It's hard to read when this could be the end.

And I know it's bad to think like this. I assured Isabelle that I'd be fine before I left the house this morning, and I'm trying not to act any different, but let's face the facts. Even with Karina Swan, there's a chance I might not make it out of this alive. Or in one piece. If my life ends tomorrow, will I have any regrets?

"Mar!" Ava calls from the beach entrance, waving her arms. She looks better today, having fully recovered from the jungle juice incident. Beside her are Rhys, David, and Declan.

I haven't seen Archer since we got back to the Veil yesterday, and Allegra has been scarce, too. Tash says she didn't come home last night. I have a feeling I know where she slept, not that it's any of my business.

I just hope they're both okay. Archer might not have wanted to marry her, but that doesn't mean he didn't have some feelings for her. Though I think he mostly felt sympathy for her.

"We come bearing food," Declan announces, setting the picnic basket down on my towel.

"The water looks amazing. Have you taken a swim yet?" Ava asks, laying down a blanket for her and Declan to share. David plops beside me, thankfully without Buck. Rhys sits at my other side, passing around plates and sandwiches.

"I might after we eat," Karina says breezily.

"By the way, a huge package arrived for you earlier," Declan says, chomping down on his ham and cheese croissant. "Uncle Richard put it in your room."

"It's probably my new saber!" Karina exclaims. "I had to special order it. Thank God it came in time."

"Really? It seems way too big to be a blade."

"You'll see" is all she says, which can't mean anything good.

"Hey, is it just me, or is that ferry speeding toward us?" Tasha asks.

I follow her gaze to the water. It's hard to make out any details from this distance, but a ship is definitely headed toward us, and it's way faster than the ferry. It's more like a speedboat.

It doesn't stop by the dock, instead halting near the shore. Someone jumps from the side, tall enough to stand in the water and walk over, not caring about getting wet, apparently. My entire body tenses and for a second, I'm not sure whether I should run away or grab a spell bag from my purse.

Karina squeaks and jumps to her feet, running across the beach and launching herself at the stranger. Instead of attacking him, however, she wraps her arms around him in a tight embrace.

He lifts her with ease, spinning her around before setting her on her feet. They exchange a few words, though I can't understand—they're speaking Chinese. Even if I knew the language, they're talking way too fast. Karina points to us, taking the young man's arm and dragging him closer.

Holy shit.

"Holy shit," Tasha murmurs, reading my thoughts exactly.

"Oh my God," Ava says, jaw dropped.

The guy Karina brings over is drop-dead gorgeous. He's well over six feet tall, and thanks to the wet T-shirt that clings to his muscles, it's easy to see he could probably bench press a car without breaking a sweat. His dark hair is perfectly styled and neat despite the wind, the color matching the deep, dark brown of his eyes.

I love Rhys, but I'm not going to stand here and deny that this guy is a treat for the eyes. And he's probably Karina's boyfriend.

That would make sense, right? They're both stupidly attractive, and with the way she's clinging to his arm, they're obviously close.

"Y'all," Karina says, her voice watery, almost like she's going to cry, "this is Jax."

The young man waves, and now that he's standing in front of me, I realize he only has one arm.

"It's nice to finally meet you," Declan says, being the first to recover. He holds out a hand. "Karina's spoken a lot about you."

Jax looks toward Karina with a questioning gaze. "Karina?"

"How did you get here?" she asks him. "Have you eaten yet? You look too thin."

Jax shakes Declan's hand. "I hope she didn't cause any trouble."

"You must be the boyfriend we've heard all about," Ava intervenes, which elicits a disgusted look from the pair.

"Boyfriend?" Karina repeats. "*Him*?"

"Gross," Jax says.

"He's my little brother."

Brother? I know she has a brother, but she told me David reminded her of her brother. I assumed he was a kid! Not...an Adonis! Though I guess it makes sense that both siblings are stunning—it must run in the family.

And "little"? He's taller than all of us!

"Does that mean he's single?" Tasha asks boldly.

Karina looks like she's going to puke. I couldn't be happier. Finally, we found her weakness! "He's in high school. Hands off."

"I'm not a little kid," he reminds her impatiently. "Never mind that. We have more important things to discuss—like where you've been for the past few months."

"I'll catch you up later," Karina promises. Turning to me, she says, "I'm going to bring my brother back to the house. We'll catch up with y'all later."

"See you," I echo, still stunned. As they walk away, Karina touches his face tenderly, shoving the hair from his forehead. I don't know what they're saying, but a warm feeling rises from my stomach.

She loves him. That much is obvious. She's already explained to me, from the moment we met, that she cares for her family. But it's more intense than I expected, the siblings having the same sort of connection that I do with Tasha and

David. Even if she hadn't blatantly said it, I can tell from a simple glance that her brother, along with the rest of her family, is her entire world.

Relief floods me, and I don't know why, but I almost feel emotional on her behalf.

At the same time, David comes walking near the beach entrance toward us, pulled along by Buck.

Buck snorts and hurdles toward us, flopping on the sand and rolling over on his stomach so Declan can pet him.

"Hey, who was that?" David asks, jerking a thumb back toward Karina and Jax. "He looked an awful lot like Karina. Was that her brother?"

Suddenly, I burst into tears, alarming Rhys and my friends.

"Maria, what's wrong?" he asks urgently.

I throw my arms around David, pulling him into a tight hug. Tasha joins me, and I can tell she's crying, too.

David, on the other hand, looks completely bewildered. "Uh, what's going on?"

"Shut up and let us love you!" Tasha cries.

Yeah, it's a pretty sorry display. But now that the floodgates are open, they're not closing anytime soon. And David, being the good little brother he is, just stands there and takes it.

I'm not good at goodbyes. I'm not good at saying "I love you," either. But I think Tasha and David already know how I feel. Isabelle, too. And once I leave tomorrow, at least I can meet my fate without regrets. That's the best any of us can hope for.

CHAPTER TWENTY-FIVE

"Thank you again for taking care of my sister," Jax says, the picture of politeness.

Apparently, he thought Karina was dead for months. Since the moment he heard about her showing up at Northeastern, he's been searching for her. He jumped on a boat with only his wallet and the clothes on his back, so Theodas has to lend him a change of clothes. He's too tall and broad to fit into anything of Rhys' or Declan's, and Archer is still MIA. So now we've got this hulking guy squeezed into Theodas' jeans and a floral shirt that looks two sizes too small.

Karina's eyes are red when she comes over for dinner. Obviously she's been crying, but no one says anything about it.

We all *just* fit at the table, with extra chairs pulled over from the kitchen: my family, the Swan siblings, and Rhys' family. Siraye will be joining us tomorrow, so she's staying at Southeastern tonight. She'll be sleeping on the floor of

Allegra's room, while Jax will take Rhys' room, and he'll be in my room. This suggestion actually came from Allegra.

We haven't talked about my relationship with Rhys, not explicitly, but she obviously knows. I take it that she's okay with it. I thought she had a crush on him, but Rhys insists they were only ever friends. Not really even that—he worked under Neil's orders to serve her.

It's a relief to know there are no hard feelings, especially when it seems she's adjusting so well to my family. Even though I haven't known her for that long, we've had a rocky past, and we're not biologically related after all...she's still kind of like my sister. In a weird way.

Theodas passes the bowl of mashed potatoes to me. "Karina has been the one taking care of us."

"She ran a very helpful bootcamp," Tasha adds.

I spoon a heap of potatoes for myself and Rhys. Due to the sizing constraints of the table, we're sharing a plate.

Jax groans, turning to his sister. They're also sharing a plate, though it's mostly because Karina insists on cutting up all her brother's chicken for him, on account of him only having one arm. He doesn't look too pleased about it, but he lets her do it.

"You didn't learn anything from cheer camp, did you?" he asks her.

Her eyes narrow and she waves the knife in his face to punctuate her words. "Cheer camp went very well."

"You made most of the squad cry. You would've gotten a suspension if Coach Harris hadn't brought up the point that you ran the camp over summer and weren't affiliated with the school at the time. That blonde girl—Jenna?—quit cheer after you humiliated her."

"She wasn't willing to do what it took to win," Karina

insists. "She just wanted to join cheer because she liked the idea of it. She liked the uniform and the football players' attention. But the girl couldn't even do a push-up. God, *you* were a better cheerleader than her!"

"You do cheer?" Tasha asks, brows rising.

"Plenty of guys do cheer! It's a competitive sport," Karina says defensively, stabbing a piece of chicken and shoving it toward her brother. "But no. Jax only helped with my routines at home; he didn't do anything in high school, except train and watch anime."

That launches Jax and David into a conversation about anime, which makes me realize they are similar, albeit at different life stages. Jax's face lights up when he talks about shows he enjoys, making him that much more appealing in Tasha's eyes. Karina snorts and continues to feed her brother.

When he's around, it's almost like Karina is a different person. She's not as...perfect, but in a good way. The affection in her eyes is clear as day from the way she takes care of him.

"I just think it's wonderful that you two are together again. Family is so important," Isabelle says kindly.

"I could not agree more," Siraye replies, smiling at her own brother.

After dinner, Rhys gets dragged into a conversation with David and Jax while Siraye and I clear the table.

"How much support should I be expecting tomorrow?" I ask her.

"Theodas and I ran the numbers. I have no doubt we'll be able to infiltrate the facility," she says, "but after that, I believe the rest is up to you."

"That's not comforting at all."

"It wasn't supposed to be." She loads the plates in the dishwasher as I rinse them off. "We may be able to handle Astaroth, but Neil Abbott and the timekeepers are…"

Too powerful. Got it. Well, as long as I can get inside, I'll figure out the rest later. Besides, if Jax is half as good a fighter as Karina, we have a shot at actually surviving this.

Theodas rents a school bus to take us to Tennessee, giving me unholy flashbacks of high school. Thankfully, the seven-hour drive goes by quickly, with all my friends on board. The nervous energy on the bus is cut by Theodas and the other elves Siraye gathered, one of whom is Ava's father. Watching Iacar grill Declan about his "intentions" with Ava is more entertaining than reality television. Declan is usually pretty laid back, but I think after this, he might get a grey streak in his hair. Honestly, if this bus ride were a reality TV show, it'd be called "The Real Elves of Elfsville: Roadtrip Edition." Spoiler alert: Declan gets voted off at the next gas station.

Archer sits next to me, asleep for most of the trip. When he finally wakes up, I gather the courage to ask about Celeste.

"We had a fight," he admits. "It wasn't pretty. But I'll be okay."

"Is your dad really letting her break off the engagement?"

"She didn't lie about that. She gets to do what she wants, and she'll claim her inheritance. My dad worked out a deal with hers. I just…I should've seen it coming. I didn't want to leave things like this, and while I know it's for the best…"

"She betrayed your trust. It's natural to be angry." I certainly am. "And your dad is still going to force you to marry someone else, right?"

"Probably. But he's too occupied with the upheaval in the Ruby Council to notice," Archer says. "Apparently, when Karina was kidnapped, a few of the leaders weren't in on the plan. Since she killed so many personnel on sight, the demons are blaming each other for formulating such a foolish plan. It's still unclear what they wanted from her, but they'll leave us alone for now."

"First, we'll have to stop Neil. Everything else comes later."

"Problems for future us?"

"Exactly!" I grin. "So you're going to be okay?"

"Of course," he says, with more confidence than before. "How are you handling things?"

"I'm distracting myself with other people's problems." But honestly, I'm a lot less anxious than I thought I'd be. Yesterday, I had my last therapy session with Dr. Jones—for the time being—and she helped remind me that I'm at peace with what's going on.

Sure, there's a lot of unfinished business I have to attend to. I'm not perfect by any means, and I don't plan on dying. But there are a lot of things—a lot of *people*—in my life I'm grateful for. And that gives me the strength to keep going.

"My loose ends are more or less tied," I tell Archer, my eyes sliding to Allegra in the front. She and Rhys are having a very boring conversation about some botany book she brought with her. "Are yours?"

Archer follows my gaze. "Yeah. Allegra and I had a long conversation yesterday night."

"And? Are you getting back together?"

"No," he says, with a small smile. "That door is closed. But we're good, Mar. I don't need to date someone to be close with them. I don't need to date anyone at all. For now, I think I'll just focus on school. If I don't get horrifically killed by a silver snake."

"And if you do?"

"Make sure they choose a good photo of me for the funeral."

"Hey, I just wanted to—why do you look like that?" Ophelia asks. Funny, she's standing outside the door to my hotel room, uninvited, and she's asking me about how I look?

"I just took a shower," I reply, stepping into the hall. Theodas rented out a floor of a hotel an hour away from Neil's lab. We don't want him to catch onto our plan; that is, if he doesn't already know about it. He might not be able to locate us with magic, but Astaroth's got a network of cultists at his disposal.

"Can I come in?" Ophelia gestures toward the door.

"I was going to get something at the vending machine anyway. Walk with me." I pat my pocket to check if I have my phone before closing the door. I'm barefoot, but there are hardly any guests in the hotel anyway.

Ophelia walks beside me awkwardly, working up the courage to tell me something. Finally, she says, "I just wanted to tell you that you can count on me tomorrow."

"What?"

"Tomorrow, when we get into the lab," she says, annoyed. I hold the door to the stairs open and we descend to the lobby, where the vending machines are tucked into a corner in the staircase.

"I, uh, know," I say. "I mean, that's why you're coming along, right? To help?"

"Yes, but if something happens, you should know that you can rely on me. I have your back, for better or for worse."

I choose a chocolate bar, because I have to buy something. Thankfully they take contactless payments via phone. "Do you want anything…?"

"Are you taking me seriously?" she accuses.

"Sort of. You're being oddly nice," I say, "and it's freaking me out."

"You little—"

"Look. We don't need to do this." I lead her back upstairs, shoving the chocolate bar in the pocket of my robe. "You and I aren't friends, but that doesn't mean I don't trust you. I know I can count on you. You're a good person."

Ophelia and I got off on the wrong foot, and we're not super close, but she's responsible and I know she won't betray us like Celeste. Besides, she's a decent fighter and she volunteered to be here, despite having no real incentive to do so.

When we reach my room again, she says, "Thanks. Try not to die tomorrow."

"I'll do my best." I use an app on my phone to unlock the door to my room. "I'll see you tomorrow, okay?"

"Wait." Her nose wrinkles, and she crosses her arms over her chest. "Were you really showering just now?"

"Yeah." My hair is wet and everything.

"Alone?"

The question hangs between us for a moment.

"I'll see you tomorrow," I repeat.

"Oh my God, are you naked under there?"

"Bye!" I shut the door in her face and empty the contents of my pockets on the table.

"Finally," Rhys says. "Is that chocolate?"

I toss him the bar and shrug off my robe, revealing a very unflattering pair of Princess Peach pajamas. Yeah, maybe I should have packed something cuter. But how was I supposed to know Rhys would sneak into my room?

"What did she say?" he asks, breaking off a row of chocolate squares.

"That I can rely on her, basically."

"How uncharacteristically kind."

"I know, right?" I hold a hand out and he breaks me off a square of chocolate. "Rhys, you're not worried, are you?"

"Not at all. I have no doubt you will manage to defeat Neil. And you appear to be confident in yourself, as well."

"Or maybe I'm just in deep denial of the reality of things?"

Rhys chuckles and pops another chocolate square into his mouth. "Either way, it ends tomorrow. We should get some rest."

"Rest, or...?"

"Rest," he confirms, putting the rest of the chocolate into the fridge. He makes sure the deadbolt is locked and closes the shades, turning off the lights as he passes by.

"Wait a sec. I have something for you." I unzip my suit-case and reach beneath my clothes to pull out a plastic bag. I probably should have worked on the presentation a little more, since it looks like I'm handing him a bag of trash. "They're, uh, letters. That I wrote. As replies to your letters."

"You wrote replies?" Rhys looks at me with surprise evident in his expression. I nod, feeling a little self-conscious about the whole thing. To be honest, I don't remember exactly what I wrote. I just went with my gut for most of them.

"Yeah," I say, holding the bag out to him. "I wasn't going to show you them, frankly. A lot are embarrassing. But I figured you should have them. Just in case, you know. I didn't want the last letter you got from me to be that email."

Rhys takes the bag from me. "In truth, I did not mind the email."

"Really? You're not just saying that?"

"Even the poem," he confirms, a playful smile tugging at the corners of his lips. "May I read these now?"

"No way!" That would be way too embarrassing. "You can save them for later. After we save the world."

"Very well. But I hope you'll consider reading them to me," he teases, settling on the bed. "It will be interesting."

I groan. "I am not doing that. You can read them in the privacy of your room or the library, or wherever you want, just not around me. And we won't talk about them either."

"Romantic."

"You know I'm still getting used to it." I hesitate. "Rhys, you know I, uh. I mean, how I feel. It's. Um."

"I know. You don't have to say it," he assures me, his eyes softening as he reaches out to take my hand. "I love you, too."

CHAPTER TWENTY-SIX

Neil's lab is in the middle of the woods, which is not suspicious at all, right?

After walking a mile to get to the gates, I'm ready to turn back around. It's humid, there are bugs biting up my arms, and I'm pretty sure my hair is a puff of frizz, despite the hair products I used this morning. More importantly, my stomach is doing that flippy, knotting thing it usually does when I get nervous. The heat isn't helping.

At least I'm not alone. Everyone else seems equally miserable, even Karina.

"Ugh," she complains, swatting at a swarm of bugs that seem to be drawn to her like magnets. "This place is the worst."

"Tell me about it," I mutter in agreement, scratching my arm where a mosquito has just feasted on me.

"Remember everyone, stay focused," Theodas reminds us, as we gather around him. There are about fifty of us, but the second group, led by Siraye and Iacar, are going around back.

We approach the lab's entrance, our footsteps muffled by the damp ground beneath us. The fence surrounding the property is electrified and topped with barbed wire. It's intimidating, to say the least. However, this is nothing compared to what we might find inside.

"Stand back," I warn, taking out a spell bag. I came prepared this time. When everyone has taken cover, myself included, I drop pig's blood onto the spell bag and toss it at the gate.

The spell bag explodes against the fence upon contact. Not the most subtle tactic, but it's effective enough, creating a hole large enough for a person to slip through. Sparks of electricity fly in all directions as the metal is twisted and torn apart. Alarms sound inside the lab, still a football field away.

The lab looks like an old hospital from the outside, with its faded brick walls and boarded-up windows. The signage outside is too rusted to be legible, but there's a big blue cross over the frosted glass doors.

"I didn't know your spells had gotten so powerful," Ophelia muses, impressed.

"Remind me never to get on your bad side," Archer says.

"Can't make any promises," I retort playfully, trying to hide the fact that my hands are shaking.

"Alright, let's split up as discussed," Provost Mathers instructs, his voice all business. "Mar, Rhys, Declan, Archer, you're with me. Siraye, you take your group upstairs. We'll meet up inside."

"Good luck, everyone," Siraye adds, her usually jovial expression somber. We run toward the entrance, parting when Siraye takes her group to a side door. My group walks right up to the front door, the alarms still blaring from within.

"Declan, use the device," Provost Mathers orders, nodding toward the security code box just inside the entrance. The tension in the room is palpable, and I can practically feel my heart pounding in my chest.

"Already on it," Declan replies, pulling out an old-fashioned phone, which looks more like a plastic box of wires, from his messenger bag. He attaches it to the number pad by the door, a determined look on his face as he begins tapping away on his phone screen. "This shouldn't take long."

"Good, because standing here like sitting ducks isn't my idea of a good time." Clearly Neil and whoever else works here is aware of a breach. And it wouldn't take a rocket scientist—or, in this case, an evil scientist—to figure out what's happening.

"Got it!" Declan exclaims, a triumphant grin on his face as the door beeps and unlocks. We waste no time pushing through, the air immediately changing from the sticky heat of the Tennessee forest to the sterile, chilly atmosphere of a hospital.

"You'd think they could at least try to make this place more inviting," I say, trying to break the tension as we step into the long hallway. It's lined with closed doors, some with frosted windows that reveal only shadows and gloom beyond. You'd think someone would have bothered to repurpose the hospital into something less...creepy.

"Considering Neil's hobbies, I doubt 'inviting' was ever part of the plan," Archer says dryly. "Let's move."

"Right," Provost Mathers agrees. "We need to locate the

security office and disable their surveillance system. Keep your eyes open for any signs of trouble."

"I'll pull up the map," Declan says. "I found the floor plan of this place yesterday night. It's old, so it might not be totally accurate, but I don't think they would have moved the control room. Neil bought this place right after the hospital closed, with all the equipment. He probably didn't bother to move the monitors in the security office."

"Lead the way."

Declan pulls up his phone and leads us down the hallway. The alarms overhead suddenly stop, replaced by an eerie silence that makes my skin crawl. We move quickly, scanning every door we pass. The silence is deafening, and I can't help but feel like something is off. We turn a corner, and suddenly we're face to face with a group of armed guards.

I don't think before pulling out a spell bag, activating it, and throwing it at them. The explosion takes them by surprise, sending them flying backward with their guns clattering to the ground. But the explosion also attracts attention, and we hear the sound of footsteps running in our direction.

"We need to hurry," Provost Mathers says, pushing us forward.

Declan leads us down another hallway, and we finally find the security office. It's like stepping into some kind of futuristic sci-fi movie, with glowing screens and blinking lights covering every inch of the walls. My eyes are immediately drawn to the monitors displaying live footage from various parts of the facility.

"Mar," Declan says. "Look."

I follow his gaze to one of the screens, and my heart

skips a beat. Astaroth is making his way up a staircase, his massive form barely fitting within the narrow space. He seems to get bigger with each step, opening a door that says "Roof Access." Right before he goes inside, he whips around, turning toward the camera and smiling. Almost like he knows I'm watching.

My blood runs cold as I watch Astaroth disappear behind the door. Karina and her group are entering through the roof. Surely Karina can fend Astaroth off, right? I've told her enough about him to properly prepare her?

"We need to head up to the roof," I say quickly.

"Right after we disable the cameras," Declan says. "We don't want Neil to be able to find out where we are. The cameras could be accessed remotely through a phone; it's possible he's watching us right now."

My eyes skim over the control panel. There are so many blinking lights, it's hard to determine what would shut off the cameras. Declan looks through his phone while he searches for the correct button, and I move to the wall of levers.

One of them is labeled "Doors." Cautiously, I pull it. A loud buzzing noise echoes throughout the building, and on the cameras, I see several doors fly open.

"Shit! What did you do?" Archer's head swivels toward me. "Mar? Maybe you shouldn't be pushing random buttons?"

Declan presses a button, turning all the monitors black. "Got it. That should create enough chaos now."

As a final step, Provost Mathers pulls a plug out of the wall and Rhys cuts it with his sword, severing any chance of using the control room again. Unfortunately, it also cuts the power for the entire building. This room doesn't have windows, so everything turns dark. The windows in the hallway afford us just enough light to make our way out of the control room.

As we sprint down the hallway, the sound of combat grows louder and louder. We need to find the stairs, fast.

"This way," Declan urges, leading us down a side hallway. The sound of gunfire and screams is echoing closer and closer.

Finally, I see a door marked "Roof Access" and barrel through it, taking the steps two at a time. I'm not even winded when I reach the top, pushing my way outside to the roof.

Astaroth stands at eight or nine feet tall, more beast than man as he throws his head back and roars. Glowing red veins cover his skin like tattoos, all over his face and bare upper body. Thankfully, he's wearing pants—even if they are kind of ripped up.

Karina and Jax stand before Astaroth while the rest of their group, composed entirely of shadowborn students, struggle to hold back black-robed cultists. Karina, in particular, looks imposing with her new weapon: a massive blade that's a terrifying cross between a meat cleaver and a saber. It's nearly as tall as she is, and I can't help but wonder how on earth she's able to swing it around with such ease. If this saving-the-world business doesn't pan out, maybe she can open a butchery.

Jax is armed with a sleek sword of his own, moving in tandem with his sister as they rush Astaroth. The two move in perfect harmony, landing deep cuts in his sides before he can react. Astaroth's skin seems to close up around the wounds almost immediately, but they keep coming at him relentlessly.

I watch in awe as the Swans dance around Astaroth, their movements fluid and graceful, like a deadly ballet. The rest of their group is holding their own against the cultists, but I can see that they're slowly being pushed back.

I can't throw a spell bag at Astaroth, because I might hit one of the Swans. Instead, I focus on the cultists, unsheathing my sword and using everything I've learned so far to kick ass.

Literally, with a kick to someone's ass, I catapult them off the roof.

I don't have a moment to savor my victory before someone else charges at me, their sword aimed at my neck. I parry the attack, but I can tell from the strength behind it that this cultist is no amateur. We exchange blows, my sword clashing with theirs as we circle each other.

I move away just in time as the cultist lunges toward me. I spin around them and drive my sword deep into their back, then pull it out in a spray of crimson before they can react.

Blood splatters across my face, and it takes all my self-control not to draw the power within me. I can't rush things. If I do, the blood magic will rebound.

Karina cries out, catching my attention. Astaroth, in his monstrous form, claws at her side, tearing open a wound at her waist. She stumbles, clutching her side as blood soaks her pink dress.

Jax runs toward her, but as he does, Astaroth's hand comes down. Everything happens in slow motion after that. Karina jolts forward, shoving her brother down and out of the way while she takes the blow directly to the chest.

Astaroth sweeps Karina directly off the roof, sending her flying over the edge with a scream.

CHAPTER TWENTY-SEVEN

I f there's anything to be said about Karina, it's that she's one tough bitch to kill.

Jax and I rush to the ledge, horrified, only to see Karina hanging onto a window ledge with one hand. Her fingers slip, coated in her own blood, as she struggles. She grits her teeth and tries to pull herself up, but I can tell it's taking all of her strength just to hang on.

"Get her," Archer says quickly. "We'll hold Astaroth off. Hurry!"

I don't know how I'm going to manage that. It's not like I can stretch my arms down and pick her up. Even if I were right there, it would take a lot of strength to lift her.

Jax looks like he's about to jump over the ledge and get her, but before either of us can do anything, the window in front of her opens. For a split second, I worry it's a guard, there to finish her off. Jax must think the same thing, shouting at her in Chinese.

However, relief colors Karina's face and she reaches out,

allowing someone to pull her inside. I let out a breath as soon as I see her feet pass through the window.

Karina should be able to take care of herself inside, despite that nasty cut on her side. Maybe one of her friends, now freed from the lab, came to help.

I turn my attention back to Astaroth, who's currently giving Archer and Declan the run-around. Rhys is holding his own, using his sword in tandem with his magic to ward off Astaroth and cultists alike. But it's not enough.

Astaroth, especially in that beastly form, is too formidable. And I can't rely on his powers backfiring like Nic's did in the cemetery. Astaroth is too experienced, too skilled, for that to work. I need to do something else — beat him at his own game.

And, like a lightning strike, I get an idea.

"Move back!" I shout, running forward. "I've got this."

The scary thing is, my friends actually listen to me. Rhys shoves the last cultist off the roof, and I point to the door.

"Go back inside," I tell him. "I need you all out of the way. No offense."

"Maria…" He hesitates, but ultimately, he nods.

The others head in, with Jax nodding at me before jogging inside.

"This is between you and me," I tell Astaroth. "I've been practicing, you know."

"I'm sure you have," he says, smoke unfurling from his mouth. "But it won't be enough, Maria Rochester."

"I think it will be. See, there's a difference between you and me: I've got timekeeper blood in me. That means I was born more powerful than you," I inform him. "And you know it, too. No matter what you do or how hard you train, you can never best me."

This is total bullshit, but Astaroth's brow furrows.

"You think you can best me, girl?"

"I know I can. So don't hold back. We'll see who, between us, is the more powerful blood magician," I challenge. "Let's end this, once and for all."

"The timekeepers need you. Killing you would be counterproductive," he muses.

"What a cop-out."

"Excuse me?"

"You know what I'm saying is true," I accuse.

"You are playing with fire," he warns.

"Good thing I'm good at fire-retardant spells," I say, taking out my dagger. "Wait. That was kind of a lame comeback. Can I try again? Er, good thing I'm not afraid to get burned. Do you think that's better? I mean, it sounds cooler —hey!" I yelp, dodging his fist from slamming down into me. He's not big enough to crush me like a bug, but any blow would certainly hurt. "It's rude to interrupt people like that!"

"Let's see what you're made of, timekeeper's daughter."

Damn, why does he get all the cool mid-battle one-liners? Maybe that's what I should have been practicing, in addition to swordsmanship. Well, too late now.

I cut into my palm, and he bites his hand. Magic is thick in the air, filling the space around me with an invisible miasma weighing down on my body.

Karina was right: this isn't a competition to see who's better at blood magic. It's about killing each other.

Do you remember what I said in the very beginning, about not liking cake? Because someone threw a brick at me? And it bounced back on my awesome (fake) boobs and hit someone else?

Well.

When Astaroth launches his spell at me, a dark shadowy spear, I activate my own spell. As soon as the spear is released, it's too late—it bounces back, directly at Astaroth's face. The magic is so great, it hits me like a spear anyway, the blow directly hitting my chest and causing me to spit up blood. It's worth it.

Astaroth is impaled on his own magic, his body shrinking. A hole where his chest should be leaks blood, and his organs splay across the roof. Okay, gross. But I won, right?

It doesn't feel like a victory, though. I sink to my knees, my legs unable to hold me. Breathing hard, I squeeze my eyes shut. Okay, super glad I only had to take Astaroth on one-on-one instead of taking him, the timekeepers, and Neil on at once.

I need a minute to compose myself, but even as I stand, a wave of dizziness causes me to stumble.

Shit. My condition is worse than I thought it'd be after one spell. I still have spell bags, I just need to recover a little bit. And I absolutely cannot let Rhys, or anyone else, know. If they think I'm sick, they might make me stay behind.

While I was mostly bullshitting Astaroth, I've known since the beginning that Neil is my responsibility. He brought me into this world, and now, I have to take him out.

Damn, does that sound cool? Should I say that to him? Or would that be lame?

Well, whatever.

Stumbling back toward the door, I open it and rejoin Rhys, Archer, Mathers, and Declan.

"Mar!"

"Are you okay?"

"You look pale, Maria." Rhys holds out a hand to steady me. "Where is Astaroth?"

"I killed him," I reply proudly. "We need to get to Neil next."

"You killed him?" Mathers asks, surprised. I don't blame him; I'm pretty surprised at myself, too.

"Yeah. Unless I'm a ghost right now."

"How did you manage that?"

"I'll tell you all about it later," I promise, using the rail to get down the stairs. The churning in my stomach hasn't stopped, but I'm still conscious, so that's something, right?

We make it back to the third floor, where the halls are littered with bodies. Not all of them are guards, unfortunately. Guilt stabs at me, but I try to keep going anyway. Neil wouldn't be out in the open; I'd bet anything that he's waiting for me.

Each step is pure agony, and my body isn't healing as fast as it normally does. I don't dare let it show on my face, powering through until we spot Ava and her team taking care of another batch of guards.

Ava lowers her bow, approaching us with a somber expression. "We've done a sweep of this floor already. Most of the more powerful guards were taken out once the test subjects were freed."

So it was a good move to open all the doors, then. "And Neil?"

"No sign of him. But I spoke with Ophelia—her team confirmed that the rest of the floors have been cleared. He's not here," Ava says. "He's probably in the basement. No one has checked the lower levels yet, and the elevators aren't working. You'll have to take the stairs."

I groan. "Oh no, more exercise?"

"Stay safe," Declan tells Ava, leaning in to give her a quick, tender kiss on the cheek. "And watch your back."

"Always," she replies with a determined nod. "We're going to make sure none of the test subjects were left behind. There are a lot more people here than I thought, Mar. Kids."

"There are gurneys on the bus. We're taking everyone we can back with us," I say.

"Let's get movin'," Provost Mathers barks. "Neil is preparin' for you, Mar. We don't want to waste any time."

We part from Ava's group and head for the stairs. I brace the railing as we descend, going first while everyone else holds onto my shoulder like a train. I'm the only one who can see in the darkness, with the power being out and all.

The basement door is marked "B1" and I push it open, revealing a hall full of glass doors. Observation rooms, probably. Green emergency lights cast an eerie glow around us as we move forward, looking in all the empty rooms. There are food bowls and cages inside, but I doubt the rooms were meant for pets. The feeling of dread heightens as we move farther into the maze of hallways until we reach two big black doors. They open on their own, an invitation of sorts.

The room is bathed in an eerie green glow, emanating from the emergency lights mounted on the walls. The light casts distorted shadows, making the rows of machines appear as hulking, misshapen figures. Their dials and gauges are fogged over, but I can see needles twitching sporadically, as if reacting to an unseen force. It's like being in a sci-fi movie, only I don't remember auditioning for the role of Girl Who Definitely Gets Vaporized First.

Pipes run along the ceiling and walls, twisting and

turning in a maze of metal. Electrical panels with frayed wires hang open, and I wonder how this place is still even remotely functional.

The air is heavy, thick with the smell of oil, rust, and something else—something indescribable that sends a chill down my spine. The room feels alive in a way that's not entirely natural, as though it possesses a malevolent energy.

Neil stands in the middle of the room, surrounded by the machines. Wearing a suit and tie, he looks polished as usual, his blonde hair slicked back with gel. Timekeepers twist about his body, spinning around his arms and legs.

"Ah, Maria," he drawls, spreading his arms wide as if welcoming us into his twisted lair. "So glad you could make it. We've been expecting you."

"Neil," I greet, trying to sound more confident than I feel. "You always did know how to throw a party."

"Indeed. And this will be one for the ages."

And just like that, all hell breaks loose.

Timekeepers spin faster and faster around Neil, glowing with a brilliant golden light. The air is filled with electricity as magic crackles all around us. He throws his hands forward, and energy slams into us like a tidal wave. I stumble backward, fighting to stay on my feet. Archer grabs me, pulling me to the side so I don't spin directly into one of the machines lining the room.

Big, leathery wings unfurl from Neil's back, tearing his shirt wide open. Horns curl out from his forehead, his true form revealed at last.

Mathers is the first to rush him, his sword held high. But Neil is quick, dodging the attack and sending Mathers flying across the room with a flick of his wrist. At the same time, the timekeepers begin to move, falling off Neil and slithering throughout the room. Definitely not a good sign.

I pull a spell bag from my pocket and activate it with a dropper of blood from around my neck, throwing it in Neil's direction. It's supposed to be a flash bang, but nothing happens. Neil stomps on it, smothering the magic under his shoe.

The timekeepers hiss in unison, their bodies writhing toward me. Rhys' back presses into mine as we hold our swords up, but the timekeepers don't make a move to attack us. Instead, they converge around Neil, their forms twisting and writhing together until they merge into a single, massive entity. The creature looms over us, its body pulsing with silver light and magical energy. It's like nothing I've ever seen before, and I can feel the fear creeping up inside me.

It's a giant snake. One giant snake, to be precise. It nearly fills the entire room, and its voice booms in my ears.

"We have been waiting for you, Maria Rochester. And now you have come to us, a choice you believe was made of your own free will."

I wince at the words, but no one else reacts. Am I the only one who can hear them? Not even Neil looks perturbed at the volume of the voices.

The massive timekeeper wraps around the room, trapping us all inside while Neil rises, his wings gently flapping behind him as spheres of fire form in his hands.

The fight begins in earnest, the intensity of it reaching a fever pitch. Mathers and Rhys battle against the giant snake while I try to contain Neil's fireballs with my magic. But to counteract his spells, I need to use my own blood, cutting deep into my palms. I can't even counterattack, merely using my magic to protect us all from getting burned alive.

We're not losing, exactly, but we sure as hell aren't winning. None of us can land a single blow on Neil, thanks to the giant timekeeper. Whenever Rhys, Mathers, Archer, or Declan try to get close, it slams its body to the ground in an attempt to crush them.

"I much prefer speaking to you, Maria," Neil calls out. "We don't need any distractions, do we? This is between you and me, after all. Let's end this farce."

The timekeeper's tail comes crashing down with a force powerful enough to shatter the ground. Declan leaps forward, desperate to block the attack, but is too slow. His sword slices its tail, but doesn't sever it completely, and certainly doesn't stop its momentum.

Blood explodes in all directions as the timekeeper sends Declan hurtling into the wall. The dual-edged sword finds its mark and pierces Declan's flesh, slicing through his body like a hot knife through butter, nearly bisecting him before he can take another breath.

We barely have time to process what's happened before Neil hurls a spell at Provost Mathers. The spell is enough to send Mathers flying through the air before he crashes into one of the machines. His head hits the metal like an arrow, but instead of piercing the machine, his neck bends.

Bile rises in my throat, but I force it down. Mathers is… gone. He helped me, and for his efforts…

Declan, too. Ava…what is she going to say?

"Maria," Rhys calls, sounding so far away, even though he's standing right next to me.

"Mar!" Archer yells, his voice distorted.

We don't stand a chance against Neil, do we?

Maybe we never did. Neil looks down at me, his expression a mix of amusement and cruelty.

The giant timekeeper slams its tail into the ground again, causing the room to shake and dust to rain down on us. Rhys and I brace ourselves, but I can tell we're both struggling to keep on our feet.

"This isn't the end," I promise both Rhys and myself. Running for the timekeeper's body, I fling myself on top of it and plunge my dagger in its tail. Blood spews from the wound, but it doesn't bother the timekeeper, who flings me away. Unlike Mathers, I don't hit a machine, instead slamming into the wall with the dagger clattering beside me. Black spots dot my vision, and I'm covered in blood, some of it my own. Most of it, the timekeeper's.

Rhys calls my name, and Neil says something, but I can't hear anything over the ringing in my ears.

"Sorry," I want to say to Rhys, but all that comes out is a strangled croak.

Using all my remaining strength, I remember everything that brought me here, like a recap from the end of the story to the very beginning: saving Karina, meeting Rhys in the past, staying at Neil's house, getting attacked on the ship...

And that goddamn car accident. I should have died, then, but I didn't. Because I'm the timekeeper's daughter.

I take the hilt of the dagger, lifting it to my chest. With a swift motion, I plunge it into me, feeling the cold steel pierce my skin and cut through muscle and bone. The pain is unbearable, a thousand times worse than anything I've ever experienced, but there's no turning back now.

As I gasp for breath and as blood pours from my wound, I can see the shock and horror written all over Rhys' face.

Time seems to slow, the world around us blurring into a kaleidoscope of colors and shapes. I can feel my consciousness fading, my body growing weaker by the second.

And then, time begins to rewind.

CHAPTER TWENTY-EIGHT

The sensation of being catapulted back into my own body sends me to my hands and knees, a wound in my chest bursting with blood. My heart beats rapidly, a telltale sign that I'm still alive.

"Maria?" Rhys asks, alarmed as he drops to his knees beside me.

"Mar, what happened?" Declan demands.

We're still in the basement. The green lights make me feel even more lightheaded. Despite the utter discomfort my body is in, I'm alive, which means I can fix things. But judging from the wound on my chest, I won't have a second chance. It's not fatal, I don't think, but bleeding so much can't be good. Thankfully, I'm wearing black. The fabric of my shirt soaks most of the blood, preventing it from dripping.

"I'm fine. I just felt...shit. I don't have time to explain," I say, looking up. "Declan, you need to go find Ava. Provost, you and Archer need to help the other students escape. Rhys, you must find your sister."

"What?" Archer exclaims. "What are you talking about? Neil—"

"I have a plan," I say, looking Rhys in the eyes. "You know I'm not lying."

"You are in no condition to fight," Rhys protests.

"Did you just time travel?" Provost Mathers asks. Thankfully, he caught on quickly.

I nod. "Just go. I know what I'm doing."

"Maria," Rhys pleads, gripping my wrist gently but firmly. "Don't do this."

"Trust me, Rhys," I say, swallowing hard against the pain. "I don't exactly love the idea of going head-to-head with Neil, but we don't have time for a debate. We need to act, and we need to act now."

The men still don't leave, so I force myself to my feet and draw my dagger.

"Be safe," Provost Mathers says finally, motioning for Declan to open the door. "We will take care of everythin' else, Mar."

"I'll find Ava," Declan promises.

"Archer?" I look to him. "I'll see you later, okay?"

"Fine," Archer grits out, clearly unhappy about the situation. But he doesn't argue any further. Instead, he shoots me one last worried look before nodding to Declan. "Let's go."

"Good luck," I call after them, injecting as much fake cheer into my voice as possible. "And hey, if you happen to run into Neil's minions on the way, feel free to give 'em a good smack for me!"

"Will do," Declan says with a grim smile before he disappears through the stairwell door with Archer and Mathers.

Rhys is the last to linger, his eyes searching mine for any sign of doubt. "Do not ask me to leave you."

"I can defeat him. I can defeat them all. Mathers told me what I have to do," I explain softly. "I just need a chance to do it. And I won't be able to if I'm worried about you."

"But you might never return," he says.

"Hey," I reply, reaching out to touch his face. "You won't get rid of me that easily. I promise I'll come back, okay? You just need to trust me."

"Please be careful," Rhys implores, his hands gripping my shoulders as if he's trying to hold onto me even as I pull away.

"I will," I assure him, forcing myself to sound confident despite the gnawing fear in my gut. "Now go. I need to do this."

As Rhys reluctantly retreats, I can't help but feel a pang of guilt for pushing him away. But right now, I have bigger things to worry about.

Making sure he's left, I turn back to the hallway and stagger through the basement. Blood drips from my chest, gushing at a steady pace onto the floor toward my final destination. Just like before, the two big doors open, revealing Neil and the timekeepers twisting around him.

"Ah, Maria," he says, just like last time. "So glad you could make it. We've been expecting you."

I stagger inside, not bothering to hide how tired I am. Neil, on the other hand, looks pristine in his suit.

"Where are your friends?"

"I need to do this alone," I inform him. We circle each other like sharks, neither of us daring to attack.

"Ah, so you've finally embraced your destiny," he says, clapping his hands together mockingly.

"Destiny?" I snort, clutching my dagger tighter. "You mean being a pawn in your twisted plans? Sorry to disappoint, but that's not how this story ends."

"Is that so?" Neil raises an eyebrow, amusement dancing in his eyes. "You act as if you have a choice in the matter."

"Everybody has a choice," I reply, my voice wavering only slightly as I take a step closer, blood dripping from my wound onto the cold, tiled floor. "And I choose not to be your puppet."

"Such defiance," he muses. "But tell me, do you really believe you can escape the fate that's been written for you? You were born for one very specific purpose."

"I was an experiment, but not a successful one," I admit, stopping in front of him. "You might have gotten the recipe right, but do you know how many times I've followed a banana bread recipe and gotten shitty results each time? There's always room for human—or, in your case, trueblood—error."

"Are you comparing yourself to shitty banana bread?"

"Yes. I didn't think it through all the way, but my point is this: I don't care what you think or what you've planned. I will never, *ever*, be under your control."

With that, I lay my sword down on the table next to me, sending a clear message: I won't fight on his terms. If Neil wants me, he's going to have to work for it.

"Such a brave little fool," he chuckles, unfazed by my defiance. "But remember, it was you who chose this path. Don't blame me when it all comes crashing down."

Neil takes a step closer, his grin widening with each movement. He doesn't even realize he's just centered himself in a ring of my blood.

I drop to my knees, closing my eyes. I made a doorway

before to get out of the Infinity Hallway. Why can't I make a trap door to go inside?

The floor falls away beneath us, sending me, Neil, and the timekeepers through the passage. I land on my back, quickly rolling to my feet as I regain my bearings. The silver hallway before me is a sight for sore eyes, and before Neil can comprehend what happened, I begin to run. Using my dagger, I cut into my palms and spread my blood across the walls.

"Running away, are we?" Neil calls after me, his cold laughter echoing through the hall. "It's a nice trick, Maria, but you've made one mistake. You've brought the time-keepers to their own domain to fight."

"Yeah, I've been thinking about that. You know some-thing I've learned from the beastbloods? Most can't create rifts. The only ones who can have claws to tear open portals," I shout as he chases me. The silver of the hallway fades to white, and I'm back in the Infinity Hallway I recognize. "Timekeepers are snakes. They don't have claws. I don't think they can make a rift with their fangs alone!"

"What does that have to do with—"

As if on cue, Jenna Cooper appears by my side, her presence an unexpected but welcome sight. "It means Mar has finally put two and two together, all on her own this time. Timekeepers can't travel through time without this hallway."

"Nice of you to join the party," I say between gasps for air.

"Wouldn't miss it," she replies with a grin, matching my pace effortlessly. "Looks like you could use a hand."

"More like a transfusion," I admit, my vision starting to

blur from blood loss. "But I have a plan, and it involves painting this hallway red."

"Sounds messy. Count me in," Jenna says, taking my dagger and cutting her own palms. Together, we create a crimson tapestry, the color stark against the pristine white walls.

"Why are you helping me?" I ask her. She's a Time Agent—she works for the timekeepers.

Jenna grins. She's the oldest I've ever seen her, probably in her forties. Her brown hair bounces in a short ponytail, and her eyes have begun to wrinkle in the corners. "I told you, didn't I? I've been assigned to help you."

"Not to sound ungrateful, but I doubt this is what the timekeepers had in mind."

"I don't do well with authority figures."

"Maria, you fool!" Neil shouts, realizing what we're up to. "You'll destroy us all!"

"Is that a promise?" I shoot back, feeling lightheaded but determined to see this through.

"You don't know what you're doing!" he bellows, his voice filled with equal parts desperation and fury.

"Story of my life."

"Let's end this," Jenna whispers, her eyes meeting mine in a silent agreement. The atmosphere around us crackles with energy as Neil races toward us, and I know it's time.

Grabbing Jenna's hand, she opens one of the doors at the same time I slam my palm against the wall. The air around us shimmers and pulses, as if the very fabric of reality is being torn apart.

"MARIA!" Neil screams, reaching out as if to grab me. But it's too late. Our spell detonates, sending shockwaves of destruction through the Infinity Hallway.

CHAPTER TWENTY-NINE

"You don't look so good," Jenna says, stating the obvious. She rolls off, having landed on top of me.

I moan, sitting up. The good thing is, the blood loss makes everything feel fuzzy. That's me, always looking on the bright side. "Where are we?"

"Looks like a forest."

I can see that. The forest is thick with towering trees, the light of the moon barely passing through the thick foliage. Pine needles carpet the soft, thick grass, specked with wildflowers. The colors here are muted, almost grey, which means we must be somewhere in the Veil.

"What door did you take us through?"

She helps me stand, looping an arm under me for support. "Uh, the closest one? I figured it would be fine."

"We could have landed in a volcano."

"We wouldn't have," she assures me. "Look. The hallway is destroyed, we're both alive, and Neil is dead."

That last part hasn't fully registered. I've spent so much

time waiting for this moment, but hearing about his death just feels…empty.

I dropped the dagger during the explosion, but the sword strapped to my belt will be enough to open a rift and get us home. As soon as I regain the strength to lift my arms, that is.

"Why did you help me?" I ask her finally. "This entire time, aside from the ship, you've been a Time Agent."

"A lot of things happened while you were gone," she answers. "Todd was decommissioned. I always knew it was going to happen, but…you saw him in the end. He wasn't himself. He died, and he was just a kid. Why? Because he wasn't part of the timekeepers' plans? Fuck that."

I didn't even get to say goodbye to Todd, to thank him for helping me. I know he was just doing what the time-keepers wanted, but he still saved me and spoke to me at my lowest points. He didn't deserve his fate.

"There's something else, Mar. It's still years away, so I can't tell you yet, but there are other things in motion. Things that you'll need my help with."

"And you being here won't create a paradox?"

"No. I worked it out with Todd and…another Time Agent. For now, as soon as we get out of here…I'm going to live my life for myself, for the first time," she says.

I look at Jenna and see the resolve in her eyes. She's been through so much, and yet she's still standing. I can't help but feel a sense of gratitude toward her for helping me when I needed it the most.

"Let's go," I tell her. "We can't stay in the Veil for too long."

Jenna nods in agreement. "Do you think you can open a rift?"

"I'll try," I say, taking a deep breath and summoning my strength to unsheathe my sword.

"Maria Rochester."

I turn a little too fast, stabbing the sword in the ground and using it for support. A cold wind sweeps through the clearing, and the hairs on the back of my neck stand up. Instinctively, I reach for Jenna's hand, knowing that something is wrong. Very wrong.

"Mar," she whispers, her grip tightening around mine. "Do you hear that?"

"Maria." The voices, a chorus of hissing, comes from the darkness.

"Great," I mutter. "The welcoming committee has arrived."

Jenna tenses, tightening her grip around my arm.

The serpentine forms of the timekeepers coil and slither around one another, their cold yellow eyes fixed on Jenna and me. Their voices invade our minds like icy tendrils, speaking as one. "Do you think you've won?"

"A little." I killed Astaroth and Neil, and I destroyed the Infinity Hallway. Things are looking good—if I don't die of blood loss before getting back to the mortal realm, that is.

"The Infinity Hallway can be repaired. And once it is, do not think you will come out unscathed."

"But you aren't the ones who built the Infinity Hallway in the first place," Jenna shoots back, which is news to me. "Mar, don't let them scare you. The time-keepers maintain the hallway, and yeah, they have a great deal of power over fate. But there are other, more powerful beings in the Veil. Don't you hear it in the name? They're time*keepers*. They aren't gods. And they needed Time Agents to help them. Without us, they could hardly act on their own. They needed Neil to conduct the experiments, too."

"I guess having no opposable thumbs is a huge drawback when you're trying to genetically modify fetuses." The indignation in their collective hiss is almost enough to make me laugh, but I'm too focused on staying conscious to truly appreciate it. I hold the sword in front of me and slash the air, the rift rippling open.

"You cannot escape your fate," the timekeepers warn.

"I believe I just did." I grab Jenna's hand, and together, we step through the doorway, leaving the timekeepers behind.

The moment our feet touch solid ground again, I collapse onto the cold tile floor. We've landed in a hospital, the sterile smell of antiseptic and the hum of medical equipment overwhelming my senses. My vision blurs, but I manage to close the rift just in time, preventing any timekeepers from following us through.

"Mar?" Jenna's voice sounds distant, but her concern cuts through my exhaustion. "Are you okay?"

"Never better," I manage to choke out between labored breaths. The truth is, I'm far from okay, but we're alive, and for now, that's enough.

I WAKE UP, MY HEAD THROBBING LIKE A BASS DRUM IN A death metal concert. The room around me is unfamiliar — sterile white walls and the constant beeping of machines that seem to share my headache. My body aches as if I've been put through a woodchipper and then spat back out.

Lifting my bandaged hands, I wiggle my fingers and toes. Everything seems to be in working order, despite the pain.

I'm in a hospital gown, so I have no idea what they did to my clothes, or my phone. I imagine appearing at the hospital with a sword was fun for Jenna to explain.

I find the nurse call button and press it, my throat parched. I could use a huge jug of water, not to mention a steaming plate of fries. But instead of a nurse, a young doctor strolls in, clipboard in hand. Her eyes widen when they land on me, and she lets out a sigh of relief.

"Ah, Miss Rochester, you're awake!" she exclaims, moving closer. "We were getting quite worried about you."

"How long have I been here?" I ask. My eyes flicker to the IV drip attached to my arm, the various tubes snaking out from beneath the hospital gown.

The doctor smiles. "Only a day. Your friends were admitted earlier. I was instructed to inform you that everyone is recovering well. I'm Dr. Hauff. You're recovering well, but we're still going to keep you under observation for another day or two. We want to make sure there are no complications from your injuries."

I nod, taking in the information. "Can I see my friends?"

"Of course. But it's fairly late, and visiting hours are over. I'm sure they can wait until the morning." Dr. Hauff scribbles something down on her clipboard before excusing herself from the room.

The moment she leaves, I sit up and swing my legs over the side of the bed. My entire body protests, muscles screaming in agony as if they've been torn apart and sewn back together by a blind, drunken surgeon.

Nothing is broken, and aside from a little blood loss, I'm lucky to have come out of the ordeal relatively unscathed. I get up, and the IV drip tugs at my arm. Unplugging myself from the heart monitor, I take the rolling IV and use it as support to stand.

I take a few tentative steps, testing my balance. The hallway is eerily quiet, and I feel like an intruder. As I walk down the hall, I look into each room.

Rhys is just down the hall, the curtain drawn so I can see him sitting on his bed. He looks a little paler than usual, and there's a bandage on his forearm, but otherwise, he looks fine.

Unfortunately, in his lap is the bag of my letters. He reads them in the dim overhead lights, his expression indecipherable.

"I thought we agreed that you weren't going to read those right now," I call out, walking inside and closing the door. Thankfully, he's in a private room.

He looks up, surprised. "You are supposed to be resting."

"I've rested enough." I sit on the edge of the bed, taking the bag of letters from his lap and placing it on the bedside table. "What are you in for?"

"I could not leave while you were still here," he admits. "Going back to the hotel felt wrong, given everything that happened."

"Did Jenna give everyone an update?"

"She did. Is Neil truly dead?"

"Yeah. He, along with the Infinity Hallway, is gone. For now. The timekeepers said they'd be back, and Jenna alluded to the fact that this might not be the end."

"Are you worried?"

"Actually, no." Neil, Nic, and Astaroth are gone. The students held at the facility are free, my family is safe, and so are my friends. Everything is as it should be, for now. "The only thing on my mind right now is how cringey those letters must be."

Rhys chuckles, and I can see the tension in his body ease. "I find them fascinating. A study in the complexities of the mind."

"That doesn't sound like a compliment."

"It is. It's like you were able to capture the fullness of your emotions in words."

I smile, my heart warming. Even if what he's saying is total bull. "Well, I'm glad you find them entertaining."

Rhys reaches out and takes my hand, his thumb rubbing circles on the back of it. "You should rest," he says softly. "We can talk more in the morning."

I nod, squeezing his hand in agreement. There aren't many guys who would do what he has, tagging along on this wild and dangerous road without any complaints.

I stand up with his help, and he guides me back to my room. At the door, I pause.

I want to thank him for everything, to tell him how much he means to me. But now that the opportunity is here, I realize there aren't enough words in the dictionary to express how I feel. Instead, I lean forward and press my lips to his.

Rhys responds immediately, his arms wrapping around me tightly as he deepens the kiss. I feel his love for me in every movement of his lips, every stroke of his tongue. It's overwhelming, but in the best way possible.

When we finally break apart, we're both breathless. Rhys rests his forehead against mine, his eyes closed.

"I love you," I whisper.

Rhys opens his eyes and smiles, his gaze locked with mine. "I love you, too."

CHAPTER THIRTY

There's no place like home. Or, in my case, my dorm house.

After a week in the hospital, our group returns to Southeastern. There are barely enough rooms to house all the Northeastern students, but we make do, with most of them couch surfing. Allegra graciously allows Ophelia to stay in her room, while her brother sleeps downstairs. The best part is, apparently Buck hates werewolves more than he hates snakes, so he barks at *them* and not me. He still doesn't like me, preferring David over everyone, but he doesn't growl at me when I walk into a room. That's progress, right?

Rhys' house is a zoo, hosting several Northeastern students camping out in the living room. He tells me that the Swan siblings haven't stopped arguing. Not only that, Karina seems to bicker with everyone, even her friends. And there's no sign of this supposed boyfriend of hers, either. I thought maybe she was talking about Blake—they're both good-looking, and I've seen them interact a few times. But when I ask him about it, he bursts into laughter. I don't think it's that funny of a question, but tears come out of his eyes and he holds his stomach, apparently dying from the hilarity of the suggestion. Even Ophelia cracks up.

"She'd chew me up and spit me out. I need a girlfriend who I'm not afraid of," he finally manages. "Thanks for the laugh, though, Mar. You're really cute, you know that?"

"She's taken," Ophelia says pointedly.

"Too bad."

"Don't flatter yourself," Ophelia snaps at me. "He flirts with anyone."

And that's the end of that conversation.

Tasha brings a suitcase downstairs and sets it by the door. Tomorrow, she, Isabelle, and David will be going back home to Douglas County. They've been away for too long, and I'm pretty sure all of Isabelle's plants are dead. But with the threat of Neil gone, there's no reason for them to stay anymore.

I'll be joining them in August, but there are a few things at school I still need to wrap up. Theodas wants me to write a testimony, or record one, of everything that's happened to me so far. He and Siraye are going to contact the High Council in the Veil to launch an investigation of the Ruby Council and all the corruption going on. This will be Theodas' final act as the Chancellor of Southeastern. No, he's not getting fired—it's just a transfer to Northeastern, to investigate the research practices of all the scientists on their payroll. Apparently, Karina's claims about Dr. Woods caught the attention of Siraye. Since she essentially funds all these schools, she's decided to become more hands-on... which means she'll be staying in the mortal realm for the foreseeable future.

Provost Mathers will be Chancellor Mathers next fall, so unfortunately he won't be teaching anymore. But he assures me there are plenty of other great professors here. Over drinks last night, he helped me, Archer, Allegra, Ophelia, Ava, and Declan choose which courses to enroll in next semester. We're all coming back, but notably, Celeste is not.

Not because they kicked her out. She's leaving voluntarily, moving west to distance herself from her father. When I asked Archer about it, all he said was, "We had a conversation, and it got…rough. But I said what I needed to." So that's something, I guess.

I, for one, am ready for a normal semester. It's still a magic school, but I imagine there will be fewer demons, cultists, and snakes. Unless, of course, Lilly Hardwicke counts as a snake. But her jaw is still recovering, even with shadowborn healing, so I doubt she'll be bothering me anytime soon. And if she does, I can always toss her through a rift.

Just kidding.

Jenna says I should cool it with the time travel and blood magic for the time being. I'm going to be taking all mortal courses next semester. I don't know what I want to do yet, but I might as well explore and get my gen eds done. Jenna will be taking courses, too, through a special adult education program Mathers is setting up for her. She's still going to be put under watch, but she says she doesn't mind.

"Provost Mathers is kind of hot, anyway. I don't mind if he's the one keeping an eye on me," she told me, wiggling her eyebrows. Gross.

With everything wrapping up and the Northeastern students leaving tomorrow, I make my way to Rhys' house to say goodbye to Karina. It feels weird to admit it, but I might actually...miss her.

When I arrive, she's surrounded by guys, as per usual. Theodas, Mathers, and Declan are among them.

"They've been at it for two hours now," Iacar says, coming up behind me. The elf's large frame fills the doorway, his steps heavy on the linoleum tiles. It's hard to imagine this burly man produced such a petite daughter. His husband, Tasar, is also quite tall. He stands on the other side of the room with Ava and Declan, smiling. "The prince tells me you've completely healed, Maria."

"Almost." I hold up my scarred palms. "I doubt these are going away anytime soon."

"Battle scars are the best kind of scars."

I look to Karina, sitting at the kitchen table. She's locked in an arm-wrestling competition with a guy from Northeastern, but it's a complete tie. I push my way forward until I'm standing right next to her.

"Ah, Mar!" Her eyes light up and she turns to look at me, as if she's not engaged in an intense competition. "There you are. I've been looking all over for you."

"I can see that. Can we, uh, talk in private?"

"Sorry, I'm a bit occupied right now," she says breezily, nodding her head toward the guy on the other side of the table. "I'm going to win in a few minutes, though."

"Like hell you are," the guy grits out.

"You are so cute if you think you're going to win."

"You're too arrogant."

"Whatever you say."

"I just wanted to thank you," I tell her. "For helping me. I couldn't have done it without you. Is your wound okay?"

"I'm good, Mar." She throws me a brilliant smile, and it's the most lighthearted I've seen her since meeting her. "After this, I'm off to find the rest of my family. There's still a lot to do, but I have my brother."

"And?" the guy asks expectantly.

"And my friends. If you want to be, like, cheesy about it." She rolls her eyes. "If you're ever in New York or South Carolina over the summer, we should hang out."

"If you need anything, just call me," I say.

"Oh, I will. We beat each other up, so now we're best friends for life, remember?"

"I don't know if I'd say we're best friends —"

"You'll never get rid of me now!"

The guy across the table snorts. "You have *got* to stop making connections that way. It can't be healthy."

"Oh please. Like you know what constitutes a healthy relationship," she snarks.

He glares at her, and I think I've found the one guy in the world who might not be attracted to Karina Swan at all. I never caught his name, but I remember his voice; they were arguing all the way back to Southeastern on the bus. Not even about the fight at the lab or anything of substance. Food, television, music — they couldn't agree on anything.

But of course, not a second passes before I eat my own words.

In one swift motion, the guy leans across the table and kisses Karina, right on the mouth. The entire room falls silent, and all that we hear is a thunk on the table as the guy slams her hand down.

He pulls back, a wicked grin on his face. "My win."

For once, Karina Swan is completely speechless.

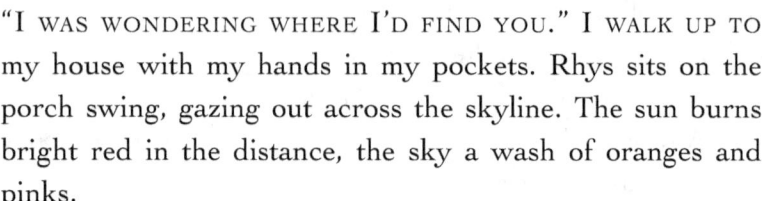

"I WAS WONDERING WHERE I'D FIND YOU." I WALK UP TO my house with my hands in my pockets. Rhys sits on the porch swing, gazing out across the skyline. The sun burns bright red in the distance, the sky a wash of oranges and pinks.

"I needed to escape the commotion," he admits, scooting over. I sit beside him, feeling the swing shift under our combined weight. We sit in silence for a moment, taking in the beauty of the sunset.

After thinking about it for a while, Rhys is going to do a gap year next fall. We're both figuring out what we want to do, but in my case, I want to stick close to home and take classes. Rhys also wants to go home—to the Veil. He hasn't been back to his homeland yet, and Iacar offered to put Rhys up for free at the bed and breakfast he owns with his husband. Rhys will travel and reacquaint himself with his own culture, which means we'll be apart for a while.

But I think it's for the best, honestly. It's a new chapter for both of us.

"Are you all packed?" he asks me.

"Not at all." But that's okay. I've always packed the night before a big trip, anyway.

This weekend, we're flying to the Bahamas for a two-week vacation at an all-inclusive. Rhys surprised me with the tickets right after we got back from Tennessee, after asking for Isabelle's blessing, of course.

"You might regret asking me to go away with you," I muse, leaning against his chest. "It'll just be us. What if you get sick of me?"

Rhys wraps an arm around me, pulling me closer. "I highly doubt that."

"No more training, or fighting, or panicking about our impending doom. You'll see who I really am."

"I already know who you are. And I love every part of you."

"Don't get mushy on me," I tease.

"Do you feel the same?"

"You know how I feel about you."

He nods. "I do. I meant, do *you* love every part of yourself?"

I pause, considering his question.

Mari was my hot-headed character. She caused a lot of trouble for me, but she also taught me how to be brave. Marilyn wasn't well liked, but she was bold and went after what she wanted. And Mary Alice? The pushover of the group? She was desperate to fit in. It was exhausting playing her. But, at the same time, I needed her to survive.

I've done a lot as my characters, and as weird as that phase was in my life, I don't regret them. Because Tasha was right all along—at my core, I've always been myself.

I may not love every single fragment of who I am—some shards are still sharp, cutting into me when I least expect it —but I've learned to gather them all up into the mosaic that is me. Each piece, flawed and imperfect, adds color and depth to the person I've become. To single one part of myself out in disdain is to compromise the integrity of the whole.

My flaws, my oddities, they're not something I have to overlook. They make up part of who I am. And when I learn to accept them, to appreciate them, I find a kind of peace that depends on having them in my life.

On the cusp of a new chapter, I recognize that everything that's happened, good and bad, has led me to this moment in time. I am, and always have been, a work in progress — flawed, yet irreplaceably me.

GLOSSARY

Astaroth: A powerful demon known for practicing blood magic. Astaroth was once imprisoned in a time prison, but due to certain events, was released. He has a cult following in the mortal realm.

Beastblood: Non-humanoid creatures originating in the Veil. They are often associated with animalistic traits and remain within the Veil, usually unable to get to the mortal realm on their own. Some examples of Beastbloods include lycans, chimera, and dragons.

Blood Magic: A forbidden type of magic that uses blood or other body parts to perform spells. Anyone, even humans, can use blood magic without many limitations. However, it is illegal to practice, and can be dangerous if used too often.

Elves: Truebloods with a distinctive appearance characterized by elongated ears. They possess the innate ability to distinguish truth from lies. In addition, Elves can wield elemental magic, enabling them to control and manipulate natural elements such as air, water, fire, or earth.

Fae: Winged truebloods who inhabit a continent alongside the elves, with whom they are in constant conflict. Fae are known for their trickery and manipulation, and they have elemental magic. They are physically incapable of lying and must always speak the truth, which often leads them to use clever wordplay and misdirection instead.

Infinity Hallway: A corridor used by time agents to travel through time. It contains multiple doorways, each leading to a different point in history or the future. However, the hallway can be dangerous to humans and may cause madness or disorientation to those who stay for extended periods.

Linguist's Orb: A fae device capable of instantly translating any language. It was created because Fae speak many different mutually unintelligible dialects.

Magician: The offspring of two shadowborn. Generally, magic weakens as the generations are mixed with human genes. Magicians can perform spells, although their abilities are not as potent as those of shadowborn. They cannot open rifts like their shadowborn counterparts.

Mortal Realm: The realm where humans and non-magical creatures live. It is separate from the Veil and lacks the magical properties and creatures that exist in other realms.

Psychic: The child of two magicians. While they cannot perform spells, psychics possess limited abilities and are born with a connection to the Veil. They are unable to open rifts, however.

Rift: A magical portal between realms that can be opened by swinging a blade through open air and concentrating on the desired destination. This ability comes easily to most shadowborn, and allows them to travel between the Veil and the mortal realm.

Ruby Council: The governing body of trueblood demons in the Veil. They hold significant political power and are responsible for maintaining order and enforcing laws among demonkind. One of the most powerful and wealthy members of the Ruby Council is Neil Abbott. As a member of the council, he wields a great deal of influence and is respected by many in the demon community.

Shadowborn: A hybrid born from the union of a human and a trueblood, possessing traits from both species. They are considered half-bloods and are often seen as shadows of their trueblood parents. Shadowborn have the ability to open rifts between the mortal realm and the Veil, and are stronger, faster, and more durable than humans. They can also perform magic, with some being born with rare and powerful abilities. Generally, the child of two shadowborn will either be a shadowborn or a magician.

Time Agent: A highly trained agent responsible for maintaining the timeline and ensuring that all events occur as they are supposed to. Time Agents use the Infinity Hallway, a special place that enables them to travel through time and space. They must be well-versed in historical events and possess advanced technology to prevent paradoxes and other disruptions to the timeline.

Timekeeper: A serpent-shaped beastblood capable of time travel. They are omniscient and can control the fates of others with bloodlines traced back to Truebloods.

Time Prison: A highly-secure supernatural prison designed to hold dangerous beings. It's a place where inmates are isolated from the rest of the world and thrown in a different time period, making it nearly impossible for them to escape.

Trueblood: A magical humanoid being originating from the Veil. Truebloods identify themselves with human-categorized monsters such as angels, demons, vampires, shifters, and more. They are not affiliated with any religion. Truebloods can only open rifts from the Veil to the mortal realm but cannot close a rift if they are in the mortal realm. They migrated to the mortal realm during the 1800s. Truebloods possess magical abilities and often hold positions of power and influence in the Veil and mortal realm.

Veil: A mystical realm imbued with magic that is filled with unpredictable and often dangerous forces. It is the birthplace of all truebloods and beastbloods, and it is separated from the mortal realm by a thin barrier that can be traversed by opening a rift.

Wisdom Tree: A sentient and omniscient tree located in the Veil, guarded by three fierce warriors. Although the tree was once thought to be a mere rumor, the grove in which it resides is not difficult to find. However, once you leave the grove, your memories of the tree are erased, making it difficult to recall any information or knowledge gained from the tree.

About the Author

Samantha Gao is a New Adult author with a passion for all things fantasy and paranormal romance. Her writing is fueled by her love for paranormal romance, and she enjoys creating compelling characters that readers can relate to and root for. After graduating from college with a degree in a completely different field, Sam decided to pursue her life-long dream of becoming a writer.

When she's not busy crafting stories that will transport readers to another world, Sam enjoys watching Asian dramas (with subtitles, of course!), listening to music, and indulging in her weakness for chocolate.

Sign up for her newsletter here: subscribepage.io/SamGao

- facebook.com/imberhousepublishing
- instagram.com/imberhouse
- amazon.com/author/samgao
- bookbub.com/profile/sam-gao
- goodreads.com/samgao